D0402191

THE SPA

AT

LAVENDER

LANE

PHYLLIS MELHADO

Black Rose Writing | Texas

©2020 by Phyllis Melhado
All rights reserved. No part of this book may be reproduced, stored in a
retrieval system or transmitted in any form or by any means without the
prior written permission of the publishers, except by a reviewer who may
quote brief passages in a review to be printed in a newspaper, magazine or
journal.

The author grants the final approval for this literary material.

Second printing

This is a work of fiction. Names, characters, businesses, places, events, and
incidents are either the products of the author's imagination or used in a
fictitious manner. Any resemblance to actual persons, living or dead, or
actual events is purely coincidental.

ISBN: 978-1-68433-464-3
PUBLISHED BY BLACK ROSE WRITING
www.blackrosewriting.com

Printed in the United States of America
Suggested Retail Price (SRP) $18.95

The Spa at Lavender Lane is printed in Baskerville

*As a planet-friendly publisher, Black Rose Writing does its best to eliminate
unnecessary waste to reduce paper usage and energy costs, while never compromising
the reading experience. As a result, the final word count vs. page count may not meet
common expectations.

*For my mother, who taught me the beauty of language,
the power of story and the joy of reading.*

Praise for
THE SPA AT LAVENDER LANE

"Phyllis Melhado has written a wonderful, lively, bitchy novel populated with a cast of women, young and old, that make the *Real Housewives* look like Girl Scouts. You'll love them. You'll hate them. You'll be glad they don't live next door to you. The perfect beach read, even if there's not a beach within a hundred miles."
~Charles Salzberg, Award-Winning Author of *Second Story Man (Down & Out Books)* and the *Swann Series (Five Star Publishing)*

"Loved my stay at *The Spa at Lavender Lane*. Felt like the pampered guest—with the delight of being a fly on the wall. Melhado understands her rich, famous, demanding and self-indulgent characters. Now, if only I can get hold of the spa's Quince Face Cream!"
~Alice Simpson, Author, *Ballroom (Harper)*

"Turn off your phone, get yourself a cup of coffee or a glass of wine, a comfy chair or couch and get ready for a riveting read. It's the perfect get-away from your daily life. This book will take you away from your problems and into the life of glamour and excitement. Oh, and get dinner ready for your family before you start the read, because once you start you won't be able to put it down!"
~Christine Schwab, Author, *Take Me Home From the Oscars (Skyhorse)* and *The Grown-Up Girls Guide to Style (William Morrow)*

"I loved the book. I REALLY LOVED THE BOOK!!! I thoroughly enjoyed every chapter, every character and all the twisting and turning plots!!"
~Paul Thomas, Broadway Executive and Artist

"What a great fun read. The characters are just wonderful and if I may say, she lets it all hang out!"
~Lyn Leigh, Co-Founder, *The Perfumed Plume*

"*The Spa at Lavender Lane* immediately drew me into a world that I wanted to be a part of. From Nadia's celebrity guests to the handsome man turning all heads when he arrived - I found myself reading every chance I could to be with them and see what was about to unfold. Ms. Melhado's ability to bring characters to life, spin a story that twists and turns and makes you long for the sequel is truly stunning."
~Vivienne Fleischer, Health and Wellness Blogger

"Destined for best-sellerdom!"
~George Christy, *The Beverly Hills Courier*

Elegance is when the inside is as beautiful as the outside.
-Coco Chanel

THE SPA

AT

LAVENDER

LANE

Part 1

Chapter One

From behind the gilded two-way mirror in her elegant atelier office, Nadia Demidova could monitor everything going on in the sunny reception salon below. Spying on her clients was a questionable tactic, she knew full well, but it had proved to be an extremely useful one, nonetheless. She had learned early on during her twenty-five-year reign as mistress of Lavender Lane, one of the world's most exclusive spas, that the difficult guests would reveal themselves practically the moment they arrived.

Nadia leaned over and peered through the glass, hoping the new ten-day session would be devoid of problems. Petite, feminine and still quite attractive at seventy-three, pressing personal issues were making it difficult to muster her legendary client concern. She was in no mood to cater to yet another batch of prima donnas.

So far, so good, she thought. Most of the women were already checked in and settled in their rooms. All seemed to be going well, unlike the last session when the wife of an esteemed senior senator arrived thoroughly inebriated and had to be restrained and sobered up before being driven to the Palm Springs airport and deposited on a flight home. Minor substance abuse was one thing. Many of her clients, most notably the Hollywood types, suffered from such problems, but full-fledged, public displays of addiction was quite another. She had created the gold standard for rest, relaxation and the rejuvenation of mind, body and spirit. As far as Nadia

1

was concerned, if a client's ability to control her serious self-destructive urges was lacking, she could go straight to the Betty Ford Clinic.

She watched as a striking, tall woman with cropped jet-black hair swept into the reception salon, followed closely by her driver struggling with several pieces of Prada luggage. Ah, dear Mavis Perkins, in the latest Armani, of course, with a limited edition Bottega tote over her shoulder. Nadia smiled as she observed the entrance of one of her regular and most demanding guests.

She thought about the time, several years before, when Mavis had first come to Lavender Lane. After having reigned as a superstar model for years, she had just given up her career to marry Tyler Perkins, one of Chicago's wealthiest and most influential real estate magnates. The stories of how she had persuaded him out of his first marriage were legion, all testaments to her ability to satisfy a man who had been famously satisfied by the best.

Mavis was always a favored topic of gossip among the guests. Her countless affairs, including one with a powerful politician who had his eye on the White House and, of course, the reckless spending of her husband's seeming limitless money, were juicy fodder for wagging tongues. Although Nadia never encouraged such conversations, the rumor mill almost always extended to her office. Current chat was about Mavis's desire to capitalize on the growing popularity of older models and return to the fashion and beauty scene in a big way. At fifty-two and still remarkable looking, she had both the connections and the moxie to make it happen.

Indeed, Nadia thought, just what our deprived world truly needs -- another dose of Mavis Perkins. She wondered how The Grand One would react when told she would not be getting her regular suite. Nadia could already feel the venom.

An angelic-faced woman dressed in a hot pink sundress, her head supporting a cascade of blonde curls, entered the salon. Nadia watched as the woman turned repeatedly to the teenager who trailed behind her, long, chestnut hair falling below her midriff-baring T-shirt, skimming the waistline of her cut-off jeans. The girl was tall and thin and a budding beauty.

"New clients from Dallas," Nadia's assiduously guarded notebook detailed. The depository of all important and personal information, the notebook was locked up in the safe each night and available only to Nadia and her long-time assistant director Phoebe Bancroft. Only the most rudimentary information was entered in the spa's computers, where it was vulnerable to hackers who, in a heartbeat, would sell her clients' most private information to the highest bidder.

"Let's see," Nadia sighed. Charlotte Tanner and daughter Lauren Fanning. Mother, 42 - overweight. Daughter, 15 - borderline anorexic. They hadn't even begun their stay and were already arguing. She wondered how the pair would survive ten days sharing a room.

Only one woman had yet to arrive. First time guest, the notebook detailed. Antoinette Etheridge, called Toni. 41. Single. Former buyer, designer sportswear, Gillam's Fifth Avenue. Extremely stressed. Another one, Nadia thought. There had been a growing roster, of late, of female executives who had made too many personal sacrifices and badly injured themselves both emotionally and physically in a relentless quest to make it to the top. She could relate, having given up a great deal in pursuit of her career. Success had not come easily.

Nadia felt the familiar flood of fatigue course through her body. She turned away from the mirror, leaning heavily on the arm of her well-worn, violet tufted Queen Anne chair. The exhaustion that had plagued her in the last few weeks was intruding once again. I cannot afford to be tired now, she sighed to herself. Simply too much to do -- lawyers, papers, Peter.

She walked slowly to the large picture window on the far side of her office, the vestiges of an injury sustained many years prior marking her graceful gait. Her damaged ankle was a constant reminder of the life she had once lived, and of the different direction her life might have taken had she only had the courage. Nearly fifty years had gone by, but barely a day passed without gut-wrenching remorse. The guilt had recently grown too great to bear. The moment to make amends had finally arrived, and if there were any doubts time was of the essence, her diminishing strength served as a constant reminder.

Time, she mused, is an adversary to us all. Nadia thought about her dear friend Dr. Eleanor Franklin, CEO of Franklin Nutritionals. Eleanor must be going mad up there in her suite all alone. She'd have to make time to see her…perhaps have dinner sent up for the two of them. Eleanor had been secluded in her Lavender Lane suite for nearly three weeks, recent plastic surgery having not quite delivered the hoped-for results. She assured Nadia she had gone to the very best, and yet, twenty-one days after the operation, she still had that pulled and pinched look when she fully expected to look rested and refreshed. The doctor promised it would ease up, but as each day went by, Eleanor feared she would remain looking more like some older sister of the late Joan Rivers than her former attractive, fifty-five-year-old self.

Nadia looked out the window and drank in the view of the lush Coachella Valley. It was especially beautiful in early spring, with the hills drenched in brightly colored wildflowers and the blue sky shining brilliantly behind centuries-old Saguaro cacti. She watched as a roadrunner darted its way across the field, crown feathers forging ahead like a sentinel in the warm, April air. Soon he would be joined by owls, hawks, hares, and jackrabbits, all answering the valley's seductive call.

She was tempted to stand there and look out all day, but it was hardly an option with a business to run. Lest she forget, the dreaded intercom buzzed to remind her. She returned to her desk reluctantly, certain the summons would mean only problems.

"What is it?" she asked, trying not to allow the fatigue to color her voice. "As to be expected," Phoebe reported in her distinctive British voice, "the difficult ones are showing their colors."

Nadia smiled at Phoebe's choice of words, language commonly used to describe the aggressive mating behavior of male creatures in the wild. Her clients were, indeed, like the inhabitants of the Palm Springs desert, each with her own agenda and unique survival techniques. Her assistant was a treasure. She always managed to put things in perspective.

"There's a situation which needs your attention," Phoebe whispered into the phone.

"Yes," Nadia said, looking down below. "Mavis appears to be in fine fettle, but nothing that can't be handled. I'll be right with you."

As mistress of Lavender Lane, Nadia Demidova had managed to tame scores of situations. This would be just one more. She smoothed her neatly coifed silver-gray hair, took a few deep breaths, and made her way toward the discreet staircase that would deliver her to the concerns unfolding in the arena below.

Chapter Two

"We're here, Miss," the driver said, jarring Toni Etheridge from a state roughly approaching relaxation. She pushed her sunglasses up into her tousled auburn hair and snapped open her bloodshot hazel eyes. She was almost sorry the ride was over. The trip from LAX had provided the first pleasant moments in an otherwise horrendous travel day which started with an insane traffic jam on the way to JFK which nearly caused her to miss her flight. Then she was assigned a terrible seat at the rear of the plane where the cabin staff were constantly rattling cans and refilling their carts. And to make the trip even more memorable, a raucous group of drag queens on their way to a competition in LA was seated near her and didn't shut up during the entire five-hour flight. But the capper was the sudden drop in altitude that put her stomach firmly in her mouth and sent her stumbling to the bathroom to make sure her body had not betrayed her like it had done a few years before. Happily, she found only the result of a leaky bladder and not the catastrophe she had dreaded.

"May I help you?" asked the good-looking young man as he opened the car door and offered his hand. He smiled broadly, gleaming white teeth set off by eager blue eyes and deeply tanned skin. Even though they were miles from the sea, Toni thought he had perfect California surfer looks, complete with thick, wavy blonde hair and a tall, well-built body.

"Did you have a good trip?" he inquired.

"Good trip!" Toni grunted, pushing her glasses back down to shield her eyes from the southern California desert sun. "Do you really want to know?

She leaned back and looked at him for a long moment, then laughed. "Of course you don't want to know. Why would you?"

There was an audible sigh of relief.

"Ms.," the limo driver interjected, appearing with two mismatched and beaten-up travel bags.

"Oh, thanks. You can dump my stuff over there," Toni said, pointing to a collection of Gucci, Vuitton and Prada bags waiting to be delivered to the rooms of other newly arrived guests.

"Now, Michael," she said, focusing on the name badge pinned to the surfer boy's neat white Lacoste shirt. "Where to?" She grabbed his arm and gave him one of her most engaging smiles.

Michael smiled politely and tried to usher Toni in through the front door. "They'll take good care of you at the desk, Ms..."

"Etheridge," Toni said, taking off her sunglasses, but making no move to walk in.

"We've got to get you checked in quickly, Ms. Etheridge. Madame Demidova runs a tight ship."

"So I've heard, Michael," Toni said, toying with his nametag. I'm sure she depends on you to, uh, keep things moving." She flashed him a coy smile. "And I certainly don't want to get you in any kind of trouble."

There was an awkward pause.

"I would sure appreciate it, Ma'am."

"Ma'am!" Toni shrieked. "Dear God. I'm not that old!"

"Of course not!" Michael said quickly as he encouraged her through the door to reception.

"Ah, Ms. Etheridge," the front desk clerk said. "Welcome!" But before Toni had a chance to reply, the cell phone buried in her huge tote bag rang. Damn, she thought, remembering the rules she read in Lavender Lane's confirmation letter: No men, other than staff, allowed on the premises. No loud talking in the public areas. And absolutely no cell phones. She began fumbling in her bag. "Shit!" she said, quite audibly. "Where is the damn thing?"

"Ah," she heard a voice say softly. "You must be Antoinette Etheridge. We've been expecting you."

Toni looked at the small, impeccably dressed woman who had silently advanced toward her. *Clearly Chanel, and definitely the real thing -- and uh-oh. It could only be one person.*

"Oh, dear. I am so sorry," she said sheepishly. Her cell, which had migrated to the bottom of her bag, somewhere between a prickly hairbrush and a plastic bag full of broken pretzel bits, continued to ring. "Guess I forgot to turn the darned thing off." *Gee-sus. Do you believe this?* Toni felt her face flower into a full flush. She rummaged around her bag and after two more excruciating rings, finally located the phone and turned it off.

The woman in Chanel stood silently, a patient smile on her face.

"My apologies," Toni said.

"Nothing to be concerned about," the woman said in a soothing tone. "You're here, now, and it's time to leave behind those dreadful little machines and all that New York stress." She offered her hand. "I'm Nadia Demidova, dear. Welcome to Lavender Lane."

■　　■　　■　　■　　■

When Mavis Perkins was shown her accommodations, her gray-green eyes ignited with slow, icy fire. Her favorite suite, with some of the most magnificent sunsets in the western part of the United States, had been given to someone else, and this was simply not to be tolerated.

"What do you mean I can't have my regular suite?" she asked, reveling in her haughtiest demeanor, making her fabled cheekbones seem angled even higher on her porcelain skin, while her chiseled nostrils arched in their most sanctimonious flare. She pronounced the word "mean" with near biblical profundity.

"I'm so sorry, Mrs. Perkins," Nadia answered, reaching for Mavis's hand. Her apology was not an empty one. She always did her best to accommodate her clients' wishes, especially those who were regulars. But as Nadia moved forward, Mavis pulled away. She simply would not be touched.

Nadia wondered how she was going to handle the situation without breaking a confidence, and for a moment she nearly succumbed to temptation. It would be so much easier to tell Mavis whom she had put in "her" suite, but she couldn't. Word simply must not get out. Eleanor was a highly visible spokesperson for her company, and if the media or the internet ever got hold of information about her plastic surgery, the perception of Lavender Lane as a retreat steeped in absolute discretion would be destroyed.

"I am terribly sorry your favorite accommodations are not available this visit. I know how much you like that particular suite."

"Like it," Mavis intoned. "I practically own it. Let me remind you I have been coming here two, sometimes three times a year for more than a decade." She glared at Nadia. "You add it up and it comes to a hell of a lot of cash." She kept her eyes fixed firmly on Nadia, not allowing her a second's grace.

"Yes," Nadia said looking directly back at Mavis, "and you know how much we love having you here."

"Well, I'm beyond disappointed, Madame Demidova. It never occurred to me I might not have my usual suite. You know how particular I am."

Nadia remained poised. "Yes, of course, Mrs. Perkins. But let me assure you that you will be more than satisfied with this suite. As you can see, it's exactly the same, only at the other end of the house."

Mavis appraised the sitting room with its familiar cream-colored sofa, graceful deep-green potted palms and delicately carved Cherrywood armoire. She turned her gaze slowly back to Nadia.

"Well, if it's the same damned thing, why couldn't you put whoever the hell is in my suite at the other end?"

Nadia studied the difficult woman accustomed to always getting her own way. Telling Mavis the real reason without going in to any details might get her to settle in.

"May I speak to you in confidence?" she whispered, summoning up a bit of the actress she had developed during a brief career as a ballerina.

Nadia's tone spoke volumes, and Mavis found herself intrigued. Usually interested only in herself, she became curious about who might be ensconced in the coveted suite. Warming to the notion of hearing something of special interest, she leaned forward. "Of course," she said, pursing her lips in a half-smile.

Nadia leaned forward as well, her petite frame no match for the regally tall Mavis Perkins. She put her hand on Mavis's arm, and looked up.

This time, Mavis did not move away. "The guest in your regular suite recently had some extensive work done," she said, "and things don't seem to be going as well as one might expect. I'm afraid she's forced to stay a few days longer than any of us had anticipated."

"I see," Mavis responded, curiosity in full throttle. "Anyone I know?"

"I doubt you have ever met this woman," Nadia said, choosing her words carefully because, in all likelihood, Mavis knew who Eleanor was. "The poor dear..." she continued. It was imperative that Nadia diffuse Mavis's curiosity. "It would be so kind to let her recuperate in peace."

Mavis arched one meticulously tweezed eyebrow, then relaxed into a measure of acceptance. She actually could identify with this problem. She lived in dread of the scalpel, having seen more than a few botched jobs among her friends in Chicago's best circles.

Nadia had taken a calculated risk, but it seemed to have worked.

"Very well then. Have someone fetch my bags. And please send a masseuse up ASAP. I'm simply exhausted from the trip -- not to mention all this unpleasantness about the rooms."

Nadia had only just checked the schedule and was quite sure the massage therapists were all booked, but it was impossible to say no to Mavis Perkins at this point.

"Certainly, Mrs. Perkins. Get yourself settled, and someone will be up to take care of you in a little while. And Mrs. Perkins, will you be joining the others for dinner this evening? Or perhaps you might prefer to dine in your suite."

"Oh, I think I'll come down to dinner. First night. I Always do." During her frequent stays at Lavender Lane, Mavis often had meals sent to her rooms, but Nadia knew she was not about to miss the first dinner, with its overview of the guests in residence.

"Then we'll see you at seven, and thank you for being so understanding about the suite. A masseuse will be up in a little while, and, of course, the service will be complimentary to show our gratitude for your kindness." She smiled graciously, then quickly summoned one of the attractive young attendants to bring Mavis Perkins's considerable luggage up to the Mariposa Suite as soon as possible.

"Whoever you have to switch around," Nadia cautioned Phoebe a few minutes later, "please make sure Mrs. Perkins gets one of the better therapists."

Phoebe peered over the top of the tortoise shell glasses which were perennially perched just below the bridge of her nose, a conspiratorial smile spreading over her angular but handsome face. "Without question. We can be sure if Mrs. Perkins's massage is anything less than celestial, we will hear about it."

They both had been subject to more Mavis Perkins incidents over the years than either of them cared to remember.

"Not to worry. I'll take care of it straight away."

"Good. And please do your best to get back here as soon as possible. From the looks of this group, re-arranging a couple of massages will be the least of our problems."

.   .   .   .   .

"Mother, I thought I was going to have my own room!" Lauren Fanning whined, glaring at her mother and twisting her pretty face into an ugly scowl.

Charlotte Tanner's ample body tensed, but she maintained her composure, determined not to allow the hurt to render her defenseless, as it had so often in the past. Lauren's outbursts had become more and more frequent and Charlotte thought this trip to Lavender Lane would help tame them. She had hoped to please her daughter, but from the way things were going, her hopes seemed dashed.

"Lauren, honey," she put her hand gently on the girl's shoulder. "I tried -- I truly did -- but I wasn't able to get us separate rooms. I didn't think you'd mind staying together. It's a very large room..." She hesitated, smiling weakly at the girl. "And we can keep an eye on each other, you know, with the food problem."

"Food problem! You're the one with the food problem, Mother. Not me!" Lauren groaned, pursing her mouth into a nasty pout. She had inherited Charlotte's full, sensuous lips and seemed to delight in distorting them, as if to demonstrate her disdain for the resemblance.

Charlotte peered at her daughter, fearing they were in for a disastrous ten days. The whole thing baffled her. Lauren had always been such a sweet girl, but this past year her warm and loving nature gave way to rudeness, snide remarks, and all-around unpleasantness. It was unlikely this drastic change had anything to do with the fact she and Lauren's stepfather were divorcing. On the contrary. Lauren disliked Jerry Tanner to the core, and rarely missed an opportunity to show it.

It had to be the weight -- both her own and her daughter's. Lauren was obsessed with being bone thin so she could become a model. The girl looked as though she hadn't ingested a single calorie in weeks while she, on the other hand, looked as though she had ingested every calorie in sight. It was ironic: Charlotte too, had once been thin with her own hopes of a modeling career.

If it were her few extra pounds that were so abhorrent to her daughter, Lauren might delight in the fact that Charlotte wasn't exactly happy with the bonus padding that had made its way to her hips, thighs and abdomen, rendering her once-slender body into a plus-size composition that distressed her each time she looked in a mirror.

The trip to Lavender Lane had been designed to boost her self-confidence and put her on a viable weight-loss track. Was it too much to hope that it might also help mend the deteriorating relationship she and her daughter shared?

"Why not have a look?" Charlotte asked, breaking a protracted silence. "The room's kind of interesting, with all the Native American decorations." She remembered Lauren having come home from school a couple of months back, enthusiastic about a class on Lakota storytelling traditions. If the girl would allow herself to, she actually might like the place.

Charlotte watched as Lauren begrudgingly turned her head and fondled the colorful masks and dream catchers hanging on the walls. She thought she saw a small smile, but, of course, Lauren would not give her the satisfaction of letting her see it.

The sun was beginning its descent for the evening and something in the distance caught Lauren's attention. She walked over to the oversized window, opened it and looked out.

"I hear there are lots of good places to run out there," Charlotte ventured. At home, Lauren averaged at least five miles a day, and Charlotte hoped Lavender Lane's beautiful paths and trails would please her daughter.

After what seemed like an eternity, Lauren shrugged her shoulders and said, "Well, I guess it won't be so bad."

Charlotte felt some of the tension finally drain from her muscles. "Why don't you unpack, honey? Then we can go down to dinner."

"Dinner!" Lauren screamed. "It's the food thing again! Mother, you have got to promise me you'll stop getting on my case about eating. I like being thin and I intend to stay that way."

"I know. You have to be thin to be a model."

"Yes, it's what I want -- to be thin and a model."

Her daughter was certainly pretty enough to be a model, but to embark on a future depending on good looks was a disastrous mistake. Charlotte was certainly living proof of that. Her own mother and father had forced her to live a JonBenét Ramsey existence, entering her in one beauty contest after another, instilling the idea she needed to use her looks to make her way in the world. Modest shopkeepers in a small Texas town, her parents sold convenience store goods to friends and neighbors. They didn't believe in higher education for girls. Such folly was for "other" people. They knew that good looks would go a long way toward helping a girl make her way in the world.

Charlotte always wished she'd had the education she saw other girls go on to have. But there was no understanding of its importance, let alone the money for tuition. Her weight notwithstanding, if she were going to accomplish only one thing on this trip, it would be to dissuade Lauren of foregoing a college education to pursue a foolish path based on looks.

Although she hated to admit it, Lauren had been dying to come to Lavender Lane. Celebs like Beyoncé and Gaga came here to veg out, and so did all the important models. She'd even heard Cosmo's newest discovery, Kerry Hudson, holed up here for two weeks a few months ago when her rapper boyfriend Caliban dumped her.

Lauren glanced back out the window. What had sparked her interest in the distance had now come clearly into view: a couple of male staffers were sprinting across the field, shirts tied around their waists, their bare, tanned chests gleaming in the setting sun.

Well, she thought, absently fondling her lower lip. While Mumsy is busy eating rabbit food and gushing sweat under those flabby arms of hers, there just might be all kinds of fun things to do around here after all.

Chapter Three

Michael helped Toni get settled in her room and, after her somewhat embarrassing introduction to Nadia Demidova, she was relieved to be safely there. She smiled at Michael. He was really very sweet. A generous tip was in order.

"Thank you. Thank you so much!" he said, a broad grin lighting up his face when she handed him a twenty-dollar bill. "If there's anything you need while you're here, Ms. Etheridge -- anything at all -- be sure to ask for me."

She returned the smile and indulged herself by letting her gaze linger yet again. Had she imagined it, or was there more than the bringing of ice or the adjusting of air conditioning included in his offer of "anything?" She should hardly be surprised. She had practically thrown herself at him only ten minutes earlier. She laughed at herself. *Hormones...*

Toni took a good look at the room: tiny, and the view overlooking the garbage collection station in the rear was hardly the one she had seen online. This is what I get for a thousand dollars a day? Her sojourn at Lavender Lane would put a nice little dent into the modest stash she'd managed to accumulate working brutal hours at Gillam's Fifth Avenue all those years.

She was whipped from the long day of travel, and the bed looked inviting. She'd rest for just a few minutes...

When the house phone rang, Toni couldn't remember where she was. She felt a cool breeze coming from an open window, and the air it ushered in was rich with the smell of newly cut grass. The phone rang two more times before she finally got her bearings.

"Christ, where have you been? I've been worried sick!"

It was the unmistakable voice of her best friend Kevin Gavelli. When he was cool and calm, his voice took on the studied tones of the mega-successful clothing designer he was. But when he was excited, which seemed to Toni to be most of the time, he practically sang his words.

"Oh, Kev...it's you."

"Bet your sweet ass, it's me. I've been calling you for hours and finally had the bright idea to call Lavender Lane directly."

"I was napping. What time is it?"

"What time is it? she wants to know. 'What time is it?'" he asked again, his voice growing louder. "It's time to de-stress, get healthy and start thinking about this serious step you're taking. Correction: serious step *we're* taking. That's what time it is!" he yelled, displaying a talent for drama that was nearly as adept as his talent for design. "What in the Hell happened to you?"

Toni leaned over and turned on the light. "Oh, it was one of those great travel days. You know, everything that could go wrong did go wrong. I'm too tired to go into it."

"Well, as long as you're there safely. How do you feel?"

"Ok, I guess. A little hopped up perhaps."

"Not on any substances, I hope."

"Of course not!"

"Well, relax. You'll be fine. It will all be fine!" It took him a complete octave to enunciate the word "all."

"Now tell me," he cooed, "have you met her yet?"

"Met who?"

"Who? Nadia Demidova, of course! I hear she's..."

"Annoyed at me is what she is," Toni said, propping herself up. She told Kevin about the cell phone ringing and, of course, he'd been the caller.

"Well, at least now she knows who you are." He paused. "Now you listen to me. Get yourself together and go down for dinner. You need sustenance -- lots of the right kind, which I'm sure you'll get. And I'm absolutely dying to know who's there! I hear The Two Donnas are regulars -- not that they would ever go at the same time. Can you imagine those two in the Jacuzzi together? TMZ, are you listening?" he asked, cracking himself up.

"Kevin, I couldn't care less who's here -- Donna Karan, Donatella Versace or Ma-donna, for that matter. What I care about, as you so astutely reminded me a few seconds ago, is getting myself on a healthy regimen. I'm spending a shitload of money for ten days of paradise. If I don't emerge a new woman with a clear picture of the future, I'll kill myself."

"Not so fast, missy. I've got a stake in this now. And besides, you can't kill yourself yet. I haven't designed your shroud."

"Very funny."

"Let's not forget who it was who had the, pardon the expression, balls to tell you that you were teetering on the brink after you freaked out at an office baby shower a few months ago."

"Yes. True. While everyone else was patronizing me, telling me I am just going through a phase and that I shouldn't take things to heart quite so much, only you told me the unvarnished truth -- I was turning into a frazzled, out-of-shape, burned-out and sexless old hag."

"You forgot over-the-hill."

"Oh, fuck you and the stilettos you came in on."

"As memory serves me, my pretty, I think I actually did -- but don't think I was wearing my stilettos."

Toni laughed. "Do you believe we actually did it -- and scored?"

"Thank God for Dr. Fishman. I knew he was a miracle worker if he was able to help that beast my partner is married to get pregnant."

"Well, at least the meds helped us score right away." She laughed. "Can you imagine if we had to do it again?"

"Now, now. Didn't seem like you were suffering..."

"Hmmm. Waaay too drunk to remember."

"Yeah. That's what they all say. By the way, you weren't my first girl. I've tried the so-called fairer sex before."

"Just as long as I'm your last."

"No worries about that, my pretty! And speaking of things in that general direction, gotta go. I'm late for the gym."

"The gym, at this hour? Isn't it past ten your time?"

"Well, there's this di-vine new weights instructor, and he has late hours, if you know what I mean!"

"I think I can figure it out. Have a good time. And Kev -- not that I don't want to talk to you -- but there's a strict rule here about cell phones."

"Right. Like you've ever been one to obey the rules."

"I've reformed, mainly because I don't want to get kicked out. But in a couple of days I'll hide behind a palm tree and call you."

"Promise?"

"Promise."

"OK. Sleep tight -- and be a good girl.

"And you have fun at the, um, gym."

"Love you lots, Antoinette."

"Love you lots, too. Kevin."

Toni laid back and closed her eyes. She had made a really big decision and there was no going back. She was nearly 41 and it was her last chance. She had always pushed away the idea of having a child in favor of career success. Her success was secure but the idea of motherhood had been gnawing at her. Her 35th birthday had been a wakeup call: now or never, kept ringing in her ears. But the guy was all wrong, a married man she had been foolish enough to get involved with when she was feeling lonely and vulnerable. Her brutal working hours had left her little time for dating, and the men who showed up on dating apps rarely turned out to who they said they were. At least Dan had been honest. She knew from the get-go he was married and unlikely to change that status, but she liked him, enjoyed being with him and there was a strong mutual attraction. After a couple of times of being together, they fell into a comfortable routine of occasional dinners and some pretty good sex. The owner of one of the most successful and still privately-owned sportswear companies. he could easily afford to take her to the best places -- Ralph Lauren's Polo, Michael's, Dirty French, Le Bernadin -- and being seen together did not present a problem. She was, after all, one of the industry's top designer sportswear buyers and it was only natural they would socialize. Almost like real dating, she had told herself.

When she found herself pregnant, she didn't know whether to be happy or sad…to tell him or not to tell him and if so when…to keep the baby or not, and if so, how…to be a single mother…to let him be involved or not …to press him to get out of his marriage. She worried about it constantly, barely able to think about anything else. She was tense, nervous, snapped at everyone and made stupid errors at work, behaviors so unlike her.

Kevin was the only one she confided in and instead of being his usual, opinionated, wise-ass self, he advised her to just quiet herself, go deep within and the answer would come to her. And it did come: she would keep the baby and somehow figure it all out. But one Saturday morning when she was about nine weeks along, she woke up with very bad cramps and barely made it to the bathroom where she deposited a wash of blood and tissue and all the hopes she hadn't been sure she had until the doctor had confirmed she was, indeed, pregnant. Then, amid a torrent of tears, she pushed the lever and flushed all those hopes away.

This time the scenario was different. This time the child would be welcome with no reservations. The arrangement might be a bit unconventional, but her beloved Kevin had long wanted to be a father and hadn't quite figured out how he would pursue it and she was sure, at this point, she would welcome motherhood. They had yet to figure out the details of how they would co-parent, but of this much they both were certain: they loved each other and their child would be loved without reservation.

She glanced at the clock, clicked off the light and drifted off to sleep. She had time for a bit more of a nap before dinner.

■   ■   ■   ■   ■

Mavis glided to the dining room in a state of total relaxation, her vintage white silk Saint Laurent jumpsuit softly caressing her thighs as she moved. That masseuse Greta certainly knew her way around a body --perhaps too well. There were a few moments when her dexterous fingers wandered too close to where they should not have ventured uninvited. Testing the terrain, I suppose, Mavis thought. Well, it's comforting to know special services are available, should the need arise. A girl can't have too many resources.

She quickened her pace as she approached the dining room, eager to see who her fellow guests were.

"Ah, Mrs. Perkins," Nadia Demidova said, greeting her at the door. "I trust your massage was satisfactory."

"Adequate," Mavis said, cutting the conversation short, hoping her relaxed stride hadn't revealed just how adequate the massage had actually been. No point in letting Nadia know how exceptional it was.

The dining room looked out on beautiful rolling hills and slopes of endless, tree-covered mountains. The tables, covered with soft peach linen cloths, were interspersed with graceful palms and flowering cacti, and the air was perfumed with the subtle aroma of lemon and lime.

Guests could choose between socializing at a group table or dining on their own. As she usually did when she came to Lavender Lane, Mavis opted to sit by herself. She didn't care to engage in useless chitchat, at least not at this point. She preferred to take in the whole panorama of possibilities. After all, one never knew who was in residence.

She had tried many times to get Nadia to let her see the guest list in advance, so she could get a fix on who she might meet, who she might wish to avoid, and with whom she might end up in the Jacuzzi. But Madame Demidova never demurred from her customary posture of correctness. The list was never provided.

On one trip Mavis spotted a woman who she thought she had known from her early modeling days, but given the passage of time and the skills of plastic surgeons, she couldn't be sure. She'd pressed Nadia for the name of the lookalike, but no dice. As it turned out, the guest was not the modeling agency booker Mavis thought she was, and by approaching the woman and satisfying her curiosity, she had gotten stuck with a tag-a-long for the entire stay. Mrs. Henrietta Schmidt of Baltimore, Md. had hardly been her idea of scintillating company, prattling on incessantly about her brilliant children and the latest Baltimore dinner party gossip. Baltimore hadn't been interesting since the last century, when Wallis Simpson went down on the Duke of Windsor and altered the future of the British monarchy.

After Mrs. Schmidt, Mavis always canvassed the guests from afar before befriending anyone. She settled in comfortably at the far corner of the room. Her view was splendid. A glass of chilled Vichy water with lime, some of Lavender Lane's world-famous gourmet low-calorie cuisine, and she'd be all set to begin her well-earned hiatus, with plenty of time to give serious thought to her newly-hatched plans for the future.

.　　.　　.　　.　　.

Charlotte struggled with the zipper on her slacks, wondering what they'd all be wearing. While comfortable, casual clothing was officially encouraged, she'd heard the first night tended to be somewhat dressier. She hoped her periwinkle Gucci pants and ombré silk knit overblouse would look all right. The blouse was a tad snug, but it should work. Her slacks however, were not cooperating. That nice Korean tailor had let them out twice, and there simply was no material left to adjust.

Charlotte studied herself in the mirror. Not only did she hate the way she looked, she hated the way she felt. Her doctor's warning of climbing cholesterol levels and elevated blood pressure had finally given her the resolve to make long-needed changes. Recently turned forty-two, she was hardly old enough to have the medical problems, not to mention the body, of a much older woman. Her husband may have wanted a divorce, but while the lawyers were haggling over terms, she was not about to make him a well-to-do widower.

She was anxious about being in the company of dozens of women who would no doubt be parading slender, well-toned bodies in addition to abundant self-esteem. They came to Lavender Lane to get pampered. She came to lose weight. But she also came to think seriously about an important question: Why did she seem unable to succeed at much of anything -- two marriages, motherhood or the discipline to correct her steadily-increasing weight gain?

She tugged at the zipper again and at last was successful.

"Come on, Mother. If we're going, let's go." Lauren had managed to mend her disposition enough to change into fresh, skin-tight jeans and yet another body-hugging T-shirt. While her daughter had repeatedly reminded her she was not hungry, Charlotte knew Lauren was anxious to get to the dining room to see who was there.

When asked by Nadia if they preferred dining by themselves or with others, Lauren quickly answered. "Oh, with other people, for sure. It'll be more fun!"

"Guess she doesn't want to be alone with her dear old mother," Charlotte said, patting Lauren gently on the shoulder.

Nadia looked at them both, doing her best not to show how sad she thought their relationship must be, and, after an awkward pause, led them to a table in the center of the room. Charlotte took a cursory look around and then turned her attention to what really mattered: food. The menu was full of dishes that sounded tempting, but which she knew were merely creative names for vegetables, more vegetables and, if she were lucky, some broiled fish and a few concoctions made from soy.

She eyed the bowl of artfully arranged crudités in the center of the table. She was starving, but the assortment reminded her too much of "the alternatives" served at the country club back home, and she couldn't bring herself to touch even one miniature carrot. She had had her share at the club's Founder's Day Dinner several months before, choosing them instead over the fattening caviar on toast points, fois gras pyramids and other delicacies that were passed around. As it turned out, she should have allowed herself the pleasure of at least a few crab cakes.

She never did get to eat dinner. While she was struggling with controlling her appetite, her husband Jerry was having no difficulty whatsoever in satisfying his own -- and it wasn't crab cakes, caviar, or fois gras that were on his menu. His hors d'oeuvres selection that evening was a size eight designer gown, draped over the perfectly distributed and willing flesh of his best golfing buddy's wife. And while the event officially kicked off the spring social season, it also hastened the end to Charlotte's second marriage. After that, she would never be able to trust her husband again.

Charlotte watched Lauren stare at the menu, knowing her daughter was not at all interested in food.

"Shit!" Lauren said as she looked up and glanced around. "There's nobody here. Absolutely nobody!"

"Please don't use that language, Lauren."

Lauren began to pout, a favorite tactic that nearly always seduced her father, Matthew Fanning, so guilt ridden at having left when Lauren was less than two years old, he usually let her have her way. Charlotte, on the other hand, was in constant turmoil about giving in so her daughter would like her, or maintaining her ground and parenting in the way she was certain was right.

"There's nothing here I want," Lauren said.

"Well, I hope these next few days will get you into some better eating habits." She reached over and patted her daughter's arm. "If I can do it, you can do it."

Lauren was about to spout another four-letter word when her eyes widened. "OMG! Look who's over there!"

"Who, dear?"

"It's Mavis. Mavis Perkins!"

Charlotte turned. "Well, darned if it isn't," she whispered with an air of near reverence. "She's actually still quite beautiful, isn't she?"

"She sure is! And can you imagine, she's old -- maybe even older than you!"

"Certainly makes her a candidate for the Smithsonian, now doesn't it?"

"Mother, stop it! I wasn't trying to insult you. Mavis is one of the first super models ever. You must remember her."

"Of course, I remember her. She was on the cover of Vogue practically every month."

"I think I'll introduce myself. Maybe she'll give me some modeling advice." Lauren pushed herself away from the table. "Thank you, Jesus!"

Charlotte looked painfully at her daughter. "You know how it upsets me when you use the Lord's name in vain." Lauren's increasing use of profanity was troubling. Even though so many teenagers spoke that way, it wasn't something she wanted coming out of her own daughter's mouth. "And please sit down. I doubt very much that Mrs. Perkins wants to be bothered."

"Oh, Mother, you're always such a downer. And how do you know what she would want? You never made it as a model."

No, Charlotte thought, the hurt assaulting her again. I never became the model I once thought I would be. A little thing called pregnancy got in the way. She silently appraised the child whose entrance into the world had caused the end of her own career dreams. She sighed. She had embraced motherhood with everything she had to offer. It was moments like this however, when she felt all her efforts had been in vain. Lauren's behavior often made it so very hard to be her mother.

"You never approve of anything I want," Lauren said, dropping back down in her chair with a thud.

"It has nothing to do with you, Lauren. I just meant that Mavis Perkins is probably here to relax. I doubt she'll want to spend time giving career advice."

The exchange was interrupted by Nadia approaching the table with a guest in tow. "Ladies, may I introduce Toni Etheridge?"

Toni smiled warily at the pair.

"The Tanners," Nadia said, smiling at Charlotte and Lauren. "Charlotte and her daughter Lauren."

"Fanning," Lauren blurted out. "She's Tanner. I'm Fanning."

"I beg your pardon," Nadia said, her voice in total control." Mrs. Tanner and Ms. Fanning."

Charlotte smiled weakly. Dear God, she thought. Did she have to correct Madame Demidova? It was absolutely mortifying.

"May I join you?" Toni ventured warily.

"Of course," Charlotte said with a warm smile.

From her vantage point on the other side of the room, Mavis amused herself watching the interaction between Charlotte and Lauren. Thank God I never had children, she thought. I can barely tolerate an occasional forced conversation with those dreadful creatures fathered by my husband. At least I don't have to deal with them on a daily basis. I'd probably be found guilty of multiple homicides.

Mavis could only guess what mother and daughter were arguing about, but she suspected it might have something to do with food. Kind of like the Jack Sprat family, she laughed, pleased with her own little joke. Too bad. Before she starting stuffing herself, the mother must have been quite a beauty, a real Miss America type. And the daughter, well, she was already a stunner: great face, long and lean body, and that mane of hair! A few sessions with some hot Argan oil and it would be glorious -- almost as glorious as her own had been.

Mavis remembered when she, too, had had a fabulous head of hair -- so fabulous, in fact, Vogue had dedicated an entire section of their annual beauty issue to images of Mavis and her waves of thick, black hair as interpreted by Avedon, Weber and Skrebneski. Black Magic, they had called the issue, and almost every hair care company on earth came after her to be their signature model. But she didn't accept any of the offers, because she had bigger fish to fry. It was time for an easier life, a well-positioned husband with big bucks and a generous-sized pocket book, among other things.

Mavis sighed as she ran her fingers through her close-cropped hair, still a striking jet black, but now kept that way with the deft touch of the priciest colorist on Lake Shore Drive. She reached into her Prada clutch for a mirror and took a quick look. While probably not yet visible to others, the tiniest lines on her face screamed out at her, made all the more demanding due to the contrast between the whiteness of her skin and the blackness of her hair. Perhaps her colorist was right. Perhaps she should consider going gray -- silver-gray, of course. It would make an incredible statement and serve her ambition to become *the* older model in an ever-increasing sea of wannabes. There was no way she would ever do a dull-looking brown or, God forbid, the clawing auburn color she saw on too many women of a certain age. And as for blond, not a chance. It had become so painfully ordinary.

Mavis turned her attention to the vaguely familiar looking woman Nadia had just introduced to the angst-charged mother-daughter table. She toyed momentarily with the idea of walking over and joining them, but the thought of possibly attracting another irritating "hanger on" put the idea to rest. No. She would pass. Better simply to sit back and observe. She took a few slow sips of water and canvassed the rest of the room.

Toni tried to make pleasant dinner conversation with Charlotte and Lauren, but found it exceedingly difficult. The pair hardly spoke, and tension infused the fragranced air. Great, she thought. I'm doing my best to nurture the growing little soul inside of me, just left a suck-the-life-out-of-you-job and am blowing a small fortune to get myself together in this over-priced sleep-away camp for spoiled women, and what do I get as my reward -- Ms. Petulant Teen USA complete with her long-suffering stage mother. She looked around the room, hoping to come up with some graceful way to move to another table.

"Did you see her?" the daughter asked?

"See who?" Toni replied.

"Mavis. Mavis Perkins. Over there in the corner."

Toni turned. Yes, indeed. There she was, one of the fashion industry's all-time, most celebrated icons -- with the unmistakable hauteur very much intact. She's still beautiful, Toni thought, but I wonder if she's also still a bitch on wheels. Aside from her no doubt well-earned reputation, Toni had had her own personal encounter with the woman while a student at the Fashion Institute of Technology. She was working as an assistant at the then prominent designer Geoffrey Beene's fashion show. Mavis had practically bitten her head off for the mortal sin of putting the tights and shoes for two of her outfits in the same plastic accessory bag.

"What have you done, you stupid girl?" Mavis bellowed for the entire complement of back-stage staff to hear. "Any idiot knows that every outfit must be accessorized separately."

"I'm so sorry," Toni managed to blurt out, fighting back tears. She had worked so hard as a mender, go-for, and general all-around, un-paid slave on the project, and now, for this one tiny error, she was being humiliated in front of everyone.

"'Sorry' doesn't cut it. They should never let any of you amateurs anywhere near a production like this. Can't they afford real help?" Mavis glared at Toni. "I'll have to speak to Geoffrey about this. Surely he can do better. Now get out of my way." She stormed off, parting a sea of open-mouthed onlookers.

"You've been 'Mavised'" her classmate Kevin Gavelli announced, coming to her side and affectionately putting his arm around her. "Don't let it bother you. She's suuuuuch a bitch." He delivered the pronouncement with what Toni would come to know as his signature drama, sending the entire group into spasms of laughter and initiating a relationship that quickly grew to best-friend status.

"Well, it certainly is Mavis Perkins," Toni acknowledged. "I met her once, years ago." Part of her wanted to tell her tablemates what a horror La Perkins was, but decided gossiping -- about this bitch in particular -- would not be prudent.

"You did? How? Lauren sat forward eagerly in her chair. "I'm dying to meet her!"

Hmm. "Well, it was actually a very brief exchange. At a fashion show."

"You saw her walk the runway?" Lauren asked, showing real enthusiasm for the first time since arriving at Lavender Lane. "Was she wonderful?"

"I recall she was...how shall I put it? Quite something."

Nadia stood near the door and slowly surveyed the dining room. She took a deep, satisfied breath. The first night was always a little tentative, but the guests seemed to be settling in nicely.

She glanced at Phoebe, who was waiting for her at the small side table they shared each evening. Nadia thought about that day nearly twenty years before at a tony Beverly Hills hair salon where she had seen Phoebe, then the salon's receptionist, diffuse a sticky situation between two demanding guests. Tall and fair with glowing British skin and the right demeanor, Nadia knew Phoebe had exactly the patrician looks and diplomatic skills needed to assist her at her then recently-opened spa.

"But my appointment with Horst was for 3 o'clock," a middle-aged socialite had pouted through doctor-plumped and Chanel stained lips when a rival of hers had shown up and somehow snagged the slot with the salon's celebrity hair stylist.

Taking the woman by the arm and gently coaxing her away from the front desk, Phoebe cooed in her ear, "I'm actually soooo pleased the appointment times got mixed up. Now you can experience the di-vine Giancarlo."

"Giancarlo!" the woman enthused. "But isn't he at Le Petite Salon on Canon? I've been trying to get an appointment with him for ages."

"Well, it hasn't been announced yet, but he's joining us here at Tiberius. I'm expecting him at any second."

The woman's eyes widened as best they could, considering the same doctor who had plumped her lips had also lifted her lids, leaving her with a look of perpetual surprise.

"We haven't booked any appointments for him this afternoon, but I know he'll be thrilled to have you as his very first client."

And as if on cue, the door opened and in strode a tall, good looking man with a tan that was a bit too deep, jeans that were beyond tight-fitting, and a torso-hugging black shirt that showed he had used his gym membership to good advantage.

"Ah, Giancarlo. Welcome!" Phoebe said with a big smile.

That earned her kisses on both cheeks.

"Grazie, cara... and who is this lovely creature I am having the pleasure of looking at?" he said, drenching the client in a wash of sexual promise both he and Phoebe knew would never be realized.

"This is Mrs. Hutchins and it would be incredible if you would fashion one of those amazing up-sweeps only you can do. She's going to a party at Lynda Rizzoli's tonight," Phoebe said, referencing a coveted invitation to the home of one of Southern California's most influential philanthropists.

"Oh, could you?" Evangeline Hutchins gushed, casting an eye at her rival, who was too busy enjoying her own image in the mirror while Horst was working his signature brand of middle-aged magic. She turned back to Giancarlo. "That would be so...so magnifico!"

"Ah, the signora speaks Italian!" Giancarlo said. *"Va bene!"* He took Mrs. Hutchins by the arm and escorted her to the chair that would be his seat of power going forward.

Phoebe smiled with self-satisfaction. The scheme had worked out beautifully. When she had seen the mix-up on the appointment calendar, she recommended that Giancarlo be brought in a day earlier than planned.

The hair stylists, as it turned out, were long-time friends, and had feigned the rivalry with a wink and subsequent pockets full of generous tips from clients whose disposable incomes easily topped what some beleaguered municipalities had in their coffers.

Phoebe's brilliant handling of the situation was all Nadia Demidova needed to witness: the woman had exactly the skills and demeanor needed to deal with the spa's difficult guests. Phoebe had become irreplaceable over the years -- a trusted right hand on whom she could always count. A meaningful reward was long overdue.

Nadia always looked forward to their daily dinner, a relaxed way to review the day's happenings and discuss plans for the next. But as much as she wanted to join Phoebe as usual, Nadia was not able to manage it. She was simply too tired. Fatigue had been tormenting her all day.

When she saw Nadia approaching, Phoebe smiled warmly. It pleased her that Nadia chose to have their dinners together. The meal was always pleasant, and the business talk productive. Tonight however, she feared it might not go as smoothly, because tonight, she planned to breach a subject that had been gnawing at her for some time.

"Phoebe, dear," Nadia said, leaning over to rest her hand on the table. "I'm afraid we'll have to skip dinner, this evening."

"Oh..." Phoebe took care not to display her disappointment.

"I'm feeling a bit fatigued and I think I'd best have something light sent up and get a good night's sleep. Tomorrow, as you know, is a full day."

Like all the days weren't full. Phoebe had finally worked up the courage to have the discussion, and now this.

"Yes, of course, but there is something I wanted to speak to you about."

"I'm sure whatever it is can wait until the morning," Nadia said quietly. "Enjoy your dinner and we'll talk tomorrow."

"Yes. Tomorrow." She gave Nadia her best smile. "I hope you have a good night's rest."

Phoebe watched intently as Nadia made her way to the door, stopping briefly at a few of the tables to chat with guests.

Bloody Hell! Of all nights. Phoebe's temples began to throb. While she was chomping at the bit to have the long-overdue conversation, Phoebe sincerely hoped Nadia was all right. She loved and respected her and would never forget that it was Nadia who had given her the opportunity to stay in the United States after her American pilot boyfriend had re-located her from London and then reneged on his promise of marriage.

When Nadia offered her the position at the Lavender Lane, she leaped at the opportunity. That had been more than twenty years ago and although Phoebe would always be grateful, she often found herself feeling resentful as well. It was a twenty-four-hour-a-day commitment, and although she was paid a respectable salary and had pleasant enough living quarters, it was a confining life and with all she had contributed, Phoebe felt she deserved more -- not only a bigger salary, but a respectable piece of the action. The thought had recently gnawed at her to the point she could think of little else. Lavender Lane had become her home and she needed insurance for her future. If she wasn't going to have the conversation tonight, she'd bloody well have it the next day.

Chapter Four

The relentless ringing of tower bells assaulted Toni's ears as she pressed through the night. She tried not to step on the lifeless bodies of tiny sparrows crowding the path in front of her, but was not successful, and waves of nausea coursed through her body. Angry lightning struck from the sky and dank rain came down in torrents. She had to find shelter -- and find it quickly. But as she moved forward, she slipped, ending up face down in a sea of slime. She was soaked to the quick and frantic.

"Get it off of me!" she screamed, sitting up with a start, her heart pounding wildly. She grabbed at the wet fabric that was pasted to her skin and wrenched it from her body -- but it wasn't slime-soaked clothing clinging to her, only perspiration-soaked sheets. The rain and lightning had stopped, and the dark had given way to morning light streaming through a large, picture window. There were no more dead birds littering a murky path and the tower bells had been replaced by the low, steady beep of an alarm. She shuddered with a huge sigh of relief. She was safe.

It was the same dream she'd had several times since finding out she was pregnant. The doctor had assured her that barring something quite out of the ordinary, she would definitely be able to carry to term. The miscarriage she had experienced a couple of years back was unfortunate, but if she took good care of herself, this time all should be fine.

Toni glanced at the clock. Nearly eight. She'd have to hurry to fit in breakfast, and a nutritious one at that. There was no question it was necessary. At least Lavender Lane didn't frown on coffee like most of the other spas. Even though she was told to drastically cut down her intake now, thank God she wasn't told she had to totally give it up. Her coffee addiction, another hazard of the retailing world, was deeply rooted.

She pulled on sweat pants and an oversized T-shirt, trying to remember the last time she had been to the gym. She wasn't in terrible shape, but hardly the same as when she worked her way through college by teaching Pilates. But that was some time ago and she needed to embrace who she was now. Everything she'd been reading told her so. And she owed that much to the little kumquat who had taken up residence in her belly.

■　　■　　■　　■　　■

By nine, Mavis had already had her tea -- Supreme Morning Blend, a delicious mix of Assam and Kenyan leaves which she had Fedexed regularly from Harrod's London Food Stalls. Not the mediocre stuff provided in the beverage basket. And forget that coffee/tea machine. She had no desire to play with it -- no matter how user-friendly it was supposed to be. At the price she was paying to be at Lavender Lane, she was not the least bit interested in do-it-yourself. She wanted breakfast brought to her room. The thought of having to look at all those women first thing, with their early-morning pusses, hair in need of a good stylist and dressed to the nines in those so-called designer velour running suits, made her want to upchuck.

The kitchen was prompt in sending her a pot of boiling water and a single poached egg in a cup. No whole grain toast. No fresh fruit. And certainly no oatmeal -- a carb catastrophe! This was her morning fare no matter where she was and she was not about to change it for anyone -- Madame Nadia Demidova included. She knew her own metabolism and what pleased it, the same way she knew her own body and from what or whom it derived the most pleasure.

By 9:30, Mavis was at her first appointment with the Hungarian Katrina, Lavender Lane's most sought-after facialist. Her fingers were absolutely magical! Mavis had tried to entice Katrina to move to Chicago, where she promised to install her in the city's most exclusive day spa and send the area's A-list socialites to her, but Katrina had not been at all tempted. A far cry from the gritty Jozsefvafos neighborhood in Budapest where she had grown up, Lavender Lane suited her just fine with its fresh air, wonderful work environment and generous tips.

While Mavis made looking great appear effortless, it was anything but. Albeit blessed with unquestionable natural beauty, expensive treatments of every sort -- short of invasive plastic surgery -- regularly contributed to her formidable freshness. She never, ever, faced the day without a generously brimmed hat and layers of La Mer's SPF 50. Three times a year, there were Juvaderm shots to plump up the lines around her nose and mouth and Botox injections to smooth out the furrows on her brow. She also underwent monthly glycolic acid face washes, bi-weekly facials, weekly manicures and pedicures and twice-weekly hair appointments with color touch-ups the nano-second one gray hair manifested.

And then there was Mavis's most costly self-indulgence of all -- a daily visit from Ingrid, Chicago's most sought-after masseuse. It was to Ingrid's ministrations, along with the liters of pricey French mineral water she consumed daily, that she attributed her body's ability to fend off the dreaded cellulite that seemed to attack the thighs of most women -- and which only she, in all of America, seemed to know how to pronounce the proper French way: cell-u-leet, *mes petites*. *Mon Dieu* - never, ever cell-u-light!

Being at Lavender Lane, with all the personal services she needed merely yards away, made the whole beautification process so much more convenient, and convenience was something Mavis had learned long ago made life much more pleasurable. Moreover, the spa provided the utmost in specialized beauty treatments, such as slimming hydrotherapy baths, detoxifying herbal wraps and marine algae-infused scalp treatments -- not to mention Lavender Lane's divine signature Rejuvenating Quince face and body treatments.

Mavis closed her eyes as the aesthetician placed a warm, lavender-scented cloth across her lids and tucked the herb-saturated fabric of the thermal wrap securely around her body. Bound up like a newly draped mummy, it wasn't her favorite treatment, but it did help to extract trouble-making toxins. With the way she had been putting the booze away lately, she feared even having Ingrid attend to her daily wasn't going to completely fend off bumpy arms, lumpy thighs and other joys of encroaching age.

■   ■   ■   ■   ■

Charlotte awoke without an alarm. She rarely needed one. The stretch of time without benefit of eating was all her body required to greet the day. Her obsession with food started during her first marriage and intensified during her second. She initially lusted for candy and sweets and then went on to crave bread and pasta, fatty cheeses and butter-drenched rice. Her weight gain over the years was easily explained: she simply ate too much of the wrong foods and did so with great gusto. Moreover, she had totally given up on exercise. She hated it.

"Lauren, honey," she called out to the other side of the room. "Are you awake?" She hoped Lauren would join her for a healthful breakfast, one from which they both would benefit. But Lauren did not reply. "Lauren?" she called again. *She must have gone for a run. Wish I had the tiniest bit of her discipline!*

But she didn't. A day of rigorous exercise and measured portions of food stretched ominously in front of her, and Charlotte felt as though she were going to the guillotine.

■   ■   ■   ■   ■

Lauren picked up speed along the jogging trail that traced the perimeter of Lavender Lane. It was invigorating to be out in the fresh air and, she had to admit, it was much prettier than her usual Dallas run. She liked all the exotic flowers and odd-shaped trees. It sure beat having to look at the dumb houses in her stupid, so-called upscale Hodges Hollow neighborhood with all the phony-looking trees they had planted by illegal immigrants. She didn't see any illegals here, and the trees all looked real.

She rounded the corner behind the gymnasium and couldn't help but laugh, thinking of Charlotte inside huffing and puffing. It didn't much matter how much exercise her mother did. She'd stuff her mouth anyway and gain it all back. That fat was sooooo disgusting.

She picked up more speed. It was never, ever, going to happen to her -- no fat, no cellulite -- no way. She ran past the Olympic-sized pool and the smaller exercise pool. There was no one in sight. What's the matter with these women anyway? Afraid the pool will wash off all that hair dye?

She ran even faster, sure she would burn more calories before noon than most of the women at Lavender Lane would manage in ten days -- and certainly more than her mother. She was so busy enjoying her own little observation at her mother's expense, she didn't notice the path in front of her suddenly dropping off. With her next step she jolted forward and, in an instant, was on the pebbled ground. "Shit!" she screamed as she reached for her ankle. It had twisted sharply.

"Are you all right?"

Lauren hated the idea of someone seeing her down on the ground in a heap, but when she looked up, she was almost glad she had fallen. Smiling at her was a really cute guy, tall and blond and great looking in his tennis whites. He might even have been one of the guys she'd seen sprinting across the field the day before.

"Greg's the name. Helping gorgeous women in distress is my game," he said grinning. "When I'm not teaching tennis, that is." He reached out his hand to Lauren.

Lauren allowed herself to be pulled up, tracing the contours of Greg's tall, athletic body in the process. She brushed the soil from her shorts, then gave him her best smile. "Thanks. Thanks so much."

"No problem. How is your ankle?"

"Hurts a little," she said, moving her foot from side to side. "But I think it's OK."

"These trails can be tricky. What you need is a guide." He smiled boyishly but looked her directly in the eyes.

Lauren decided he was about twenty or twenty-one. She also decided he might make getting through the next totally boring ten days bearable.

"My name's Lauren, Lauren Fanning. And I'm jail bait. Do you think you can handle it?" She tilted her head and practically purred the words, letting her tongue rim the circumference of her full, well-glossed lips.

Greg's mouth dropped open, but he recovered quickly. Lauren could tell she had surprised him with the boldness of her remark. She could also tell he liked what he'd heard. And even as she was thinking of the next totally outrageous thing to say, Lauren was also thinking of ways she would successfully escape from the watchful eyes of her no doubt sex-starved mother.

■　　■　　■　　■　　■

Walking to the gym, Toni was filled with anticipation. It was as though she were going to meet a lover she hadn't seen for a long time. Would it live up to her expectations and be as good as it always had been? Would she be able to coax her body into nearly-forgotten postures and routines? And would working out still give her that feeling of satisfaction and accomplishment she had always experienced? She hoped so, because now it was more important than ever to be fit and in shape with a body that was the best it could be to prepare her to be the best mother she could be.

Once through the doors, her anxiety dissipated. The gym was bright and sunny and light years away from some of the dark basements where she had taught while working her way through college. It was enclosed on three sides by filtered glass and on the fourth with mirrors, and there were terra cotta-potted flowering cacti and lush desert palms sprinkled throughout. Every vantage point offered a wonderful view of the valley and all the exercise stations were equipped with personal monitors, earphones and bottles of chilled spring water.

Several women were in the throes of various workouts. One fit-looking guest in her late twenties was using the Nautilus, well-honed muscles expanding and contracting in labored rhythm under her skimpy, black and white two-piece Spandex. She was killing it! Next to her on shiny chrome

Stairmaster machines were two plus-sized, middle-aged women with large gold earrings and big, frosted hair. They were wearing matching bright fuchsia sweatshirts and pants, and they breathed heavily in unison as they struggled through their paces. Toni smiled. They had a long way to go.

A woman on a treadmill on the other side of the room caught her eye. Overweight and bulging out of her white Donna Karan exercise suit, the curly, blonde ponytail on the back of her head bobbed rhythmically as she concentrated on an iPad perched in front of her. On closer inspection, Toni saw that it was Charlotte Tanner, her tablemate from dinner the night before.

"Hi! How's it going?" she asked.

"OK, I guess," Charlotte chirped.

Toni hopped on the treadmill next to her and poked a couple of spots on the panel, attacking it with true New York impatience. After a few frustrating moments, she finally succeeded in activating the machine at a snail's pace.

She turned to face Charlotte, smiling at her small victory. "As you can probably tell, patience is not my strong suit, and to be honest, I haven't been on one of these things for quite some time."

"Well, you're certainly one up on me. At least you've been on one. This is my first time."

"First time? Well, you'll get the hang of it. As for me, I'm totally out of practice. Used to do five miles every day before work began leaving me no time for anything else."

"Five miles every day!" Charlotte said, slowing down to a complete standstill. "Can't imagine!" She tucked her iPad under her arm. "What kind of work do you do, Toni? I never did ask you last night."

"Did. Not doing it anymore. Designer sportswear buyer at Gillam's Fifth Avenue. Just left my job."

"Gillam's. Oh, that's exciting! I love to go there when I'm in New York, not that it's all that often. Why would you ever want to leave such an exciting job?"

Toni punched up the speed a bit more, wondering how much personal information to reveal. She wasn't about to talk about her pregnancy. This woman was a stranger, after all, and she wasn't ready to answer questions about who the father is and how she would handle it all as a single mother and on and on. She frankly didn't know herself. Plus, there was the fact she was still in the first trimester and everything was frankly iffy. She would keep it all about her work.

"My job was exciting, all right," she said a bit out of breath. "If you can call eight-day weeks, zero social life, never being able to get away for a vacation, a windowless office the size of a mouse hole complete with a resident rodent, exciting." She paused. "And, oh, lest I forget -- a bitchy boss to round it all out!"

Even talking about work agitated her. She slowed her speed a bit.

"Oh, dear!" Charlotte said. "Was it really that bad?"

"Trust me. It was," Toni nodded.

"That's too awful, but I'd still love to hear about it."

Toni and looked at Charlotte's sweet face. It had "good soul" written all over it. "How about this? Let's have a go at the treadmill for twenty more minutes and then we can have one of those yummy green juices and I'll tell you all about it."

Charlotte scrunched up her nose. "I don't think I can get one of those things down this chubby throat of mine." She shook her head vigorously. "They look absolutely repulsive."

Truth was, Toni, too, was not looking forward to trying the stuff -- a blend of spinach, kale, beets, watercress and celery -- but everything she read in the spa workbook was convincing: weight-controlling fiber, detoxifying chlorophyll, anti-aging antioxidants. All conspiring to make her fit for what was ahead, and to provide nourishment for the kumquat.

"Well, "Toni said, "looks like you didn't do your homework."

"Homework?" Charlotte asked.

"You know -- the workbook. You did get one, didn't you?"

"I must confess, I did," Charlotte said. "But when I had the choice of reading the latest Nicholas Sparks novel or plowing through that thing, you know which one won out." She shook her head. "Guess I'm still a die-hard romantic, even after two failed marriages." She inched up the speed ever so slightly. "Maybe you can give me the Cliff Notes."

"I'll see what I can do," Toni said. "You'll get to hear about my job and the glories of green juice, but in return, you'll have to let me in on some of your secrets!"

"You may have to book out for the day."

Toni laughed. "See you in twenty…" She wondered how she would ever be able to explain to Charlotte the love/hate relationship she had had with her job. How she went from graduating from FIT and thinking that being in the fashion industry would be a slice of heaven, to working in the training squad at Bloomingdales and eventually making it to sportswear buyer. And how, after her stint at Bloomie's, she took a great offer to be Gilliam's Designer Sportswear Buyer, only to find that when she got to Nirvana, it was basically going to Hell, just in better clothing.

Memories of frantic calls because merchandise hadn't arrived in time for the expensive ads in the Sunday papers, meetings that were called by the Divisional Merchandising Manager when they were told everyone would be working Sundays from Black Friday until well into the new year. And then there was the uplifting news that there would be no wage increases for the fiscal year, and once again the fiscal year following. Toni recalled the announcement informing an already overworked staff about Gilliam's decision to no longer take on student interns, the drones who did so much of the grunt work. Could they have made it any more difficult for her to do her job?

Could she possibly reveal more and tell her about how she broke down crying uncontrollably at a colleague's baby shower, not quite understanding why until some difficult sessions with a therapist helped her realize that after her earlier miscarriage, she had been suppressing her desire to have children, sublimating it under her demanding career?

"Wherever do they get these gorgeous boys?" Toni asked, when they were at the café, staring at glasses of juice set in front of them by an attractive young man. "Your daughter will have a ball here!"

"Exactly what I'm afraid of."

Uh, oh, Toni thought, as she fingered her glass filled with sludge that was more brown than green. Better not to go there. "Well, shall we give this stuff a try?"

"Don't know if I can get it down," Charlotte said.

"Be brave. It's only veggies. How bad can it be?"

Charlotte took a swig, and gagged. "Bad," she said as she took a fast gulp of water. "Really bad!"

It was Toni's turn. She brought the glass to her mouth and took a sip. "Beyond bad!" she blurted out, quickly following suit with water.

"Ok. So much for that stuff! Toni said laughing. "I promise not to proselytize anymore about the virtues of green juices. I'll segue to the work drama.

Omitting her crying jag at the baby shower, Toni went on to tell Charlotte about the rigors of retail life and how the idea of leaving her job had been brewing for some time. "Gillam's ate up my life," she said. "The hours were horrible. I never had time to get things done for myself or go to the gym or get to the theater before the curtain went up. Except for my nearest and dearest Kevin, my friends have all but given up on me. When I had a date for dinner, I'd have to call at the last minute to explain that something had come up and I couldn't get out of the office. And when I got a rare day off, I was so exhausted I stayed in bed and ate junk food. Hence this state-of-the-art body." She grabbed at the modest roll of flesh perched on top of her waistline. "Lady Gaga does not look to me as a role model!"

Charlotte laughed. "Honey, that ain't nothin'! She grabbed her upper arm flab. "When I lift my arms, these things flap so hard I would surely take flight -- if only I had the energy to lift off."

What started as giggles quickly graduated to full-strength belly laughs. Toni and Charlotte laughed to the point where they both started gasping for air, prompting one of the handsome young staffers to come check on them.

"Oh, we're fine," Charlotte assured him in between howls.

"Yes, we are," Toni concurred, then proceeded to laugh even harder.

"If you need anything," the beautiful young man said, "be sure to let me know." He gave them a gorgeous smile and walked away.

"Now what do you think he meant by that?" Toni asked.

"You are a naughty girl," Charlotte said, and they both broke up again. You'll never know how naughty, Toni thought as she eyed the server's cute behind. *Damn hormones again.* "Can't remember the last time I laughed so much," she said when they finally calmed down. "Let's have more of it this week!"

"For sure," Charlotte said. "But now, please, go on about that job."

Toni took another drink of water. She couldn't tell her the whole story without telling her about the baby shower and she wasn't ready to share everything at this point, and probably not at any other point while at Lavender Lane.

"Simple, really. One day I woke up and I knew it was the day I was going to resign. I simply didn't want to do it anymore. Not for one more hour, one more day, one more minute. I got myself dressed for work, walked into my bitch-of-a-boss's office and resigned. And frankly, she wasn't surprised. Guess I had been wearing my stress on my face for some time. I was always going to fix my situation tomorrow, or next week, or the week after that. When I finally did it, gotta tell you, it was a huge relief.

" It all sounds so dreadful I will never shop at Gillam's again!" Charlotte said indignantly. "Not even online!"

"I assure you it was dreadful. On-line shopping has really thrown a wrench into the retail business. The hours were getting longer, the pressure greater, and the rewards fewer. And my so-called office was a claustrophobe's idea of extreme punishment. I looked old and tired with colorless skin and dull-looking hair and my body was a total disaster. How did I ever let this happen? Was this going to be it for me? No husband, no children. There had to be more to life than this. I had even started fantasizing what they would put on my gravestone when I died a premature death slumped over my shithouse of a desk: *She was the Designer Sportswear Buyer at Gilliam's Fifth Avenue. Big Fucking Deal.*

Charlotte winced at the language. "Well, you look fine right now," she said. "Even glowing."

Glowing? She'd heard that said about pregnant women so many times.

"Even if it was as awful as you say," she said, still with a hint of envy, "it still seems interesting to me. I never had a real job. Got married straight out of school. And then got married again. I always thought having a career -- especially in the fashion business -- would be amazing." She looked down for a moment and dabbed at the corner of her eye. "I know it's hard to believe, seeing me now, but there was a time I wanted to be a model."

Toni looked at Charlotte's still-lovely face with her creamy skin, small, straight nose and cornflower blue eyes which were quickly filling up with tears. She touched Charlotte's hand. "It's not hard to believe at all."

"That's so sweet of you to say." Charlotte dabbed at her eyes again. "I gave up on my own modeling ambitions years ago. Now it's my daughter who wants to be a model. But that's another story."

And a difficult one to boot, Toni thought. "She's certainly pretty enough."

"Thanks. But she's also a very smart girl and I think she'd be much better off doing something else."

"From what I've seen of some models, I'd have to agree with you."

"Oh...maybe you could talk to her."

Toni didn't welcome that opportunity. The girl might be pretty, but judging from dinner the previous evening, being pleasant was not one of her strong points.

"I'm certainly no authority."

"Do you think Mavis Perkins would talk to Lauren? Last night you mentioned you'd met her. Did you ever work with her?"

"In a manner of speaking, when I was in college. But I doubt very much she'd remember me."

"Well, it was a thought," Charlotte said. "Thanks, anyway. I'll try to find some opportunity to chat with her myself."

Toni wondered how welcoming Mavis would be to an overweight housewife from Dallas with a petulant teenage daughter who harbored modeling ambitions, but she didn't want to be a downer.

"Give it a shot," she said to Charlotte, forcing sunshine into her voice. "You never know until you try." She paused for a moment. "You know, I've spent all this time trashing the job which gave me enough money to come here in the first place, and I really want to know more about you. For starters, you were reading The Wall Street Journal on your iPad. Now don't expect me to buy your 'I'm just a little 'ole housewife' routine!" She gave Charlotte a playful nudge.

"You are too funny," Charlotte said. "I guess you'll have to have dinner with me tonight to hear all my secrets." She gave Toni a little poke. "And I suspect you've got some secrets of your own you are dying to share with me!"

Toni felt a twinge in her stomach. *Indeed…*

"But right now," Charlotte continued, "I'm off to a massage and then I'm going to try the Jacuzzi. After all, if I'm going to starve myself, I deserve a little reward -- don't ya think?"

Toni watched Charlotte leave. She was easy to talk to and clearly in need of a friend, but even as she was thinking that, she realized it had been a very long time since she had indulged in delicious, soul-satisfying girl talk. Perhaps she, too, was in need of a friend as well.

Chapter Five

Mavis let the generous-sized bath towel slip from her still enviable body. The towel formed a graceful, peach mound as it fell to the gleaming cream-colored tile floor. The lighting was warm and low and the seductive melodies of Rimsky-Korsakov's Scheherazade streamed softly from unseen speakers. She breathed in the lavender-infused air and let the sensuous surroundings envelop her. It was four-thirty, and she had been looking forward to this private time all day. She should be safe, at least for fifteen minutes or so. Most of the others were probably on the massage tables, trying to relax while practiced fingers explored their tense bodies, priming them for a quiet dinner and an even quieter evening. Mavis preferred her massages at night, when she could totally let go and prepare for a good night's sleep.

She stepped down into the bubbling, warm water of the Jacuzzi and looked at her reflection in the mirrored wall a few feet away. She had posed for an ad for outrageously expensive Italian bath salts when she was a young model. "Bring out your own Venus," the tagline had read, with a nod to Botticelli. Well, she still looked damned good. Maybe when she was ready, she would get in touch with the company and see if they wanted to reprise the campaign.

She waded slowly to the other side of the pool, allowing the delicious, warm water to swirl around her body, then slid down and situated herself on the bench. The water from four strategically placed jets flirted brazenly with her, tantalizing her to move closer. She closed her eyes and slowly rode the wave, arching her body forward, helping the flow to find its target. But then the waters played with her, receding for a maddening beat, only to come forward again. She continued moving toward the source, heightening her pleasure with each shift. She turned and leaned back against the side of the pool, closed her eyes and languorously stretched her arms out along the perimeter. She adjusted her position, and a soft moan escaped from her throat. It would be mere seconds...

"May I join you?"

"What?" Mavis grunted. Her eyes flew open. *I don't believe this!* She watched as a plump woman in what, she had to admit, was a rather attractive deep violet, strategically draped bathing suit, stepped down into the Jacuzzi. *Well, at least she has the sense not to wear some bright colored thing that calls attention to all the wrong places -- not that there are any right places on that body!*

Mavis moved away from the jet. She tried to place the woman, then realized she was the senior half of the mother-daughter duo she had seen the previous night in the dining room. "Of course, you may," she said, as pleasantly as she could. *Of course I don't mind your ruining the moment for me.*

"Thank you. It will be nice to have some time to chat with you," the woman said.

Nice, my ass. A chat is hardly what I need right now.

"My name's Charlotte. Charlotte Tanner."

Mavis nodded. "A pleasure. I'm Mavis Perkins."

"Yes, I know. I recognized you. My daughter and I saw you in the dining room last night. She knew all about you and, of course, I remember when you were on all those magazine covers." Charlotte smiled sweetly. "You haven't changed a bit."

Mavis studied the woman, wondering how someone with such a pretty face had allowed herself to put on so much weight. It would be a damn shame if the same thing happened to her kid. "You're very kind to say that. Thank you." Mavis slid her body down more deeply into the water.

"Unfortunately, we all do change. Isn't it why we're all here, after all, to fight that change?"

"Well, as you can see, I've got a lot of fighting to do," Charlotte said, laughing nervously at her own expense.

Mavis liked such self-awareness. It appealed to a rarely evidenced generous side of her nature. "You really don't have so much to do. A little dieting and exercise, perhaps."

Charlotte slid down into the water as well and sat on the bench. "Unfortunately, my relationship with food is not a good one." She sighed deeply. "It's completely taken over my life."

Mavis cupped some water in her hands and splashed it on her face. It was apparent the Jacuzzi would not have the opportunity to deliver its usual satisfactions that day. She'd have to wait until later to take care of her very special needs.

She gave Charlotte one of her most practiced smiles, the kind she had delivered on cue for adoring cameras for so many years. "I guess I've been lucky, never having to diet."

"You can't imagine how lucky!"

Mavis smiled. "I noticed your daughter is very thin."

"Yes, she is."

"Beautiful girl. It doesn't look as though she has a problem with food."

"I wish that were the case. Truth is she does have a problem -- the opposite one from mine. She doesn't like to eat at all."

Mavis thought for a moment. "Well, that's certainly not good, but she could put her thin body and good looks to excellent use as a model." Mavis laughed to herself as she remembered growing up skinny in Kensington, a tough, blue collar Philadelphia neighborhood with no taste for aesthetics, whatsoever.

As a youngster, Mavis had been odd-looking, with very white skin, a rather mature face and too much unruly black hair. She looked nothing like the other girls her age, who had already begun to develop breasts. She was way too flat chested to suit the tastes of the local bullies, who regularly targeted her with their under-aged, beer-infused taunts. But those bullies, rather than instilling fear, had inadvertently helped Mavis build resilience, prompting her to resolve that one day she would have the upper hand. None of them, of course, knew how nature would ultimately take Mavis's side, and not only would she fill out in all the right places, she would go on to use her unusual and startling looks to become one of the world's most famous and successful models.

Mavis thought about Lauren and what a privileged upbringing she must have. The girl surely never has to worry about bullies of any kind at the pricey private school she no doubt attends. *I may just have to help her toughen up.*

"From what I saw of your daughter from a distance," she continued, "she's a natural."

"She'd be absolutely thrilled to hear you say that, but I'm not so sure it's a good idea."

"Why not? Modeling can be very, very lucrative."

"But the life. Aren't there lots of men and drugs and fast living?" Charlotte blanched. "Oh, I'm sorry. I didn't mean to insinuate..."

"I'm sure you didn't dear," Mavis said, trying to sound sincere. "And don't believe everything you hear. There are a lot of very nice, normal girls living terrific lives as models. You travel, meet all the right people. You can really do well. I certainly did." Mavis extended her long legs and kicked the water in front of her, raising a froth of bubbles and barely missing Charlotte's generous left thigh. "So, where is that lovely daughter of yours anyway?"

"Oh, she's off on her own. Doesn't want to hang around with her dear old mother. She said something about a tennis lesson."

"Tennis. How lovely." Greg. Of course. Mavis knew, first hand, how adept that young tennis pro was in finding his way around other places besides the court. She wondered how long it would take him to find his way around Lauren's lovely young body.

"I'm sure she's having a splendid day, whatever she's doing. Lavender Lane has so much to offer." Mavis stood slowly, not bothering to wrap herself in the towel which was within easy reach.

"Oh, my," Charlotte gushed. "You look exactly like you did in that ad! Shorter hair, of course."

"So nice of you to remember. It was quite some time ago."

"Will we see you at dinner? You can join our table," Charlotte offered eagerly.

Hmmm. One never knows. Might be interesting. An idea of what could be a most interesting project, highlighting her own beauty of course, already beginning to germinate. "Why, what a lovely invitation," Mavis said, finally wrapping herself with the towel as she glided slowly toward the stairs on the opposite side of the room. "All right, then. See you at dinner. About seven."

"Wonderful!"

Yes, I'll see you and that beautiful daughter of yours this evening. In the meantime, you can have these miraculous waters all to yourself, but I doubt you would have the foggiest notion of some of the more pleasurable things they can do for you.

■　　■　　■　　■　　■

By four o'clock, Nadia found it necessary to lie down. It had been a full day, like most days when Lavender Lane was totally booked, and that, thankfully, had been the case almost from the beginning. She remembered the first season well and how worried she'd been the spa wouldn't take off and she'd be in debt to the bank for the rest of her life. It was hard to believe it had been twenty-five years ago.

Twenty-five years! There should probably be some kind of anniversary celebration, but she was too fatigued to even think about it. At this particular moment, she was so tired she didn't think she would even be able to make it down to dinner. She hated missing her time with Phoebe two nights in a row. She also hated missing the opportunity to stop by the guests' tables to show her personal interest. Her attentions made the women feel important, and that, she had learned, was a form of pampering each and every one of them craved, and, at the prices she charged, felt they so richly deserved.

She laid down on the embroidered Chinese silk brocade spread that had graced her bed for decades. Persimmon red and ornate, it was always a special comfort to her, and so unlike anything else at Lavender Lane, a veritable bastion of natural color and soothing calm. The bed covering, created for her by the old wardrobe mistress at the Ballets Russes, was one of the few vestiges of a life gone by. The company's babushka had made it from material left over from their sumptuous production of Petrouchka. Nadia stroked the fabric lightly, letting her fingers experience their own fading memories as they traced the raised stitching of the once magnificent cloth.

Bars of Stravinsky's strident music filtered through her head. She flexed her ankles and sighed. Decades ago, her life had been so different. Nadia had toured from city to city, obsessed with the excellence of her own body. Now her geography was Lavender Lane, and her mission, other people's bodies; but she had done well, and there was much to be said for that. Her only real regret was the person who should have been so present in her life had never been able to see her there, had never known pride in what she had accomplished. Nor, for that matter, had she been able to take pride in the triumphs and joys in his life.

Nadia shifted to her side and gratefully closed her eyes, pulling the bedspread over her still-clothed body. Thinking about him and about her plan both electrified and terrified her and made it necessary to lie down in the middle of the day, leaving little doubt in her mind: the check-up she had been planning to have had better be sooner, rather than later.

She felt a chill but did not have the wherewithal to get up and adjust the air conditioning, choosing instead to wrap herself more tightly in the bedspread. Yes, she thought, opening her eyes. She planned to accomplish two missions when she made it into Los Angeles. After the appointment with her lawyer, she would definitely see Dr. Brendel.

Comfortable with her plan, Nadia closed her eyes again and allowed herself the tonic of drifting off to sleep.

.   .   .   .   .

Salmon steamed en croute with Herbs de Provence, tiny new potatoes drizzled with fragrant extra-virgin olive oil, freshly-picked green peas laced with flavorful pearl onions. Eleanor Franklin allowed herself a faint smile. Even though she wasn't in the mood to eat, she had to admit it was a spectacularly elegant room service offering. Regardless of its low-fat content and meager calorie count, not only was the dinner highly nutritious, it could have held its own against similar fare at any four-star restaurant. She had to hand it to her friend Nadia. The woman was a pro.

In earlier years, when the pounds crept up, Eleanor would escape to Lavender Lane for a ten-day session and, without ever feeling deprived, emerge looking and feeling light years better. But maintaining slender, youthful looks had become more and more difficult of late, and no number of spa visits or mega-watt dosages of the most efficacious Franklin Nutritionals formulas had been able to stave off the inevitable hallmarks of time. She was looking every bit her fifty-three years, and then some. Her chin length, dark blonde hair was coming across dull and matronly and her skin was not faring well. Lines were cropping up around her mouth and giving her brows a furrowed look, and it was becoming increasingly difficult to cover the discoloration that had taken residence under her eyes.

In addition to her regular presence as a nutrition expert in a variety of women's magazines, and in the Tweets and Facebook and Instagram posts her PR girl so dutifully churned out, she was often quoted in the financial press and featured as a guest on CNBC and CNN financial shows. Her visibility had been good for the company's stock, but the fact she was looking so awful lately spelled looming disaster.

She had hoped to avoid plastic surgery, but ultimately it had not been possible. She didn't need any detractors on her board to tell her what was so obvious: The company was selling youth and vigor and even though she was hardly ancient, she no longer represented Franklin Nutritionals in the way she should. She knew they wanted to replace her. Worse, she also knew that Albert Macklin, the CFO whom her husband had gifted with stock when the company went public, owned enough to garner support and swing the vote against her. Formerly an ally, he was currently in the clutches of one of Franklin Nutritionals' pretty and ambitious young lab associates who saw herself as the company's next spokesperson, and who had no desire to wait until Dr. Franklin exited on her own terms. An aging, widowed accountant, Albert was easy prey. Loyalty to his late patron's wife was less urgent then firm, twenty-eight-year-old breasts and a mouth which knew how to do a lot more than talk about the benefits of Selenium, Vitamin D3 and Probiotics.

Eleanor was determined not to be pushed out of her own company, and although she had always vowed she would never submit to the knife, what she saw in the mirror had been a powerful impetus to contact Beverly Hill's pre-eminent plastic surgeon. Dr. Kashani had assuaged her fears and assured her he had "done" many, if not most of Hollywood's aging stars and notable philanthropists. Eleanor had nothing to fear. On the contrary, she had much to look forward to -- years of looking refreshed, younger and at the top of her game. What he had delivered however, was what she had, indeed, feared most.

She didn't want to think about it anymore at the moment. Tomorrow and another day of worrying would come soon enough. For now, she would lie down and enjoy the oblivion one of her little white tablets blessedly delivered. She reached into her handbag and retrieved a generous-sized bottle of Ambien. She quickly washed one pill down with mineral water, wheeled the room service cart into the hallway and hung the "Do-not-Disturb" sign on her door knob. Oblivion would be most welcome.

Chapter Six

Phoebe surveyed the packed dining room, savoring the bountiful cast of colorful characters much more than the exquisitely prepared, aromatic tarragon chicken sitting untouched in front of her. The guests were animated and happy and seemed glad to be there in a stew of female companionship, sharing confidences and shedding pounds. She had to hand it to Nadia. Lavender Lane was *the* place to come -- but then again, Phoebe had helped make it so. Soon she would share more meaningfully in its success. She was nervous about speaking to Nadia, but was determined to do it now, over dinner, this very evening.

She looked at her watch. Twenty minutes past eight. It was not like Nadia to be so late. She was about to signal the waiter to take her food back and put it under the warmer, when one of the staff approached.

"Yes? What is it?"

"Ms. Bancroft, Madame Demidova asked me to tell you that she's a bit tired this evening and won't be able to join you for dinner."

"Oh, dear." *Again?* "Is anything wrong?"

"She did sound somewhat fatigued, but I think she's OK. She said not to worry. And to be sure to look after the guests."

"The guests, of course. Always her first concern." Phoebe gave the young woman her most practiced smile. "Madame Demidova is definitely working too hard. We'll just have to do our best to help her out a bit more, now won't we, dear?"

"Absolustely," the young woman said with near reverence. She, like most of the staff, held Nadia Demidova in great esteem.

Damn it to Hell! Phoebe fumed to herself, trying her best to keep the smile on her face. I need to get this conversation with Nadia over with or I will absolutely burst. She gritted her teeth, frustration winning the battle over her waning smile. I suppose now it will have to wait another day.

"Can I do anything for you Miss Bancroft?" the young woman asked earnestly.

"Excuse me?" Phoebe was so absorbed in her own thoughts she hadn't been aware the help was still standing there.

"Do you need anything?"

"Oh, no. Thank you for bringing me the message."

"No problem, Miss Bancroft. Any time."

Phoebe returned her attention to the cooling food in front of her. She poked her fork around the perimeter of the still moist chicken breast and then jabbed at its center, releasing a stream of fragrant juices.

Damn it! I was so ready to get this over with tonight. She let herself brood, for a moment, then slid her fork to the edge of the chicken, eased off a generous piece and deposited it in her mouth. I've waited nearly twenty years to get what should be mine, so I suppose one more day won't make much of a bloody difference.

■　　■　　■　　■　　■

One day had made all the difference however, at the table near the tall cactus at the far side of the room. The two women seated there, who had barely known one another twenty-four hours before, had clearly bonded and were careening with laughter.

"I wish you could have seen some of the women in my investment club," Charlotte said, trying not to laugh. "Remember those old women who did a calendar a few years back -- The Beardstown Ladies? They were a bunch of spring chickens compared to the old cluckers in my group!"

"Lots of old dames have plenty of money," Toni said. "You should see them when they come to the store, all decked out. They spend a fortune on the most ridiculous things, like five hundred-dollar scarves and three-thousand-dollar handbags, not to mention outrageously priced costume jewelry. Who in their right mind lays out two thou for fake stones?"

"The Texas crowd spends even more!" Charlotte countered. "You know, everything's bigger in Texas. Well," she said devilishly, "almost everything." She paused. "Oh, dear. Did I actually say that?"

Charlotte's feigned prudishness set Toni off again, and they both got to laughing so hard they didn't even see Lauren approaching.

"Mother," Lauren said through clenched teeth, leaning down to whisper in Charlotte's ear. "I could hear you out in the hallway. It's disgusting. The whole place is staring at you."

"Are they now? Well, I do believe most of them are too busy staring at the pathetic little wads of tofu on their plates, wishing some genie would come along and turn them into juicy, medium-rare Big Macs."

"With fries," Toni piped in, covering her mouth to stifle yet another outburst. "Lots of fries."

"And double chocolate milkshakes to wash it all down!" Charlotte added.

Lauren shook her head. "Is food the only thing you ever think about, Mother?"

"Aren't you joining us for dinner, Lauren?" Toni quickly asked, hoping to ease the tension.

Lauren didn't respond. Her attention had been diverted elsewhere. Mavis Perkins was gliding regally toward their table. She approached and put her hand on Charlotte's shoulder, her freshly manicured fingers pressing down as though greeting a dear, old friend. "You ladies were having so much fun, I thought I'd come join you."

"That would be lovely," Charlotte said, glancing at Toni. "Wouldn't it?"

"Lovely," Toni replied. *Just lovely.*

Mavis had already slid into the chair next to Charlotte. "I don't think I've had the pleasure," she said, extending her hand across the table.

"Toni Etheridge."

"Mavis Perkins."

Toni did her best to smile politely.

Mavis returned her own saccharin version of a smile and then turned her attention to the still standing Lauren. "And who is this beauteous young creature?" she asked, smiling at Lauren.

Charlotte was clearly pleased at the compliment. "This is..."

"Lauren. Lauren Fanning," Lauren blurted out, interrupting her mother's introduction.

"You must be Charlotte's daughter, of course. I can see the resemblance."

Lauren smiled wanly.

"Won't you be joining us for dinner, Lauren?" Mavis inquired.

"Actually, I came by to tell my mother that I'm going out for pizza." She drew the word out slowly, clearly trying to annoy Charlotte.

"And who is providing this fabulous, balanced meal?" Charlotte asked.

"The tennis instructor. Greg"

"Really?" Mavis asked, eyebrow in full arch.

"Oh, he's cute!" Toni exclaimed. "I'm going to book a lesson with him.

Charlotte looked up at her daughter. "How old is Greg?"

"What difference does it make?"

"He's probably too old for you, that's the difference."

"He's about twenty, I guess."

"Twenty!" Charlotte exclaimed.

"Oh, let the kid go," Mavis said. "God knows, if you can't have fun when you're young, when can you? Don't you agree, Toni?" Mavis looked Toni pointedly in the eye, urging her to complicity, but Toni said nothing.

Charlotte thought for a moment then reluctantly gave her blessing.

As Lauren turned to leave, she quietly spun back around and mouthed a silent "thank you" to Mavis. Mavis smiled back at her -- barely a full smile, but one which made Lauren feel she had received a very special favor.

"Well, ladies," Mavis said. "I think I'll call it a night. Got to get that beauty rest, *n'est-ce pas?*"

"*Bien sûr,*" Toni answered easily, then continued sipping her mineral water.

"Aren't you going to have dinner?" Charlotte asked Mavis.

"I ate a little something before. Don't want to overdo, you know."

"Of course not," Charlotte said, quickly putting down her fork.

"Enjoy your meal," Mavis said. "Ta-Ta…"

Ta-Ta and good riddance, Toni thought as she watched her walk away. "The woman is a certified bitch."

"Really? I haven't seen that side of her, but I supposed I'm naive. Heavens knows, I've been fooled before."

"Really? Care to talk about it?"

"Are you sure you want to hear? It's not a pretty tale."

"I'm from New York City. I ride the subway. I even read The New York Post, on occasion. Nothing shocks me!"

Charlotte looked away for a moment, then back at Toni. "Well, all right then." She took a deep breath. "It was at the Spring Gala, at our country club, about this time last year. It's the highlight of the season, you know, and I had been looking forward to it for weeks. I was going to be such a lovely party! The night was so beautiful and Jerry looked so handsome in his Hugo Boss tux. I had squeezed into my fabulous new midnight blue Oscar. I thought we were a great-looking couple."

"I bet you looked gorgeous! Blue is a perfect color for you with those beautiful eyes."

"You're sweet, Toni. Really… Anyway, Jerry was in unusually good spirits and the waiters kept our champagne glasses filled. The band was playing all those wonderful American standards…those great songs when music was actually music. You know, show tunes and ballads Sinatra and Tony Bennett used to sing."

"My faves, too," Toni nodded.

"I so wanted Jerry to be proud of me that evening, I practically existed on grapefruit and steamed vegetables for weeks so I would fit into my dress. What a waste of time and effort! I might as well have gone right on eating my Godiva, for all it had mattered to him. He had one drink with me, then made some excuse and disappeared."

"Oh, no!"

"I was so frustrated standing there alone that I lost my resolve. I gorged on every hors d'oeuvre that came my way -- especially the buttered toast points with smoked salmon and Beluga caviar."

"Hard to pass those up," Toni commiserated.

"After my third one, I decided I should freshen up before dinner. I figured the closest powder room would be over-the-top busy with those skinny belles primping before going in to dinner. I wasn't in the mood for all that happy chatter, lip glossing and hair spray so I decided to walk down to the ladies' room near the billiards parlor. Hardly anyone ever used it."

Charlotte stopped for a long drink of water.

"As I approached," she continued, "I heard moaning. I thought someone must be in pain, so I hurried, but when I opened the door, I couldn't believe what I saw: Jerry, my so-called husband, one of Dallas's most respected and successful dentists, was splayed out on the floor like some dumb penguin, and the whore Elaine, the wife of his best golfing buddy who was supposed to be my friend, was riding him for all she was worth. She was going at it so hard I thought for sure she would hit him with a horse crop any second."

"Wait! She had a horse crop?"

"No, but I'm sure she wished she had. Would have been perfect. If I hadn't been so angry, I would have sat down on the floor beside them and laughed, because the bitch had her ten-thousand-dollar, yellow polka-dot Carolina Herrera lifted up ever so neatly and pushed to the side so she wouldn't get it messed up."

"What a sight it must have been."

"Of course, my husband and his Jezebel were so involved in what they were doing, they didn't even notice me coming in."

"'Is Jerry baby happy now?' she asked him. And he was all over those surgically-amplified boobs of hers, but she was pushing his hand away. 'Sweetie,' she cooed at him. 'Gotta be careful of my dress.'"

"'But angel, Jerry grunted.'"

"Couldn't you just vomit, Toni? I mean…really?"

"Awful. It's like something out of a bad soap opera."

"It gets even better. She promised him he could have everything next time. Like she wasn't giving him everything already. I'll never forget the look on his face. He never looked so happy with me," Charlotte sighed.

"At any rate, she was moving even faster now and he was breathing even harder and those moans! Part of me wanted to scream at the top of my lungs, but another part of me wanted to stand there and take in the whole glorious spectacle."

"So, you really watched," Toni said.

"I did. 'Does Jerry baby want more?' The Whore of Dallas was drawling at him. He could barely get the word 'yes' out, he was breathing so hard. I half-wished he would have a heart attack."

Charlotte shook her head. "You know, after my first divorce, I felt like such a failure. It took lots and lots of soul searching, but I finally came to realize only God could help me. I started going to church and even with everything that's happened, I'm grateful to the Lord every day for my blessings. I know He doesn't condone violence or profanity, but I know He will forgive me for my language and for what I did. Jerry's betrayal was just too much."

"What language do you need to be forgiven for?" Toni asked. "I haven't heard anything all that awful."

"Oh, but it was. 'You son-of-a-bitch!' I screamed, at him. 'You God-damned son-of-a bitch!' Then before I even realized what I was doing, I walked over and kicked the bastard in the ribs. With my pointy-toed Jimmy Choo's."

"Ouch!" Toni grimaced. "Must have hurt -- big time."

"I sure hope so," Charlotte said. "Jerry let out a yell, and would you believe he actually had the audacity to look at me like I was the one doing something wrong?"

"'Does Jerry baby want more?' I said, kicking him again. The bitch, meanwhile, was quick to roll off him and adjust that expensive dress of hers. She tried to get up but I pushed her down hard. I was proud of myself at that moment. I didn't know I had it in me."

"I could have guessed you did," Toni said.

"But wait, it gets even better!" Charlotte said. "'Oh, is there a roach on your dress?' I asked her. 'Ooh...nasty. Wouldn't want it climbing up into that amazing cleavage of yours, now would we?' She screamed, looking for the bug, and then I immediately ground my shoe into those beautiful Herrera polka dots. 'Oh,' I said. 'My mistake. There was no roach. Just a piece of shit -- you!'"

"Go, Charlotte!" Toni cheered.

"'He's all yours, now,' I said to her. 'You can take him home with you tonight. I'm sure my husband and your husband will have lots more to talk about now than nine irons and sand traps.' Jerry, meanwhile, is lying there groaning. The only move he made was to put his pathetic thing back into his pants. 'And in case you're too stupid to read between the lines, Dr. Tanner,' I said, 'you can forget about coming home tonight or any other night. I know God will forgive me a second divorce. I'm absolutely sure he doesn't want me spending my life with you, such as sorry excuse for a man -- but I don't think He will forgive either of you for your adultery. You are both going to rot in Hell.'"

"OK, Charlotte!" Toni said. "That's my girl!"

"I stared at them for several moments, before leaving them there on the floor. Then I left to go and find her husband and give him the news that he was about to be identified as the cuckold, I think that's what it's called, in the scandal of the season at Dallas's most elite country club. And here I am, one year and a couple of lawyers later, about to become a divorcee yet again." She wiped a tear from the corner of her eye.

Toni studied her new friend for a moment. "You acted pretty ballsy in the country club bathroom. I've got good vibes about you, Ms. Charlotte. I think this little trip to Lavender Lane is going to change your life."

"That would be nice 'cause it sure could use some changing."

"Stick to your diet and get in some good exercise. You'll see."

"Sure hope you're right."

"I know I am. Now, my soon-to-be-slim-again friend, how about some fabulous dessert? Let's see," she said, picking up the menu card. "There's sugar free Jell-O, assorted flavors of fat-free ice milk and an absolutely sinful plate of finely separated South African Kiwi slices delicately sprinkled with a soupçon of Splenda."

∎　　∎　　∎　　∎　　∎

Lauren suspected when Greg invited her to go out for pizza, it was hardly food he had in mind. But as she ran along the dark, winding path leading to the tennis office, the unmistakable aroma of tomatoes, cheese and pepperoni wafted in her direction. In an instant, a wave of nausea overcame her. She winced as she stopped in her tracks, nearly stepping on some small desert creature which darted out in front of her.

Food -- she had conditioned her body to reject it at the first hint of temptation, never allowing it to make even the slightest positive impact. Not even pizza, which she had once loved, aroused a desire to eat. She had managed to skip the entirely natural process of enjoying food, food which motivated most people and controlled so many others, like all those fat women she saw around the malls -- fat women like her mother. Pizza. God. Big old Charlotte would love inhaling a few greasy slices. She would probably eat the whole friggin' pie.

She picked up her gait and moved swiftly down the path. As she approached the cabin, Lauren could see Greg's tall, lean form draped in the doorway. His shirt was off, and his sculpted chest gleamed, illuminated by the room's dim light. She was taken by the sight of him, and slowed her pace, wondering what the rest of the night would be like.

She watched as he put a cigarette to his lips. It surprised her to see him do that. Smoking was definitely not cool for an athlete, but when he struck a match and lit up, she recognized the distinct aroma. She had smelled pot plenty of times around school and at all the hottest parties, but she had never tried it. She had seen her friends high, and thought it was kind of scary. She never, ever wanted to be out of control.

But she had been tempted. Everyone always talked about how smoking pot made everything else a lot more fun -- especially sex. She wouldn't know about that either. She was way behind most of her friends in the boy department. Making out with Bobby Neihauser was all the experience she'd ever had, and it hadn't been all that great. He kept wanting Lauren to put his thing in her mouth, and she wasn't about to do it. Gross. No way. Lots of the guys had tried to get her to do the same thing, but what they had probably wasn't been much better than stupid Bobby Neihauser's.

Greg was cute, that's for sure. Even from several feet away she could see his warm, welcoming smile. Maybe his was different. She moved her eyes up along his body and caught his gaze. She moved closer and watched as he slowly breathed in the smoke and let it work its way to the base of his throat, savoring it for several seconds before letting go. They were face to face now and he reached out his hand and traced the outline of Lauren's full lips. She felt strange, kind of weak, but she wanted him to touch her.

He traced her mouth again and then probed her lips slightly. "We'll do pizza later," he murmured. "But first, I need to do this." He moved his index finger back past her lips and searched for her tongue. When he found it, he circled the tip, withdrawing his finger seconds later to put it in his own mouth. He sucked his finger slowly, groaning, clearly savoring the taste. "Yes, definitely lots better than pizza."

He licked his own lips equally as slowly and took another long drag. Then he offered the joint to Lauren. With some hesitation, she ventured forward and grasped his hand. It felt warm, alive, and she was sure he wanted her. She laughed to herself. Like what did she expect? She had practically promised her body to him that morning. Well, OK. She needed to try the sex thing some time. She should just go for it now. Greg was nothing like Bobby, or any of the other boys at school. He was different.

Lauren bent down and drew guardedly on the joint, taking in the barest amount. The smoke registered strangely in her mouth, and she felt awkward, but good.

"Breathe it in," Greg instructed. "You've got to let it get deep down inside of you."

She did as she was told and a tantalizing funnel of anticipation burrowed its way into her core. She wasn't sure if it was Greg's words, the drugs, his great body or a combination of all three, but she certainly felt something she had never felt before -- and she liked it. She liked it a lot.

"Again," Greg coached. "Inhale again but take more this time."

"I really shouldn't."

"Of course you should." Greg insisted. "Suck it in." He breathed heavily into his words, doing nothing to mask his own anticipation.

Once again, Lauren did as she was told and she got her reward. She felt an awakening throughout her entire body, like little rushes working their way through her legs up through her thighs and definitely in *there*. It was kind of cool. Cool? Shit. It was great! She looked up at Greg. What the Hell? She was feeling good -- really good -- and she had to start doing this kind of stuff sooner or later.

Sooner turned out to be right then, as Greg moved forward and pulled her towards him. He drew in deeply on the diminishing joint and then put it to her lips.

"One more drag, go on."

Lauren obeyed, once again, and as the magic heightened in her body, Greg moved his hands from her shoulders down her back and all along her torso. He grabbed hold of her rear. It felt great, but she stood motionless, not quite sure of what to do.

"You're a tad too skinny, but you've got a good ass."

"What? I didn't hear you." Lauren was lost in a newly found world.

"Not important," Greg managed to get out as he put his mouth on hers. He reached around and drew her body more tightly towards his.

She could feel her nipples standing up against the silky material of her bra. She wished she was not wearing it. Her entire body was flushed with heat. She wished she was not wearing anything at all.

Greg kept his hold on her with one hand and moved the other hand under her T-shirt. He worked his fingers around to the front and settled them on her breast. She quivered when they passed over her nipple.

"You like it, don't you?"

"I, uh...yes..."

"I knew you would, and judging from those ripe, little nipples of yours, I'd say we were ready to get down to some real business." He moved the other hand up to her waist, and then burrowed it down inside her skin-tight jeans.

"Help me out here, Lauren," he breathed. "Un-zip these damn things."

"OK," Lauren mumbled, surprised at her own slurred speech. She withdrew her arms from behind Greg's neck and grappled with her jeans. The zipper wouldn't budge though. She wasn't able to get her fingers to work effectively.

Greg began running his tongue down the side of her neck, and that made it worse. Worse, but better. She felt herself sliding, melting, descending into a world of sensations over which she had no control. She hated it, but loved it at the same time.

"Greg . . ."

His mouth covered hers and his hands grazed to the front of her jeans. "That's OK, princess," he whispered. "Glad you're feeling no pain." He nudged her hand out of the way and deftly worked open both the snap and the zipper of her jeans. Then he took her hand and put it under the elastic of his shorts.

Lauren began to move her hand down Greg's smooth, flat stomach. She felt a sizable bulge in the front of his shorts and froze. Jesus. Greg's was nothing like Bobby's. His thing was enormous.

"Don't be afraid. It won't bite you."

"But I've never..."

"Oh. Come on. You can handle it."

"No. You don't understand."

"Understand what?"

"I've never really..." she hesitated." I've never, you know, been with anyone."

"Shit!" Greg's head jerked back. "You gotta be kidding."

"No. No, I'm not."

"But the way you came on to me."

"All the girls must come on to you, Greg. You're fucking irresistible."

The voice came from the path behind the cabin. They quickly let go of one another, straining to make out the source.

"Irresistible or not, Greg, act a little responsibly." The voice moved closer. "This girl's a baby. And from what I can see here, it's not baby food you've been giving her."

Greg was the first to realize who it was. "For chrissakes!"

Mavis emerged from the shadows, her perfectly taut midriff set off by a black organza shirt tied up under her bosom, her porcelain skin glimmering in the ambient light.

"Oh my God!" Lauren shrieked. "Mavis!"

"You bet that sweet ass of yours it's Mavis. And make no mistake about it, my little chickadee, you'll thank me for this."

"Jesus Christ, Mavis. What the fuck are you doing here?"

"What I am doing here is looking after the welfare of a minor, and the daughter of a friend at that."

"Friend?" It took a second to sink in. "Oh God, you're not going to tell my mother, or anything!" Lauren blurted out. "She's on my case enough as it is." She reeled, almost losing her balance. "Shit. I've got to sit," she said, dropping to the ground.

Greg stepped away and looked down at her. "Is she really a friend of your mother's? Somehow, it doesn't compute."

"I don't know about real friends or anything," Lauren said, her mouth feeling like it was stuffed with cotton. "Like, they met yesterday."

"Now Greg," Mavis said, placing her hands on her waist and letting them slide down the silky fabric of her clinging black tights. "You know how quickly we females..." she hesitated, "bond in a special place like this."

Mavis breathed the word "bond" with an almost religious fervor. "So, lay off this kid."

"I didn't force her to come here, Mavis. She came because she wanted to." He turned to Lauren. "Didn't you, Lauren?"

"Well... yes."

"No matter. She shouldn't have come, and that's that. And by the by, Gregory, we won't be mentioning either your foolish attempts at child seduction or my fortuitous rescue of lovely young Lauren. I am not about to allow you to ruin her reputation, or we'll be discussing a whole lot more than you bargained for, like a little dope trafficking right here on the hallowed grounds of Lavender Lane."

"You know damned well I don't sell the stuff. Shit. It's hard enough to buy it for myself."

Mavis moved closer and glared at him. "I'm not convinced, Gregory, so I suggest you play it my way."

Greg glared back at her. "I thought I had," he blurted out. "All those times when we got it on."

Lauren shot forward, wide-eyed. "Greg? You...you and Mavis?"

Mavis bent down and caressed Lauren's hair, smoothing it back from her temple. "Don't be shocked, my pet. Greg does have his charm -- about eight solid inches of it. It's just that I don't think you're quite ready for what he has to offer. Not at fifteen. Much too young. You never know when you might need to prove you're still, how should we say, intact. Like when they want to marry you off to some holier-than-thou Bible thumper from one of the Lone Star State's best families. Why jeopardize that? And besides, if I am any judge -- and we know I am the best -- I am sure you have a marvelous future ahead of you, so why take the chance?"

Greg was incredulous. "You are an amazing piece of work, Mrs. Perkins."

"And you, my dear boy, are every grown-up girl's late-night dream, but for now, hands off the babies."

Mavis reached for Lauren's hand.

"Come on, my pet. It's time to go."

"Shit! I hate this," Lauren said, withholding her hand.

"You'll hate a lot more if you don't get out of here. Trust me. I know what's right for you."

Mavis reached for Lauren's hand again, and this time Lauren allowed it to be taken. Mavis pulled her up smartly.

"This is all too weird," Lauren said, tripping over her own feet. Mavis strengthened her grasp.

"There's nothing weird about it all, my dear. You have an itch and you need it scratched -- that's all. But this is neither the right time or place, or male, for that matter. So, let's get you back to the room safe and sound and no one will be the wiser for it." She turned to Greg and shot him an icy look. "Isn't that right, Gregory?"

"Oh, for sure, Mavis. For fucking sure."

Lauren stepped back and put her hand on Greg's arm. "I'm sorry."

"It's OK, Lauren. But don't be so quick to jump into her pool. You might find yourself drowning."

Mavis tugged on Lauren's arm and pulled her in the direction of the path. "That's enough philosophy for tonight, kiddies."

Lauren smiled weakly at Greg and then turned and allowed herself to be led away.

Chapter Seven

Toni charged into the dining room, eager to plunge into the day. She was energized from her foray back into exercising and she was so much more relaxed than she had when she arrived a little more than a day ago. The environment, the activities, the healthy food, and perhaps most of all the time she had spent with Charlotte, were invigorating. There was nothing like good old-fashioned girl talk to give a woman a boost, and Charlotte sure could tell a story. What a shit that husband of hers was. And a tasteless one, too. A bathroom floor at a country club! Could he be more disgusting?

She looked around the room. The tables were decorated with green centerpieces in honor of Saint Patrick's Day. Seeing tiny leprechauns everywhere made Toni smile and think about the promotions she was certain were in full frenzy at Gillam's. She breathed a huge sigh of relief. Happily, she no longer had to deal with those special events — for the immediate future, at least. As for her long-term future, she had so much to figure out.

She sat down and toyed with the leprechaun in the floral arrangement in the center of the table. It had been two weeks since she left her job, and she was finally beginning to fully comprehend the magnitude of what she had done: walked out on her hard-fought career -- a career with many highs and probably many more lows, but a career that was rewarding, overall. But as each day passed and her pregnancy held, she was more and more confident that she had made the right decision. A healthy pregnancy and the kind of stress she experienced on a daily basis were mutually exclusive. With her credentials and experience, she always would be able to get another job, but with the window on becoming a mother nearing a close, she was absolutely sure she had made the right choice.

"Good morning," Charlotte said, plopping down in the chair next to her. Charlotte eyed the small tray of mini gluten-free carrot muffins which had been placed on the table and scowled. "Why couldn't I have been born skinny instead of merely a plump, but devastatingly beautiful and, may I add, a natural blonde?" She toyed with the curly ponytail that skimmed her shoulder.

"'Devastatingly beautiful!' I like that, Charlotte. Nice self-esteem. I'm impressed."

"Don't be. Got it an hour ago at the 'Sense of Self' seminar."

Toni laughed. "So early? I have to hand it to you. I needed that extra hour of sleep. I'm only now starting to decompress."

"Well, whatever you're doing is working. You're still glowing!"

Glowing. There was that word again. Even though she wanted to, she couldn't share the information. She was just entering her tenth week, and besides, there was her somewhat unusual story. She did not care to be judged. Not that Charlotte would. She was so sweet -- but she *was* religious.

Toni gestured toward the iPad Charlotte had placed on the table. "Maybe if I hang around you long enough, some of your financial prowess will rub off on me. God knows, I could use it."

Charlotte grabbed a tiny muffin and ate it in one bite. "You never know, Antoinette," she said, licking her lips to capture every speck of muffin. "You know, I love your full name. It's so lovely. Does anyone ever call you Antoinette?"

"Not much anymore. Only my friend Kevin and..." Toni turned her head and looked off into the distance.

"Oh, dear. Have I said something to upset you?"

"No. It's just that it brings up memories."

"Care to talk about it?" Charlotte asked softly.

Toni's eyes welled up. "My fiancé Eddie used to call me by my full name."

"You were engaged?"

"Yes…almost," Toni said, brushing away a tear. "We fell in love as kids. While the other girls were collecting dolls and playing house, I preferred to be with Eddie, climbing trees and exploring the creek that ran along the back of the houses in our neighborhood. There was never any question about our getting married when we grew up. He even gave me a dime-store engagement ring when we were ten-years-old."

Toni laughed. "Said it was a down payment on the real thing he would get as soon as we grew up and he started earning money. I still have that ring…in a box with my grandmother's cameo."

"Eddie sounds adorable,' Charlotte said.

"He was," Toni said as a tear rolled down her face. "He absolutely was, but he never got the chance to earn the money and buy me the real thing. One night when we were sophomores in high school, Eddie and his friend Alex, who was always going to be Eddie's best man at our wedding, were in a head-on collision with an 18-wheeler. I was supposed to have gone with them but stayed home at the last minute to help my mother with some things around the house. Alex was driving and was seriously hurt, but he survived. Eddie was in the passenger seat and was killed instantly."

"Oh, Toni," Charlotte said, grasping her hand. "I am so, so sorry."

The tears flowed freely now and Toni struggled to regain her composure. "A big part of me died that day. Eddie and I were so completely bonded. It was years before I even went out on a date."

"I wondered why no one had scooped up someone as wonderful as you," Charlotte said. They looked at each other for a very long moment.

"I pretty much put all my energies in my career."

"What about now…now that you're taking a breather. There's gotta be someone terrific out there for you!"

She so wanted to tell Charlotte about Dan and the first pregnancy and Kevin and their crazy, unconventional decision, and the precious life that was growing inside her, but she didn't want to jinx herself. "Whether I'll connect again remains to be seen, I suppose." Toni smiled sadly, sure at this stage of her life and with the decision she had made, the proverbial man of her dreams was not to be. "At any rate, after I lost Eddie, I threw myself into exercise, and it served me well. I worked my way through college as a fitness instructor."

"Ah, ha!" Charlotte said. "That explains why you're so good at that stuff. Just looking at the gym makes me want to run. And I don't mean run a marathon! Guess you could see that yesterday."

Toni perked up. "I hope you can get into it. It's a great stress reliever. Wish I hadn't let it go when my job took over. It would have helped me cope."

"You make it sound so necessary," Charlotte said.

"It is, and I hope I can help you to learn to love it."

Charlotte laughed. "You've got your work cut out for you, girl!"

"Coffee, ladies?" A bouncy young waitress, brandishing two steaming carafes, approached the table.

"Yes, puleez. High-test." Charlotte barely gave the waitress time to finish pouring before she moved the cup to her lips.

"Me, too," Toni said. "Thanks. And if I could get a hard-boiled egg and whole grain toast quickly, that would be great."

"No problem." The waitress turned to Charlotte who had already popped another muffin into her mouth.

"She'll have the same," Toni said.

Charlotte puckered up and gave Toni her best Lauren-like pout.

"No time like the present, right?" Toni asked.

"Be back in a jif," the waitress said, as she turned and walked away.

"Great pout. Did you learn that from your daughter?" Toni asked, laughing.

"For sure," Charlotte said. "She's pretty much perfected it, don't you think? She shook her head. "Wish she'd come down to breakfast. My girl needs to start eating properly. She's way too thin."

"But she *is* very pretty."

"Yes, but I'm afraid her disposition isn't."

"I hadn't noticed."

"LOL, as the kids say!"

"Where is the lovely, young Ms. Lauren this morning? Getting her beauty sleep?"

"And more."

"Late night?"

"Not really. It was about eleven when she got in, but she didn't want to get up this morning, and it's not like her. Lauren's usually out running by six."

Toni stole a glance at her watch. "Damn. I can't wait for that egg." She grabbed a muffin and wrapped it in a napkin. "Got to get going or I'll be late for my class. Can I leave you here alone with all these muffins?"

"Not to worry. I'll do my best to restrain myself. And anyway, Mavis should be showing up any minute. She did say she would see us at breakfast. After all, she didn't even finish her dinner last night. She must be hungry by now!"

"I wouldn't worry about the nutritional needs of that one, my dear. I'm sure she's already eaten a generous serving of freshly-honed nails."

"You are wicked!"

"You have no idea!" Toni said, getting up from her chair. "Now for the treadmill, some yoga, a spinning class, and a two-hour Pilates. See ya!"

Charlotte watched Toni leave, and without thinking, reached for another muffin and put it to her lips. This time it was a large one, a mélange of pineapples and cherries and the flaky dough crumbled and fell to the table as though programmed to self-destruct at first contact with a hungry mouth. One large chunk dropped into her coffee cup and promptly began to decompose, rendering the contents undrinkable.

Guess the universe is trying to tell me something…

She shooed the crumbs away and fired up her iPad, making sure first that Madame Demidova was not in the room. She knew using "those machines" while at Lavender Lane was frowned upon. She clicked on The Wall Street Journal app to see if there was any relevant news. In addition to the $45,000 she had in the Dallas Savvy Gals Investment Club -- which, during the last four years of her membership had grown from an initial $15,000 -- she had an additional $450,000 invested in blue chips and mutual funds. But it was the $150,000 invested in some small start-ups and riskier stocks that got her juices going. Her soon-to-be-ex-husband Jerry had staked her to $100,000 a couple of years ago, saying it would provide something constructive to do, instead of eating. The money was hers to keep, no matter how high the total climbed. But now Charlotte understood it had really been his way to quell his conscience for the lack of attention he was paying to her. Had she known how their relationship would end, she sure would have asked for a heck of a lot more.

Thanks to a long bull run, both her individual portfolios and club account had grown handsomely. Jerry never asked her about her investing, or anything else for that matter, so she never bothered to tell him about her online trading account and the new issues and other speculative stocks she bought.

Charlotte loved sitting at the computer, buying and selling, making her money grow with the click of a mouse. It was really a form of legalized gambling and if Jerry had known how good she was at it, he probably would have been furious. It was supposed to be something to keep her busy, not an occupation. But so what? Her financial prowess gave her the satisfaction she lacked in every other aspect of her life.

She looked over the front page of The Journal, then turned to the "Money and Markets" section to scan for news about her core holdings.

She skimmed the usual stories of upcoming treasury auctions, earnings digests and insider trading until there, tucked in between rumors of another stock split for Microsoft and the latest misdeeds at a prominent Wall Street brokerage house, was an item she nearly missed: "Lincoln Labs Wins FDA Approval on New Depression Drug."

She lurched forward. "Lincoln Labs, a small bio-tech firm located in Bangor, Maine, has quietly developed a new approach to serotonin uptake that is bound to shake up the pharmaceutical industry. Phase III trials were successfully completed yesterday on Zeltor, and news of imminent FDA approval quickly began to spread. Speculation is gathering on a bidding war among the giants. Most likely to buy out the recently-taken-public firm is industry monolith Merck. Shares on the Nasdaq soared a record-breaking 30 points in the last hour of trading to close at 50."

"Oh-my-Go…," Charlotte breathed, stopping short of saying the word "God," which, in that context, was definitely contrary to her sincere religious beliefs. She tried doing some quick calculations in her head but she wasn't able to get the numbers to compute. She dipped into her bag and found a piece of scrap paper, then rummaged around for a pen. The best she could come up with was an eyebrow pencil. She ripped off the cap and quickly jotted down the numbers, barely visible in the soft, light brown cosmetic lead. 10,000 times 50 equals...No. it couldn't be. Equals...oh my God...500,000!

She had nearly forgotten about the Lincoln stock. The last time she checked, weeks ago, it was doing nicely and had gone up another 3 points. But 50! It was astounding. She had gotten really lucky late last year and was able to get in on the ground floor of the IPO, paying only $4 a share. If she were to sell today, she would make a $460,000 profit!

In addition to haranguing her about her weight, Jerry had often berated her for her lack of sustaining interests. Ha! Wouldn't he be surprised? All those hours spent poring over Value Line, Investors Business Daily and Morningstar reports, endless glaring at CNN Financial and CNBC, listening to every fund manager, analyst and long-winded guru and all the time she had spent surfing the web for every obscure financial site. And she, Charlotte, had come up with this winner all by herself. This was proof she could make things happen...proof she could succeed!

She leaned back and squared her shoulders. It had been so long since she genuinely felt positive, she had nearly forgotten what it was like. It felt good, darned good. She tucked the iPad under her arm, pushed her chair away from the table and resolutely stood up.

I can make the last half of the 9 o'clock aerobics class, she thought, and do the stretch class and the treadmill, and after that, Pilates, too! She strode away from the table, a long-overdue and very welcome confidence in her customarily defeated gait.

Chapter Eight

The shutters were closed, allowing only modest rays of light to suffuse the warm, intimate room. Mavis lay in wait, head resting on the small, soft pillow, lips moist and slightly apart. Screw those women. She didn't want to eat breakfast with them, or any other meal for that matter.

The slightest bit of guilt tainted the moment as she remembered she had promised to join Charlotte that morning. Well, all things considered, it could certainly wait until tomorrow.

She closed her eyes and allowed a delicious flood of anticipation to course through her body. Her breath quickened and she could feel her heart beating. The waiting was exquisite -- a familiar sensation that always visited her before such a meeting.

The woman approached, and Mavis readied herself for the pleasure she was sure would ensue. Her nostrils quivered at the first touch of the woman's fingers. She breathed in slowly, reveling in the sensuous, warm air around her, redolent of quince and lavender, and the fingers that danced on her skin with ease and grace. The fingers were well practiced. They moved lightly, deftly, but with sufficient pressure to ensure they would satisfy.

Mavis relaxed into willing receptivity. In many ways, she found a facial even more pleasurable than a full body massage. The intimacy was immediate, the terrain to be traversed was neatly circumscribed, and the knowledge of what the well-practiced touch could accomplish in the quest to keep her beauty intact made the exercise even more meaningful. Her looks were still her mantra, her most prized possession, her personal security in an insecure world and she would spend any amount of time, invest any sum of money, and endure any treatment -- short of the surgeon's scalpel -- to keep those looks in prime condition.

As she surrendered to the fragrant cleansing cream that gently nourished her already spotless face, Mavis thought about Lauren...the tall slim body, the elegant narrow hips, the small but exquisite breasts. The girl could have a great career, and it would serve both of them beautifully. "Oh dear. Am I hurting you, Mrs. Perkins?" Trudy, the aesthetician asked, alarmed this notoriously difficult client might find even a modicum of fault in her work.

"No. Continue, please," Mavis answered curtly, annoyed her nearly perfect state of reverie had been so unceremoniously interrupted. She moved her head a bit, giving Trudy additional pause. Mavis waited for the fingers to return, and when they did not do so instantaneously, she snapped open her eyes and found those of the nervous aesthetician looking directly into them.

"Is this a facial or a god-damned eye examination?" she barked.

Trudy jerked away, clearly stung.

"A fa..."

"I can assure you," Mavis said, abruptly cutting her off, "I have 20/20 vision, so there's absolutely no need for optometry."

"Of course not, Mrs. Perkins," Trudy said flinching. "I am so sorry,"

"Of course you are. Let's get on with it, then. If you can still manage, that is."

The woman stiffened, then smiled weakly and tentatively began to remove the cream from Mavis's face. Mavis closed her eyes and returned her thoughts to Lauren -- the age, the attitude, the bountiful hair and lovely, unspoiled face with the eyes of an angel and the mouth of a courtesan. What possibilities! She felt a rush of warm, moist air envelop her head and shoulders as tiny drops of water settled on her brow and upper lip. Trudy was steaming her face, opening the virtually non-existent pores to encourage detoxification.

Mavis grunted her approval, then settled in to pondering on what to do about Lauren. Should she make her move now, or should she wait? She wasn't quite sure, and that unnerved her. Certainty was practically her birthright. She always knew when to move on something. But this was different. There was too much at stake.

Trudy patted the excess moisture from Mavis's face and began to massage in Lavender Lane's signature Rejuvenating Quince Face Crème. Mavis drew in an extra breath. Alarmed, Trudy lifted her fingers again, afraid she had, once more, inadvertently hurt her client.

"No problem, Trudy," Mavis said, opening one eye and closing it just as quickly. She did not want any more of the woman's histrionics.

Trudy smiled nervously and continued her massage.

Mavis breathed in deeply, yet again. She liked the aroma and, even more, what the creme did for her skin. She went home with a half a dozen jars every time she visited. Why Nadia had never marketed the stuff outside of Lavender Lane was a mystery, but that was fine with her. Mavis wasn't ready for the entire world to learn of its miraculous benefits. Not yet.

Trudy passed an ionizer over Mavis' face to sanitize her skin, then dabbed on a freshener. She continued with a slathering of a thick, silky paste, slowly swirling it on Mavis's chin and cheeks and up through her temples to her forehead. When she was finished, she whispered to Mavis that the quince and papaya mask had been applied. She would leave her alone with it on for twenty minutes. Did she care for the mittens and booties?

Mavis detested the smell of papaya but would tolerate it because it did a hell of a job as an exfoliant. As for the mittens and booties, no way. Keeping your hands and feet in electrified hot socks and gloves might go a long way to making them smooth, but being confined like that was not for her. No, she would spend the next twenty minutes with feet, and especially hands, unfettered, machinating on the girl and all the extraordinary possibilities the future might hold.

Trudy quietly left the room, leaving the mask to do its good work -- and leaving Mavis to her own devices.

■　　■　　■　　■　　■

Lauren had never been in a sauna before, but she had heard it could help with weight loss, so she thought it was worth a try. She stretched out on the bottom bench, a large, peach towel under her slim thighs and torso. The air wafted gently over her body, soothing her with its unique, dry warmth and comforting her with the balm of fragrant eucalyptus. Being alone in the small, dimly lit cabin was fine with her. She didn't much feel like talking to anyone.

It was already mid-afternoon, and she had wasted most of the day. She had wanted to get out of bed early and go running, but there was no way she was going to budge an eyelid until after her mother had left the room. She was not about to answer any questions about the previous night or listen to any of her mother's advice about dating -- or, God forbid, discuss what was on the menu for breakfast and lunch.

Not today. No way. And, besides, she had a crummy headache. Staying in bed late wasn't a crime and skipping the run for one day wouldn't kill her. And as for marijuana, she would be skipping it permanently. It had been kind of fun, but it made her feel out of control, and she hated that.

Lauren stretched her arms out behind her head and yawned. *The night had sure been confusing. Greg was cute, and it felt good when he touched her -- but Mavis Perkins! What was that all about? Seemed like she was trying to protect her. Weird. Whatever. I still want to ask her about modeling. I may never get a chance like this again.*

Lauren closed her eyes and let the sauna's warmth envelop her. She tried to put the whole thing out of her head and had just begun to relax when she heard the door open. Shit. She liked having the place all to herself. Well, I can't stop anyone from coming in, but that doesn't mean I have to chat. Whoever they are, they can climb up to the top shelf and sweat their fat little ass off all by their lonesome. I couldn't care less. She turned her head, closed her eyes and laid perfectly still.

Mavis, a towel wrapped around her body, had opened the sauna door and quietly entered. She gazed down at the reclining beauty. Her hair was fanned out behind her head, and her flawless skin wore a faint flush from the heat. The girl's beauty was really beginning to ripen. The timing couldn't be more perfect to talk to her about the future.

She bent down, her towel brushing lightly against Lauren's body.

Lauren stirred and shot up, nearly knocking Mavis down in the process. "Mavis!" she screamed. "You scared me."

"Sorry, my dear. I didn't mean to."

"Well, you did," Lauren barked.

Mavis backed away and glared at Lauren. She paused for a moment, eyes blazing. "I don't especially like your tone of voice, Missy. I should think you would be a bit more grateful. After all, I did save you from near disaster last night."

Lauren reached for the towel she had hung on the adjacent wall and thrust it awkwardly in front of her chest.

"There's no need for modesty, my dear. If you want to be a model, you'll have to get used to prying eyes. It's part of the business."

Lauren relaxed her guard a bit and managed a smile. "How do you know I want to be a model?"

Mavis sat down on the bench and put her arm around Lauren's shoulder. "Your mother mentioned it."

"Really?"

"Yes, but I must tell you, she's not especially keen on it."

At that moment, the door opened, revealing a fully clothed and totally frazzled Charlotte. "And what is it I'm not especially keen on?" Charlotte was clearly not ready for a sauna in her turquoise blue warm-up suit and barely used Nikes. Perspiration rolled down her face.

"Mother! You're letting all the steam out!" Lauren screeched.

"Well, damn the hot air and pardon my language! I've been frantic looking all over the place for you. I thought you might have gone out running and gotten lost somewhere." She moved forward, dabbing her forehead with a tissue. "I'm relieved to see you're safe. Safe here with Mavis. Thank God."

"I can take care of myself, Mother. I'm not a child, you know. I am fifteen."

Mavis squeezed Lauren's shoulder and gave Charlotte one of her more practiced smiles. "She'll always be safe with me, Charlotte. You can be sure of that."

Charlotte was about to respond but before she could say anything, a scream from somewhere down the hall pierced the stillness in the air.

"Oh, dear," Charlotte gasped. "What was that?"

"I don't know," Mavis replied. "And frankly, I don't care. This place is supposed to be quiet."

Lauren jumped up. "Let's not just sit here," she said, adjusting the towel to completely cover herself. "Don't you want to see what's going on?"

"Not especially," Mavis sneered, leaning back against the honey-colored, cedar wall.

"I do!" Lauren said, eager for the opportunity to exit. She got up and bounded for the door, practically shoving her mother aside in the process.

"Mother," she said, pushing open the door.

"Well then, we'll see you later, Mavis," Charlotte said, as she followed Lauren into the hall.

"Yes. See you later," Mavis replied, studied smile intact.

Lauren knew the remark was directed at her. She also realized she should probably be nicer to someone who could be so helpful. Truth was, she wasn't really anxious to get involved with anyone who made her feel so uncomfortable, but after thinking about it for a moment, she realized she would be really stupid to screw up the chance of possibly getting help from Mavis. She turned, smiled and waved her would-be mentor a guarded goodbye. Mavis, of course, smiled back. It was all falling nicely into place.

Chapter Nine

The last scream came from the locker room, and it was one of many, the final domino to herald the news throughout every corner of the traditionally silent Lavender Lane. It had taken mere minutes to pass the unimaginable information through the entire work force, and less than half an hour to all of the guests.

Eleanor Franklin was the first to scream. She had been expected at Nadia's apartment for tea at 4 p.m. and arrived promptly. When Nadia didn't respond to several raps on the door, Eleanor pushed it open. For a number of seconds, she stood there motionless, gasping for breath, before any audible sound came from her throat. And then a low whimper rumbled and grew and took on power until her entire body was wrenched in its thrall.

Eleanor had been delighted that morning when Nadia called to invite her to her apartment suite for afternoon tea. Though she had sounded tired, she had also sounded happy and eager to spend some time with her old friend.

"I've located him, Eleanor. I've finally located him!"

"That's wonderful news! You must be thrilled."

"I am, but also very nervous. It has been a long, long journey. I'll tell you all about it this afternoon."

Eleanor had always liked visiting Nadia's apartment, with its French antiques and ballet memorabilia. Over the years, she and Nadia had met dozens of times, sharing freshly baked miniature scones or small, perfect cucumber sandwiches with fragrant, rich black tea served Russian style in generous sized glasses with cubes of sugar on the side. They would spend hours trading observations on world affairs, discussing books and the films Nadia barely got to see and, of course, praising the merits of nutritional supplements.

As the friendship deepened, they went on to share private thoughts and confidences, each coming to deeply value the other's friendship. Neither woman could count many close friends, and their yearly or sometimes twice-yearly fellowship worked to satisfy both of their marginal needs for female intimacy.

Nadia learned of Eleanor's early marriage to a fledgling pharmacy student, the tragedy of her husband's premature death at the age of forty and, of course, the fabulous success of Franklin Nutritionals, which he had founded and which Eleanor had gone on to so successfully shepherd.

Eleanor learned of Nadia's early work in ballet, her coming to America, her struggles to develop her new career and ultimately to create Lavender Lane. She also learned of Nadia's single most private struggle -- a story no one else but her attorney knew. Eleanor had considered it a privilege to be taken into Nadia's confidence in such an important way.

She had been cooped up for days and was glad to get out of her room, if only to go down the hall and around the corner to Nadia's apartment. She put on a full-length, silk jacquard caftan and draped a long, chiffon scarf over her head, wrapping it loosely across the lower half of her face. No one would pay her that much attention should they spot her. She would be just another client going from one end of the floor to the other. She could silently slip into Nadia's sitting room with no notice whatsoever.

But that hadn't proved to be the case. Phoebe, who had been close by, down the hall, was the first to reach the source of the scream, and soon she was joined by the guest in the nearby Field Mallow room, followed quickly by the chambermaid who had been turning down beds a few doors away.

Phoebe stood paralyzed as the small group watched the tableau in front of them. Eleanor, her face strangely distorted, was wailing uncontrollably and there, in front of a dark walnut Louis Seize table, with a Victorian tea service beautifully laid out, was Nadia Demidova, totally motionless, slumped in her chair, her head drooping lifelessly to the side.

Phoebe immediately grabbed her cell phone and connected with 911.

"Quickly, please," she whispered. "Lavender Lane. It's Madame Demidova. I am fearing the worst…"

Eleanor darted forward and shook her friend. "Nadia. Nadia dear. Please…"

But Nadia did not stir.

"Nadia," Eleanor cried out again and then collapsed to the floor, the scarf around her head dislodged in the process. She moved close and laid her head gently on Nadia's lap.

Additional guests and employees arrived to find the slumped-over, Nadia Demidova, with a strange-looking woman crying uncontrollably in her lap.

"My God, can you believe it?" one of the guests said too loudly. "I think it might actually be Eleanor Franklin!"

And then another, equally as loudly, "You mean the vitamin lady? Good Heavens! What's happened to her face?"

Then another, "Oh, dear. But what about our Madame Demidova? What's happened to her?"

Phoebe gently pushed her way through the small group. She smiled weakly at Eleanor then felt for Nadia's pulse. It was weak, but if the ambulance arrived promptly, she might make it.

The news began to travel, from floor to floor, from the main house to the pool, from the tennis courts to the gym, gathering with it fresh screams as it made its morbid rounds. Nadia Demidova had apparently had a heart attack and was either dead, or soon would be…and Eleanor Franklin, a prominent health and nutrition authority, as well as one of the country's most attractive and successful female CEOs, was a beauty no more. In the bastion of rejuvenation, preservation, and enduring good looks that was The Spa at Lavender Lane, which tragedy was the more difficult to accept?

For Phoebe, the answer was easy. If Madame Demidova were dead, that would be the insurmountable catastrophe. Love, admiration and respect notwithstanding, the death of Nadia Demidova now, before she had secured her financial stake in Lavender Lane and insured her future, was an unmitigated disaster. She knew she should take command, clear the room, get Eleanor out of the way, and attend to poor Nadia, but she was not able to think straight. She stood transfixed, unable to move, feeling the blood drain from her face and sensation leaving her body.

Toni had been nearby when the screaming began. When she arrived at Nadia's suite, she couldn't just stand there and watch. She had to do something. She was adept at handling difficult situations. Years of salvaging near disasters in the retail business had proven that. Poor Phoebe looked pathetic and was clearly in need of help. And that woman with her…wasn't she the vitamin queen Eleanor Franklin? She had seen her interviewed on The Closing Bell not that long ago. What in God's name had happened to her face? She looked absolutely bizarre.

She pushed past the several women who were gathered in the doorway and moved quickly ahead. "Ms. Bancroft," she asked softly, "is there a doctor on the premises?"

Phoebe looked at her with fearful eyes and managed a weak "no." "I called 911. I certainly hope they sent someone quickly."

"Ok good. Meanwhile, let me see if I can get a pulse. Hope it's not too late."

Toni walked over to Eleanor and gently coaxed her up from Nadia's lap. A chambermaid who had attended Eleanor during her many visits over the last fifteen years, quietly moved forward from the gathered crowd and helped her into a chair.

Toni knelt and reached for Nadia's wrist, but even in the reaching realized the effort would be useless. There was no sign of life. She shot Phoebe a look and discreetly shook her head "no."

Phoebe gasped, covering her mouth with a shaking hand. The on-looking women buzzed audibly.

"Ladies, please," Toni said, "please go on about your business while we wait for help."

"Is she dead?" one of the women called out. There was a collective gasp and the group's nervous chatter careened to an abrupt halt.

Toni looked directly at the insensitive woman. "I do think we should give Madame Demidova the dignity of not having everyone standing around gawking, don't you?" She asked the question as politely as she could. "Help is on the way."

"Of course," one of the guests called out.

"Prayers for our dear Madame Demidova," another said quietly.

The group quietly dispersed and Toni remained to stand vigil with the now softly weeping Eleanor and the silent Phoebe, whose face had drained of all color. No one spoke, choosing instead to be alone with her thoughts and to glance at the others from time to time for some measure of reassurance that she was not as solitary as she felt at this terrible moment.

A few minutes passed before the faint wail of a siren began to shatter the customary silence of late afternoon in the tranquil Palm Springs desert. The hawks and the owls, the moles and the rabbits, the saguaros and the palms were surely taking notice. The patron saint of the valley, the one to whom so many had turned to correct their misshapen bodies and to mend their troubled spirits, would reign no more. Nadia Demidova, the indomitable mistress of Lavender Lane, was gone.

Chapter Ten

"Toni, you were so very kind to me this afternoon. I don't know what I would have done had you not been there." Phoebe dabbed at her eyes with a lace-edged handkerchief, leaving an occasional drop or two to be wiped away.

"No thanks needed, Phoebe. I wish there might have been some way to help her."

"I can't believe she's left us…"

They were seated on the sofa in Phoebe's modest studio apartment, sharing a bottle of dry California white wine. It wasn't exactly spa fare, but it was blessedly right to ease the trauma of the day. The sun had long since set, and the heat of the desert day had given way to the cool breezes of the valley night.

Phoebe threw open the windows and the night air filled the room. It felt good -- a much-needed balm and life-affirming counterpoint to the day's events. She smiled at Toni. "I noticed you this morning at the Pilates studio. You looked splendid doing the routines. Awfully professional, I must say."

"Well, not quite. Not anymore, that is. Time was…but thanks for the compliment." Toni took a sip of her wine, clearly relishing its crisp taste, as well as its powers to soothe. "Good stuff," she said, realizing she should not be drinking at all. She would sip very, very slowly, and take in as little as possible.

"Yes," Phoebe sighed. "And never more welcome."

"Amen. You know, it's funny, because I noticed you at the studio, too. You weren't doing so badly yourself."

"That's very kind, Toni."

"No, really. I was going to come over and introduce myself, but you finished before I did and left pretty quickly."

"I had to get back to the office straightaway. I can only indulge myself so many minutes. Madame Demidova is... I mean was...always so kind in allowing me to use the facilities. I never tried to take advantage. At least, I don't think I did." Phoebe sniffled and then patted her reddened nose, tender from hours of crying, with her now well-used handkerchief.

"I'm sure you didn't take advantage at all, but you were lucky to have the privileges."

"Yes, indeed I was."

A thoughtful look crossed Toni's face. "What will happen to Lavender Lane now?"

Phoebe shook her head. "I really don't know."

"Won't you be running it?"

"That's the million-dollar question, as you Yanks would say. I would certainly like to."

"Who else is there? Did Madame Demidova have any children?"

"I doubt it, but God only knows. She was such a private person. Never spoke about any family, or much of anything personal, for that matter. All the years we were together, I knew her, but didn't, if you know what I mean."

Toni smiled in recognition. "Yes, I do know. I worked for someone like that once. Saw her every day for years but didn't know the first thing about her. But tell me about Eleanor Franklin? Did you know they were friends?"

"No, I didn't. Beyond the usual client rapport. I must say, I was absolutely astounded to see her there, and to see her face!"

"She was such an attractive woman," Toni said. "Should have left well enough alone."

"I her case, I would certainly agree, but most face lifts don't all turn out that badly. You would be surprised at the number of guests here at

Lavender Lane right now who have had work done." She smiled. "Don't get me wrong: I would never reveal any names. That would be beyond unethical."

"I'm glad to hear it, in the unlikely case I ever decide to do a little number on myself, and come here to hide."

"As long as I am at Lavender Lane, you will always be welcome here to hide, or otherwise. But I don't think you'll even have to contemplate a visit to the surgeon's office anytime soon."

"I hope you're right. I was an absolute disaster when I arrived, but these last couple of days have done wonders. I feel ten years younger. Madame Demidova certainly created a remarkable place."

"Yes," Phoebe sighed. "Without question, but I like to think I am somewhat responsible, as well." She regarded the surprised look on Toni's face. "I don't mean to take undo credit, but frankly, I helped her make Lavender Lane what it is. I have been her closest colleague for more than twenty years." Her words were stated as simple fact, with not a hint of rancor in her voice.

"Twenty years? I didn't know that."

"There would be no way you would."

"It would be wonderful if you could get a shot at owning Lavender Lane."

"There is certainly nothing I would like more. But there's not much chance of that. My expenses here have been minimal, and I do have some savings of course, but hardly enough to even allow myself to think about purchasing the place."

"You just never know what the future will bring," Toni said.

"I suppose you're right." Phoebe smiled wistfully and closed her eyes for a moment, luxuriating in the strong breeze that had wafted into the room. "I love the nights here." She rose from the sofa and drifted toward the window. "Look," she said gesturing for Toni to join her. "You can see the Big Dipper, the Little Dipper, Orion and all the others. Pretty soon, the stars will all be shining down on Madame Demidova." She pointed to the left. "Over there, at the foot of the mountain. That's where she'll be buried. Day after tomorrow."

"Did you make the arrangements?"

"After I collected myself -- with many thanks to you -- and after they finally took poor Madame Demidova away, I had a chat with Eleanor Franklin. She had finally gotten hold of herself and seemed intent on getting involved. Suggested that I call Madame Demidova's lawyer in Los Angeles, a Jake Meyers.

"I found it curious she knew the name, but she definitely did. She came with me to the office and we found his number in Madame Demidova's phone book. Dr. Franklin placed the call. As it turns out, she had only recently revised her will, so the lawyer had the information about Madame Demidova's wishes properly at hand. I'm told her instructions were that she be buried with a simple, private, graveside service right here on the property. I heard Dr. Franklin offer to take care of the arrangements, which presumably she has done."

"Other than yourself, who else will attend?"

"Dr. Franklin, of course, and this Mr. Meyers. And it seems there is someone who may be coming from the east coast, but she didn't elaborate."

"I'm sure all of this is very difficult for you, Phoebe, so if you need a friend, I'll be here at least until the end of next week -- assuming the spa remains open."

"Oh, it most definitely will stay open. Apparently, Madame Demidova had specified that, under no uncertain circumstances, should Lavender Lane close. She said she had faith in her staff to run it properly if she were sick or indisposed." Phoebe's voice faltered. "She said she had faith in me…"

She began to sob and Toni came to Phoebe's side and gently put her arm around her shoulder.

"Of course, she had faith in you. You'll do a wonderful job."

"But what if I don't get that chance? I have put my life in this place. What if, when Lavender Lane is sold, and the new owners don't wish to keep me on?"

"Maybe the new owners will be smart enough to realize they need you. Let's wait and see. In the meantime, what you need most is a good night's sleep. You've got a difficult few days ahead of you."

"You're right." She took Toni's hands in her own and smiled. "Again, Toni, I cannot thank you enough for your thoughtfulness."

"Don't worry," Toni said, injecting a note of cheerfulness. "You'll pay! For my next visit, I'll hit you up for free room and board."

"Then, I will just have to factor it into the budget," Phoebe said with a genuine smile.

After Toni left, Phoebe returned to the window and fixed her gaze on the spot near the mountains where Nadia Demidova would soon rest, watching over Lavender Lane in peace for all eternity while she, Phoebe Bancroft, although alive and well and with many productive years ahead of her, would be unable to rest or grieve or find a moment's peace until she was certain how her own future would unfold.

Part 2

Chapter Eleven

Peter Culvane admired the rich patina and clean lines of his Biedermeier credenza as he sipped coffee from an old mug. He certainly had access to the best china money could buy, but somehow coffee always tasted better in the chipped and discolored Stamford classic he had used since college days. He breathed in the aroma and smiled. He had brewed it himself, earlier that morning, from a blend of Sumatra, Java and Ethiopian beans gathered from various specialty importers in Boston. Not one to follow the crowd to Starbucks, or any other destination for that matter, he had prided himself, from an early age, on being self-assured and every inch his own man. This singular focus had served him well. A standout in debating competitions as an undergrad, as well as the lead runner on the track team, he continued on to Columbia, where he made Law Review. And it was his confident mindset which also fueled the extraordinary entrepreneurial success he went on to achieve in the tough, highly competitive world of mergers and acquisitions.

But these very same qualities had also assured his failure at marriage -- two times over. While he wasn't proud of his inability to make either of his marriages work, he was confident he could handle just about everything else. There were very few things that could throw him. This situation however, was different. It had grabbed him by the gut and left him stunned.

And yet, he had to admit, the news had not been totally unexpected. On a completely visceral level, he had almost always known -- an uncertainty, a faint longing, and now here it was, the most minute of feelings fully blown and totally realized. Here was irrefutable confirmation of all the simmering doubts and foreshadowing he had long endured.

He gazed out at the panoramic view of the historic Boston Harbor he had from his 37th floor office. It was a view which had always soothed him, helped him clear his mind, and helped him think strategically, but at that moment, the infinite ocean beyond the harbor seemed to mock him. Why couldn't he have found out sooner, years ago, when it might have meant something, made a difference? Why now, when it was abysmally too late?

Peter drew his fingers through a head of salt and pepper hair, no longer raven but still blessedly thick. He brushed away the strands that habitually fell in his eyes, favoring him with the look of enduring boyhood.

He had been the only one of four children to have black hair. His sister Margaret, the youngest, was a carrot top like their mother. His twin brothers Sean and Patrick, two years his junior, were dark blonde, mirroring their father's coloring. Growing up, Peter's siblings had always teased him about being the Black Sheep, the maverick who took after the part of the family descended from the Roman invaders of many centuries prior. He smiled at the thought of the large Culvane crew. They had all been together the previous evening for their annual St. Patrick's Day festivities -- all twenty-three members of their extended clan.

St. Patrick's Day rivaled Thanksgiving, Christmas and Easter on the list of favorite family holidays, as it was also his brothers' birthday. It was a long-standing Culvane tradition to eat a bit too much corned beef and cabbage, and drink a tad too much fine Irish stout. The festivities always gave his now seventy-five-year old mother another opportunity to reproach him for being the only Culvane who had not provided her with grandchildren.

"What in the world are you waiting for, Peter?" she would ask, with the slightest hint of a scowl on her still lovely face. "Time's a' fleeting."

"I know, Mom. I know," he would say, then craftily change the subject.

When the call came, he thought it might have been the opening foray to yet another high-profile business deal.

"Dr. Eleanor Franklin is on the phone for you, Mr. Culvane," his assistant informed him via the intercom.

"Franklin?"

"Yes…you know, the vitamin lady."

"Franklin Nutritionals, of course. Interesting. They're still privately held. Guess they're thinking merger. Or acquisition." He cleared his throat. "Put her through."

"Dr. Franklin, good morning. A pleasure to speak to you. What can I do for you?"

"Mr. Culvane?"

"Peter. Please call me Peter."

"Thank you, Peter."

Eleanor Franklin paused, for what seemed to Peter, an interminable amount of time.

"Peter, we do not know one another and honestly, even if we did, there would be no easy way to explain the reason for this call."

Strange way to begin a business conversation, Peter thought. "Go on, Dr. Franklin."

"Eleanor. Please call me Eleanor."

"Certainly… Eleanor."

"Late yesterday afternoon, I lost a very dear friend."

"So sorry for your loss. Losing someone close is never easy."

"My friend was someone I admired and respected a great deal." Her voice began to crack. "I'm so grateful she didn't suffer."

What the Hell does all of this have to do with a deal? Peter was growing impatient. He had an important meeting later that morning and needed to start preparing for it.

"My friend, Nadia Demidova…"

"Demidova. I know the name. Isn't she the woman from the spa -- the one in Palm Springs?"

"Yes, Lavender Lane."

"That's it. Lavender Lane." Peter had heard about the place from some of the women he dated. Alexis, in fact, the woman he was currently seeing, had been there just a couple of months before and had raved about how wonderful the place was. He recalled how she had described Nadia Demidova as being absolutely formidable.

"My condolences, Eleanor. Your friend had a fine reputation. Wonderful that you had a personal connection." He could hear Eleanor drawing in her breath, hesitating.

"My friend, Nadia, also had a connection to you."

"A connection to me?" Surely his women friends hadn't taken Nadia Demidova's valuable time to discuss their various levels of dismay with him, but then again, knowing Alexis, she just might have.

"Really? How so?"

"She was..."

Peter could hear Eleanor Franklin's breathing becoming more labored. She was struggling.

"She was," Eleanor cleared her throat. "Well, there's no other way to say this, Peter, so I'll come right out with it." Eleanor swallowed. "She was your mother."

Peter did not respond.

"Peter, did you hear me?"

He still did not respond.

"Are you all right?"

"Yes," he whispered, his voice barely audible. "I'm quite all right," he lied. *My mother?* He reeled, a tornado funneling through his abdomen. He lurched forward and jostled his coffee cup, spilling a good portion of the contents on his desk. "But I don't understand," he breathed, turning to grab a handkerchief from the breast pocket of the jacket draped around the back of his chair. He quickly stabbed at the liquid which was seeping onto several important papers.

My Mother. What in God's name was this woman talking about? This Nadia person could not possibly be his mother. He already had a mother - - a wonderful mother -- Mary Bernadette O'Brien Culvane, the woman who had bathed him and burped him and sung him to sleep. The woman to whom he had gone running when his world was all wrong, to whom he brought pride when school and sports afforded him a place to shine, to whom he crowed when he took the business world by storm and to whom he made excuses when both of his marriages failed. "I guess I couldn't settle for someone not as wonderful you, Mom," he would say to her.

But somehow, he knew it wasn't impossible that some woman he had never even seen, much less met -- some woman who had absolutely no connection whatsoever to his world, to his life, someone totally alien to him -- might actually be his mother. Maybe it was the secret glance his parents so often gave one another when he was young. Or the way his Aunt Kathleen always seemed to greet him a bit differently from the way she greeted his sister and brothers, giving him a little too much of herself in every hello and goodbye, as if trying to make up for the lack of something.

He had always experienced feelings of disquiet, separateness…an unspoken difference and indiscernible element he could never quite congeal in his conscious thoughts. And now, at forty-eight years of age, the effect had found its cause.

Hair had settled on Peter's forehead and he brushed it away, letting his hand linger while he collected his thoughts. "I must say, this is astonishing. Frankly, it's quite difficult to absorb."

"Certainly. I understand."

"What about my parents, the Culvane's… the people I've known and loved as my parents all these years?"

"Nadia told me they did not know her, nor she them. She had been assured they were a lovely couple who, at the time, were unable to have children of their own. The adoption was done through a private attorney in New York, and the records were sealed by the authorities."

"New York?"

"Yes. Manhattan. Apparently, that's where you were born. Nadia told me the story some time ago, and aside from her lawyer, I believe I am the only person to know it…until now, that is."

"This is all quite unbelievable," Peter said haltingly. "And the father?" He faltered. "My biological father?"

"Your father was a man with whom Nadia was in love when she was quite young. She had been a ballet dancer and he was a fellow dancer -- also Russian."

Russians…dancers, artists, free spirits -- not at all like the very traditional and wonderful people who had raised him! The Culvane's were devoted to God and family and solid American values. He adored them.

Eleanor sighed. "I'm sorry to say he deserted her. They had been touring the U.S., and when she was five months pregnant, he left her and returned to Moscow. Apparently, he already had a wife and a couple of children back home." She paused for a long moment. "I'm certain this must be an extraordinary shock."

"Shock doesn't begin to cover it."

"It's so dreadful I had to tell you in this way, but there was simply no choice, under the circumstances. What makes it even more unfortunate is the timing, because after years of trying to find you, she had only recently been successful. Poor Nadia was at the point of making contact with you."

"How did she find out who I was -- or where I was?"

"She finally found someone who knew all the right people and how much it would take to get the job done."

Peter felt himself regaining his bearings and was relieved. As emotionally unsettling as the news was, he did not want come across as weak.

"Well, Eleanor, this is one of the more remarkable telephone calls I have ever received in my life." He cleared his throat. "Thank you for getting in touch with me. I'm sure this was not an easy call for you to make."

"No, it wasn't. And Peter, you will most likely be contacted later this morning from Jake Meyers, Nadia's lawyer. Unless things have changed, and I don't think they have, he'll tell you that Nadia has left her entire estate, including Lavender Lane, to you."

Peter felt his bearings begin to slip once again. "You've got to be kidding."

"Not at all. She told me some time ago that those were the provisions she had made, depending of course, upon her ability to find you."

Peter's head was throbbing. He had so many questions. Did his parents know that their secret had been revealed? That the woman they had unburdened of her charge so many years ago had found out who and where he was? The Culvane's were his parents. He loved them dearly and would never want to hurt them. And what about his sister and brothers? Were they adopted too? Probably not. Unlike him, they looked so much like their mother and father. And they were all younger. He had read that frequently when couples seemed unable to have their own children and adopted, childbirth frequently followed.

"You poor dear. You must be reeling," Eleanor said softly.

"I have to admit, I am. This is all quite astonishing." Peter paused. "And what about the arrangements?"

"The funeral, you mean?"

"Yes."

"I told Mr. Meyers I would take care of it, and I have. Oddly enough, Nadia and I had discussed such things." She sighed. "We'll be doing it privately, right here at Lavender Lane. Those were her wishes. Mr. Meyers will be coming, and I would guess Nadia's long-time assistant Phoebe will want to be there. There are no immediate survivors, except you. I suppose it would be rather awkward for you, but I'll email you the information, should you decide to come. It's been orchestrated for tomorrow afternoon."

"So quickly?"

"Yes. She wanted it that way."

Nadia Demidova. Lavender Lane. Funeral. None of it made any sense. Burying a mother he'd never known -- never even known he had.

"Good-bye then, Peter. If not at the funeral tomorrow, then perhaps we shall meet one day."

"Yes, perhaps."

Peter hung up the phone and turned to face the window. The sea, listing gently against a clear blue morning sky, shimmered with tiny jewels of light. He leaned back and focused on a sailboat heading out of the harbor, watching it as it grew steadily smaller and then slowly disappeared into the horizon. He needed to lose himself, if only for a few moments, to be soothed, calmed by the tranquility of the water, but the intercom jolted him back to reality.

"Are you engineering a merger for the vitamin lady? Jeannie asked. "Hope you can get me some free samples. That stuff is expensive!"

"Forget the samples, Jeannie, and listen carefully." His assistant was good, but she constantly inserted herself inappropriately and, at this moment, he was in no mood to pander to her. His mind was fully engaged and there were things to do. "Jeannie, are you listening?" he asked impatiently.

"Yes. Yes, of course."

"Good. I want you to hold all my calls and cancel my 11 o'clock meeting."

"But it's already 10:30. Mr. Culvane."

"I realize that, but something unexpected has come up. Now do as I say. Please."

"Yes, sir. Shall I reschedule for tomorrow?"

"No. All my meetings will have to be put on hold. I'll be going out of town for a few days and I'm not sure when I'll be back."

"Sounds important. Shall I make some reservations for you?"

"Yes. I'll need a flight to Palm Springs first thing in the morning."

"You're going to Florida?"

"No, Jeannie. That's Palm Beach. I'll be going to Palm Springs. In California."

"California, of course. Sorry. Will you be needing a hotel room?"

"No. I own a place out there."

"I didn't know you had property in California, Mr. Culvane."

"Well, Jeannie, as it turns out, neither did I."

Chapter Twelve

The sun had just risen from beyond the mountains, as it had done for an untold number of mornings, but this was no ordinary daybreak at Lavender Lane. The hush in the valley was audible, enveloping the lush grounds like a fine, primordial mist. Somehow, even the birds had refrained from their routine chirping at day's first light.

Phoebe began the day by making sure the notice she had spent half the night writing was reproduced and slipped discreetly under the door of every guest. Even though it was unlikely that word of Nadia Demidova's passing had not already spread to every soul within a five-mile radius, she called a 5:30 a.m. staff meeting. The hour was wretched, but necessary before any of the guests might go for an early morning hike up the mountain or a pre-breakfast jog around the property.

While she had long wanted to be more adequately rewarded for her part in the success of Lavender Lane, Phoebe never anticipated losing Nadia who, in many ways, was her protector. The complexities of running Lavender Lane were vast, and she felt less than prepared to manage it entirely on her own. She had always envisioned a "someday" scenario in which she was a partner and, with Nadia advancing in age, an orderly transition allowing ample time for her to learn everything she needed to learn. She had hardly been prepared for that someday to come so quickly - - to be now. She would press on, of course, but the prospect terrified her.

She wrote then rewrote the message for the guests three times before she was satisfied.

It is with the deepest regret that I must inform you of the sudden and untimely passing yesterday of Madame Nadia Demidova, beloved founder, guiding light and proprietress of Lavender Lane. She will be sorely missed by all those who knew her and loved her.

It was Madame Demidova's most cherished wish that, should anything happen to her, Lavender Lane would continue as always. I will do my best to carry out those wishes with the greatest respect and regard for her memory.

Lavender Lane will come to a standstill at sundown today when private funeral services are to be held. Normal activities will resume at 8:00 this evening, with apologies that our dinner service will be later than customary.

Phoebe Bancroft, Acting Director.

Phoebe read the note to the assembled staff, hoping it answered their questions, and if there were any, so wishing she would be able to handle the answers without breaking down. Usually quite in command of herself, she was afraid the tears would come, and that wouldn't do. She should never let the staff see her in less than total control of herself, even in a dreadful circumstance such as this one. As it turned out, however, there were no questions. The silence in the meeting room reverberated, creating an energy of its own. The cooks, chambermaids, grounds keepers, pool attendants, hairdressers, manicurists, masseuses, facialists, gym coordinators, tennis instructors, and the golf pro had all sat quietly, listening intently to what she had said. They all looked stricken, bereft at the loss. Beyond that, however, Phoebe was quite sure each and every one of them had concerns about their future at Lavender Lane.

The uncertainty was palpable. Phoebe assured the staff that, should the decision be hers, their jobs were certainly secure. The simple question no one wanted to ask, but the one everyone wanted answered, hung over the room like a brooding, dark cloud waiting to let loose its singular disruption. Would the decision, indeed, be hers? No one, of course, wanted the answer to that question more urgently than Phoebe herself. To the others, Lavender Lane was a job. To Phoebe, Lavender Lane was a great deal more. Lavender Lane was her whole life.

■　　■　　■　　■　　■

Lauren stepped on the notice when she left the room for her customary 6:30 a.m. run. She didn't even bother to bend down to pick it up. Bet the rumor's true: the old woman's dead, she thought, glancing down at the funereal-looking, black-rimmed paper, text now smudged by the soiled ribbed sole of her running shoe. How old was she anyway? Sixty? Seventy? No biggie. Nobody lives forever.

Lauren was anxious to get going. It was just another day to her and she was not about to give the newly departed Nadia Demidova even one more thought. She kicked the paper aside and sprinted off down the hall, her eager, young body in full gear, decades away from even the slightest inkling of its own mortality.

■　　■　　■　　■　　■

How sad! Charlotte thought, as she read the notice on her way to breakfast. God rest Nadia Demidova's soul, the poor dear. Imagine going just like that. And such an attractive woman, too. Her skin was amazing. Not a line on her face. And she always looked so composed, so serene. She couldn't have been that old, even with that gray hair. No more than in her early sixties, I expect. And to think she made health a way of life. It's a pity, but I suppose it's better to die quickly of a heart attack than to suffer with some drawn-out and painful disease. Sorry I didn't have a chance to get to know her. And only yesterday I was thinking of asking her if she might be interested in opening an outpost in Dallas. My friends would absolutely adore it and it might have been a really great investment for me. Well, The Lord has His plan and I guess it was not meant to be. God bless her soul. I'll certainly say a prayer.

■　　■　　■　　■　　■

Even though Toni had seen it for herself, it was jarring to read in print the words proclaiming Madame Demidova's death. How was it possible Nadia Demidova had heart issues? Surely she had taken good care of herself. She had been the creator of one of the world's premiere health spas and, by all visible accounts, was the epitome of health. She should have lived to a very ripe old age. Guess there are no guarantees in life, even for someone like Nadia Demidova. *Carpe Diem.* You never know, she thought, putting her hand on her belly, hoping she would pass on the best of genes to life growing inside of her.

Toni read the notice a second time. Phoebe had done a good job, showing respect for the fallen leader while assuring the troops that life would go on. And, she noticed, Phoebe had positioned herself nicely in the process. She had her work cut out, though. Must be a really difficult time for her. She could probably use some help. Someone with solid business experience. Something to think about...

Since finding out she was pregnant, Toni hadn't given too much thought about her business future. Somehow, it would all come together. Millions of women had careers and children. The thought of being involved in Lavender Lane was surprisingly tempting, but there was no way she could re-locate. She wouldn't do that to Kevin. They had made the decision together, and they would be the best, best-friend, co-parents ever, living close to one another and sharing like family -- birthdays, holidays, doctor visits, dental appointments, school activities, camps -- everything and anything having to do with bringing up their child...the whole, beautiful adventure.

But perhaps it was possible to do it long distance? There was really no need to physically be on the Lavender Lane premises, except, of course, for a visit a couple of times a year. So much of business was done remotely at this point in time. There was no reason it wouldn't work for her involvement in the spa. Definitely something to think seriously about.

Then she took her thinking a step further. Maybe even get investors to buy the place. There were lots of people in Kevin's circle with money to spare, starting with his business partner. And being a part owner of the spa would sure appeal to that wife of his. The idea was beginning to sound more and more feasible.

▪ ▪ ▪ ▪ ▪

"*Merde!*" Mavis shouted as she slipped on the notice while rushing out the door. "*Merde*" was one of the French words she had picked up modeling in Paris, and she preferred it to its more pedestrian Anglo-Saxon counterpart. It had so much more style, so much more panache.

She was anxious to get to her loofah scrub at the Beauty Center. It always made her body gleam and feel so incredibly soft. She slipped as she lunged for the paper. What is this damned thing? She asked under her breath as she steadied herself. Nearly made me break my neck. She had not put in her contact lenses and didn't feel like fishing in her bag for glasses. She strained to read the text. "... beloved founder, guiding light and proprietress of Lavender Lane. She will be sorely missed by all those who knew her."

"*Merde en plus!*" she barked, startling the woman across the hall who was leaving her room.

The woman quickly composed herself. "Terrible, isn't it?" she intoned.

"Yes, just dreadful," Mavis shot back. She turned quickly, not wanting to engage in conversation. She lingered, pretending to be having trouble locking her door, and by the time she turned around, the woman was gone.

Yes, I know she dropped dead. And I cannot believe this timing. Just when I was ready to move on everything! She gritted her teeth and continued reading. "...cherished wish that, should anything ever happen to her, Lavender Lane continue as it always had, and she would do her best to carry out those wishes ..."

Phoebe! Well, well, well. Now that's very interesting, indeed. No heavyweight there. That woman has about as much authority with the crew of Lavender Lane as the Vice President of the United States has with Congress. Machiavelli had it right: "A man who is used to acting in one way never changes; he must come to ruin when the times, in changing, no longer are in harmony with his ways." If I were you, Ms. Bancroft, I'd be looking over my shoulder.

The idea had begun to gel the last time Mavis was at Lavender Lane, when Gretchen, one of the facialists, offered to sell her the spa's signature Lavender Lane Rejuvenating Quince Face Creme under the table for $95 -- much less than the official $375 price. Gretchen apparently had a quite a lucrative, don't ask-don't tell business going. Women loved the stuff, and Mavis knew very well why. Whatever was in it -- lavender, quince or otherwise -- she couldn't live without it. Her skin looked light years better than the skin of other women her age, and even women fifteen years her junior. Nadia Demidova, whose own skin was flawless, had always said: "Start using my creme when you're young, and you'll look young forever."

The stuff was more powerful than anything Mavis had ever tried, and she had tried everything. She never understood why Nadia had not marketed her product outside Lavender Lane. She could have made a killing. Nadia's loss might very well be my big gain, she thought. And, why not? She was damned bored doing nothing but charity work and waiting for Tyler to kick the bucket so she can collect on the will. She longed to be back in the spotlight again, to see her face on billboards and magazine covers, on TV and of course on the internet. She would be divine on Instagram! The timing for a comeback was perfect. She was ready and the public was ready. These days, consumers actually wanted to see beautiful middle-aged women. Of course, they would not settle for merely any middle-aged woman. They wanted to see the one and only Mavis, back with the secret of her glorious looks – and perhaps with her, the gorgeous Lauren.

The sales pitch would echo exactly what Madame Demidova had preached about starting to take care of your skin when you are young. She could see the campaign perfectly. It would feature Mavis, the beautiful older woman who had been using the creme for years, sharing her wisdom with Lauren, the gorgeous teenager. The first time she had laid eyes on Lauren, she knew this girl was the right one. They would be absolutely unstoppable together.

The only question was how to proceed? Approach Lauren directly? She hadn't seemed too friendly in the sauna. Perhaps she was still reacting to the rescue mission of a couple of nights ago. Perhaps Lauren had misinterpreted her motives. She'd simply been trying to do the girl a good deed. Lauren shouldn't get mixed up with cocky, well-endowed boys like Greg. Such talent was best left for the big girls, like her, as he no doubt saw for himself once again last night. Aah, yes. It had been an especially creative evening.

Maybe Charlotte is the way to go. She's got to have a bit of the stage mother in her. Christ knows she hasn't achieved much of anything herself. I'm sure I could convince her that Lauren would be a lot better off if I took her under my wing. It might put her more at ease about Lauren's modeling aspirations.

Mavis spotted Phoebe walking briskly down the path in her direction. She was wearing a large beige straw hat and over-sized sunglasses, both of which seemed at odds with her tailored, navy blue business suit.

"Miss Bancroft..."

Phoebe looked up.

"It's Mavis. Mavis Perkins." Mavis momentarily lowered her own sunglasses to reveal her easily recognizable eyes.

"Yes, Mrs. Perkins. Of course."

"I was so sorry to hear of Madame Demidova's most untimely passing. It must have been quite a shock for you."

Phoebe smiled wryly. "Indeed, it was."

"Miss Bancroft, Phoebe," Mavis said, putting her arm on Phoebe's shoulder, "there's something I'd like to talk to you about."

Phoebe looked at the hand resting on her shoulder, its long, beautiful fingers fanned out, each perfectly manicured tip laying claim to its own domain of linen-covered flesh. It unnerved her. Over the years at Lavender Lane, the singular lack of men had led Phoebe to alternative means of expression, and various guests had made themselves available. This guest, however, was one she should stay clear of, of that there was little doubt. This one was lethal.

"Let's get out of the sun so we can…" Mavis favored Phoebe with one of her most dazzling smiles, "chat."

"I really have to return to the office, Mrs. Perkins," Phoebe said stepping back. "I'm running dreadfully behind schedule."

"I promise it will only take a moment, and I think you'll find my, shall we say, 'proposition,' of interest."

Proposition? Phoebe froze.

"It's business," Mavis said coyly. "Strictly business."

Business. Phoebe's body relaxed. Business was quite another story and, at the moment, she could use all the help she could get. She was on the verge of losing her twenty-year investment and Mavis Perkins was a very rich, very well-connected woman.

"Let's go and sit," Mavis said, pointing to a bench beneath a grove of large oak trees a few feet away.

"I never go out in the sun without one of these on my head," Mavis said, removing her large, dramatic hat as she sat down. "And judging from your marvelous English skin, neither do you."

"Quite right," Phoebe concurred, taking off her own hat, clearly a bit more at ease. "Madame Demidova taught me many years ago that large hats, sunscreen and regular applications of Lavender Lane Rejuvenating Quince Face Creme can go a long way toward warding off Mother Time."

"She is -- she was -- so right," Mavis said, leaning forward. "And that's precisely what I want to talk to you about. The creme! It's quite extraordinary, as you know. And marketed properly, it would make money --tons of money." Mavis looked Phoebe pointedly in the eye. "I can help you do that. Market the stuff and reel it in."

Phoebe leaned back into the bench, her sense of unease returning. "I'm quite sure you're right, and I would certainly welcome your help, but there's one small problem."

"And what would that be?"

"The creme is not mine to market."

"Really?" Mavis asked. "I assumed you would be taking over Lavender Lane now that Madame Demidova is gone."

"I am running the spa, at least for the moment."

"'For the moment?' I don't understand. Won't you be continuing here?" Mavis shot off, gears in full grind. "Who are the heirs?"

"Actually, I don't know. I was advised by the attorney to keep things going, but I suspect my position here is precarious, at best. I hope to know more after the funeral tomorrow."

Mavis peered at Phoebe from behind her darkened lenses. "Yes, I expect you will." She rose abruptly from the bench, her interest in Phoebe and their conversation clearly evaporating. "Well, my dear, stay out of the sun. You don't want to damage that perfect complexion." She turned and strode down the path, moving with a tilting, measured gait, as though the tiny stones and assorted pebbles beneath her feet had been transformed into the runway at the paparazzi's favorite A-list designer fashion show.

Phoebe sat back in disbelief. The bitch. The blatant, bloody bitch. There isn't a decent bone in that miraculous body of hers.

A gentle breeze rustled the leaves of the trees overhead and a nearby brook sang its soothing, rhythmic song. Phoebe looked out into distance and drank in the beauty surrounding her. Lavender Lane was her home, and she never wanted to leave, but how was she going to secure her future? Without knowing the details of Madame Demidova's will, there was no way of planning anything. And it was apparent Mavis Perkins was not going to help her. Well, Mavis Perkins be damned! She would continue to do her job to the best of her ability, nonetheless. She owed that to Nadia. She only hoped her long-time employer had felt equally beholden to her.

Chapter Thirteen

Phoebe opened the door to the gym and spotted Toni on the treadmill, going at a moderate clip.

"There you are!" she said brightly. "I've been looking all over for you."

"When in doubt, you can usually find me either here or in the Pilates studio."

"I thought perhaps we might have a bite of lunch. I would love to have your advice about something."

"Sounds great. Give me a sec and I'll be right with you. I've been on this thing for nearly forty-five minutes anyway."

Toni wound down her pace and did a couple of quick stretches, letting out a loud groan. "I don't know, Phoebe. This stuff never gets any easier."

"I'm afraid nothing ever does, does it?"

"Speaking of things not getting any easier -- how are you coping, being in charge and everything?"

"Brilliantly, I would like to report, but frankly, I'm not sure."

Over lunch in the gym's Salad Bar Café, Phoebe revealed her fears about her future at Lavender Lane, as well as her discomfort at her earlier conversation with Mavis Perkins.

Toni listened intently. "I have to agree. It sounds like the infamous Mavis is definitely on the prowl. And I wonder what she has up her sleeve, because while the creme is amazing, it's Lavender Lane itself that's the real prize."

"Without question."

"Knowing Mavis, she'll probably start small and then maneuver for the whole package. My guess is she figured you were going to inherit a piece of the place and were her in."

"Would that were the case -- the inheritance part, I mean."

"Do you have any idea who Madame Demidova willed Lavender Lane to?"

"Not the foggiest," Phoebe said shaking her head. "She was so totally reticent about her private life."

"Well, I suspect it won't be long till you'll find out. Chances are, some relative will come out of the woodwork. They always do." She reached over and patted Phoebe's arm. "Not to worry. Anyone inheriting this place would be an idiot to try to go forward without you. If I owned Lavender Lane, I'd never let you go!"

Phoebe smiled weakly. "That's sweet, Toni, and now I feel absolutely terrible about what I'm about to say -- but Madame Demidova died at the worst possible time, before I had the chance to plead my case, so to speak. I was just at the point of having a discussion with her about being given at least a small percentage…I was thinking ten percent was fair…when…" she lowered her eyes, "when it happened."

"It's truly awful that Madame Demidova has passed, but that has absolutely nothing to do with your wanting a piece of the pie. That's natural and, from what I can see, you've more than earned it."

"I like to think so."

"Don't just think it, believe it! Take it from someone who spent her whole career slaving for other people. There's a better way to live!" For a split second, she was going to tell Phoebe about the big decision she had recently made and the little kumquat, but decided against it. She would keep it strictly business. If she were going to share the information with anyone at Lavender Lane, it should be darling Charlotte.

They looked thoughtfully across the small table at one another for a few moments, and then started to talk at the same time -- not once, but twice, propelling them into fits of laughter.

"You first," Phoebe blurted out, barely able to speak.

"No. You first," Toni managed. "I insist."

Phoebe took a deep breath. "Well, then..." she said, looking playfully at Toni, "are you thinking what I'm thinking?"

"Entirely possible," Toni responded, "if you're thinking we might run the spa together."

Phoebe's eyes sparkled. "Precisely!"

"I was envisioning that very thing, just this morning. We'd be a great team!"

"Indeed, we would, with your retailing background and my work here at the spa, not to mention your athleticism."

"Thanks for the compliment, but haven't we forgotten a few small details?" Toni asked.

"Such as?"

"Such as who owns the place now, and will they want to sell it to us?"

"Sell it to us? I thought you only meant we could run Lavender Lane. How could we ever buy it, Toni? It's worth millions, many times over. Where in the world would we get that kind of money?"

"I haven't thought it through but my nearest and dearest friend Kevin Gavelli is close to lots of people with tons of money."

"Kevin Gavelli, the designer?"

"The very same."

"He's marvelous! Not that I get to wear any of his clothing."

"Well, you might. Haven't discussed it with him, of course, but he is very well connected and I am sure he would help me -- help us -- raise capital." Toni wondered what Phoebe's reaction would be to learn how connected she and Kevin actually were.

"Well," Phoebe said. "Sounds like we've got a glimmer of a plan."

"I think we do," Toni responded. "*Et maintenant*, as a certain older mannequin might say in model-speak French, let's get started. You get to work on finding out who actually owns Lavender Lane now, and I'll get to work on the finances."

"Good. Then let's drink to it!" Toni lifted her glass of carefully blended green juice. "To the future of Lavender Lane."

Phoebe lifted hers and returned the toast. "To the future of Lavender Lane."

. . . . .

Toni spotted Charlotte lounging by the pool in a shaded cabana, a fluffy, queen-sized peach towel covering her from chin to toes, her iPad in one hand, an ornate magnifying glass in the other. Sure enough, Charlotte was checking numbers on her favorite financial app.

"Hey, Charlotte, where did you get the spyglass? The court of Louis the Sixteenth?"

Charlotte looked up slowly. "As a matter of fact, I got it at an auction a few years ago. And, Miss Smarty Pants, you've got the wrong Louis. This one's the fourteenth." She patted the chair beside her, shifting her legs to make room.

"Those damn Louies were never my strong point, nor unfortunately, is the stock market. How are you doing? Still making a killing?"

"At the risk of jinxing myself," Charlotte beamed, "I'm riding the proverbial bull. Another one of my little gems has started moving up."

"How would you like to invest in another sure winner?"

"Don't tell me you've got a hot tip for me? I thought you said you didn't know a thing about the market."

"I'm not talking about stock. I've got something better."

"What could be better than the market?"

"Lavender Lane."

"Lavender Lane! As in here, this place?"

"The very same."

Charlotte looked at her wide eyed. "My dear, I must say you have succeeded in gaining my attention."

"You know I have no desire to go back to retailing, or anything remotely like it. And I've gotten a bit friendly with Phoebe Bancroft, you know, Nadia Demidova's right-hand. The English woman."

Charlotte nodded.

"We started talking about running Lavender Lane together, and before we knew it, we had a plan."

Charlotte studied Toni. "That's a pretty big deal."

"True, but Phoebe and I would be a good team. Our skills are complementary, and she's devoted to Lavender Lane. Did you know she's been here for more than twenty years? As a matter of fact, she was just about to discuss the possibility of some kind of partnership with Madame Demidova, but..."

"That's too bad, but what about poor Madame Demidova? Now everybody's wondering why she died that way. Makes you wonder if any of this health stuff really works."

"Apparently, she had some congenital problem that couldn't be overcome, no matter how healthful the lifestyle."

"Still, it's kind of strange being here at a time like this. There's a pall over everything, don't you think?"

"Without question! But life does go on and fortune favors the prepared. This is a really good chance to invest."

"Invest?" Charlotte was taken aback.

"It's a once-in-a-lifetime opportunity."

"Oh, I don't know."

"Would you at least sleep on it?"

"How much is involved?"

"At this point, we have no way of knowing. And to be honest, we don't really know if Lavender Lane's for sale yet, because we don't know who's inheriting it."

Charlotte threw her head back and laughed. "Kind of important information, don't you think?"

"Of course. But we're just getting our ducks in a row."

Charlotte paused. "Some expensive ducks! Well, it does sound intriguing. And I suppose if I owned a piece of the place, I would have an excuse to come here often."

"Not to mention receiving first-class treatment."

"Everyone who comes to Lavender Lane gets first-class treatment, Toni. It's part of the draw."

"See, you're talking like an owner already!"

"I admit it's a very interesting possibility," Charlotte said, leaning forward "But Lord's sake, the woman isn't even buried yet. I don't feel right about discussing it. Not yet. It's much too disrespectful."

"I understand. You'll be more comfortable talking about it after the funeral."

Charlotte nodded. "Are you going?"

"Oh, no. It's a very small, private ceremony." And besides, Toni thought, I can't go near any funerals. She couldn't risk a bad case of the Evil Eye. She laughed out loud.

"What's so funny?"

Toni needed to recover quickly. "Oh, just thinking what fun it would be if we actually owned Lavender Lane had the power to tell Mavis Perkins there was no room at the inn."

Charlotte tried to suppress a laugh.

"Oops. Sorry for the religious allusion."

"No problem. I'd be the first one to say "Sorry. Full up, Mrs. Perkins. Try Motel 6 down the road."

"That would be too delicious!"

"Speaking of delicious, I'm absolutely famished. Care to join me for some lunch?" Charlotte asked.

"Thanks, not really hungry. Think I'll sit out here for a few minutes and then hit the Nautilus machine."

"Not really hungry! How I wish I could say the same!" Charlotte swung her legs over the side of the lounge. "See you later."

Toni felt a twinge in her belly and she nearly called Charlotte back. She really did want to tell her about the kumquat, but she had read the literature: don't talk about it until after the first trimester. The pregnancy may not hold. And the funeral thing. That one was hardly medical. It was one of the many superstitions she heard from her grandmother while growing up. And certainly don't let a snake cross your path, Nonna had said to her pregnant older sister. Well, she would not be at Madame Demidova's funeral, so she would not be able to control that one, but not so in with the second. She was in the desert, after all, and there were plenty of snakes everywhere -- not to mention the slithering, human variety.

She doubted that Mavis, a long-time client and actual acquaintance of Nadia Demidova, was out lighting candles for the poor woman's soul. On the contrary, The Grand One was probably well on her way to getting those beautifully pampered claws firmly sunk into the much-desired prize of the Southern California desert.

.   .   .   .   .

Charlotte sat down at the poolside café and scanned the salad menu with every conceivable kind of lettuce known to humanity. In another day or so, she would surely turn into a rabbit. But she had to admit, it was working. The scale had already begun to move.

She ordered water-packed tuna over a bed of mixed greens, then leaned back and thought about the discussion she and Toni had just had. Imagine trying to buy Lavender Lane! It was a thrilling idea, but she couldn't allow herself to think about it. Not until poor Madame Demidova was at least buried. It simply wasn't right.

Still, the notion kept finding its way back into her head. The stock market was very risky, and her winning streak had to come to an end one of these days. An investment in something like Lavender Lane could be quite lucrative, and one heck of a lot safer. When the time was appropriate -- very soon -- she'd give it some serious thought.

At the moment, Charlotte's relationship with her daughter needed attention. This little vacation was doing nothing to bridge the gap between them. On the contrary, their disconnect seemed to be widening, if that were possible. The girl was more headstrong than ever. And this fixation on modeling! Charlotte hated the idea: the men, the sexual abuse she'd read so much about, the drugs and the distorted values. There had to be a way to dissuade Lauren.

The sounds of a familiar laugh interrupted Charlotte's thoughts, and she turned to see Lauren stretched out on one of the poolside lounges. She was face down, wearing the bottom of her skimpiest bikini, with the tiny top dangling provocatively from her outstretched arm. Mavis Perkins, covered head to toe in a mauve silk caftan, allowing nary a spec of sun to even flirt with any part of her flawless skin, was seated next to Lauren, rubbing sun lotion on her back.

This was the second time she had come upon Mavis in an especially familiar situation with Lauren. She got up from the table and quickly walked over to the pair, a salad suddenly seeming to have less urgency. "Hello down there," she said in her cheeriest manner.

Mavis looked up from under her hat. "Charlotte! Well, hello -- again."

Lauren's body flinched at the arrival of her mother, but she did not dignify her by looking up.

"I see you're covered up, Mavis. I keep telling Lauren the sun will ruin her skin, but she never listens to me. I thought she might see you as an example."

Lauren suddenly flipped over, her breasts completely exposed in the process. "I do see Mavis as an example, Mother."

"Lauren, cover yourself up!" Charlotte said a little louder than she would have liked.

"Why? There's nobody here but us girls."

"That's not entirely true," Mavis interjected, letting out a low, throaty laugh. "That absolutely awful tennis boy might be lurking around."

Lauren giggled and reached for a towel. "No need to get all nervous on me. This is the last time I'll be doing sun. Contrary to what you see here today, Mavis has convinced me not to sunbathe anymore." She looked at Mavis and flashed her a huge smile. "It wouldn't be good for my career."

"Really?" Charlotte asked.

"Mavis has this amazing plan about how to get me top model status right away, without having to go through all the shit first. Isn't that unbelievable?"

"Unbelievable," Charlotte sighed. *Why did she have to use that language?* She glanced at Mavis who seemed to have no reaction to it whatsoever.

"You know how I feel about modeling, Lauren."

"Yes, mother. I know how you feel. It's always about how *you* feel. But have you ever given a damn about how I feel?

"I'm only interested in what's good for you."

"How in the world would you know what's good for me? You don't know anything," Lauren whined, scrambling to her feet. She glared at Charlotte and then bounded off.

Charlotte slumped down on the lounge, her eyes welling up with tears. Her child had done it to her yet again. She was losing the war to a point beyond any conceivable return. "You must forgive me, Mavis," she said, as the tears began to fall. "My daughter and I have a bit of a communication problem."

Mavis reached into her pocket and withdrew a neatly folded tissue. She pressed it into Charlotte's hand and affected her most sympathetic smile. "I can see that your daughter might be difficult, but I also can see she does have the kind of looks that could make her a very successful model."

Charlotte dabbed at her eyes. Her carefully applied eye makeup had smeared onto her full, flushed cheeks. "You really think so?"

"Yes. And if she's so hell bent on doing it, your trying to prevent it will only create a wider gap between you."

"I suppose."

"Why not take this opportunity to let her have what she wants, but in a way that has lots of safety valves built in."

"Safety valves?"

"What I'm proposing is a chance for her to get to the top without having to go through all of the, shall we say, 'more difficult' beginnings of the novice."

Charlotte continued dabbing at her eyes. "I don't understand."

"Have you had a facial here yet?"

"Yesterday. But what does that have to do with any of this?"

"Plenty. Did they use the Lavender Lane Rejuvenating Quince Creme?"

"Yes. It's so nice I bought two jars to take home." She patted her moist cheek.

"Precisely! The Crème is exceptional. Trust me, I know about these things. And with the right promotion, it could be beyond an enormously successful product."

"What does that have to do with Lauren?" Charlotte asked. "She's certainly too young to use skin creme."

"*Au Contraire.* Not only is she not too young, she's the perfect age to begin. Madame Demidova's advice has always been: 'Start young and you'll look young forever.' Lauren would be the ideal role model for girls her age."

"Lauren, a role model?"

"Charlotte, don't even think twice about it. She's a natural."

"It's awfully nice of you to take Lauren's interest at heart."

"Well thank you, but I must admit I do have an ulterior motive."

Oh dear.

Mavis laughed at the expression of horror that had overcome Charlotte's face. "My dear woman, whatever it is you're thinking, I can assure you, it's nothing the least bit irregular, in any way. The time is right for an older model to trend, and that older model is me. I've had it with retirement."

"Forgive me if I'm being dense, Mavis, but I still don't understand."

"It's simple: Your daughter and I are the two ends of the spectrum. Lauren represents the young woman who uses the product and I, Mavis, am the older woman. Like Madame Demidova said…"

"Yes, yes: 'Start using the creme when you are young, and you will stay young forever.'"

Charlotte sat back and stared at Mavis. She knew approximately how old she was because of her fabled career, but the woman hardly looked a day over forty. "It's certainly an interesting idea, but I don't know."

"Lauren would catapult right to the top, Charlotte. She won't have to start down and dirty like the others. Why deny your daughter this chance?"

"Do you have the rights to market the creme?"

"Not yet. But that shouldn't be a problem."

I doubt anything is ever a problem for her, Charlotte thought.

"Word is Madame Demidova didn't have any relatives, so Lavender Lane will probably be up for grabs. I've decided to buy the place."

Toni was right! "My goodness! Buying Lavender Lane." Charlotte suddenly blanched. *Oh dear. It really is an incredible opportunity for Lauren. But what about Toni? There would be no way I could get involved with her plan now.*

"You were saying?" Mavis said with marked impatience.

Charlotte cleared her throat. "Won't it be complicated, the business arrangements, and all of that?"

"Shouldn't be. My husband will handle all the financial details. It's the least the old bastard can do for me. And I'll take care of being the spokesperson for both the spa and the crème -- with Lauren, of course."

With Lauren.

"What do you think?"

"I think," Charlotte said haltingly, "it would be a very unique opportunity for my daughter."

"Unique? It's the proverbial chance of a lifetime!"

"I suppose it might be."

"Then you'll agree to let her do it?"

Charlotte studied the woman across from her -- the woman with the face that had graced the cover of every fashion magazine from the Far East to South America and the body that had walked the runway of every major designer in New York, Paris and Milan. She was still an extraordinary beauty. The story would be very believable, and the creme would probably be an enormous success. And Lauren -- her Lauren -- would be a part of it all. How could she deprive her daughter of this opportunity? It most certainly could be the chance of a lifetime. If she said 'no,' it would drive a wedge in their relationship that would be so deep, it would be irreparable.

Charlotte caught her breath, waited a moment, then said, "Yes. I'll let her do it, assuming you'll legally secure the rights and everything will be on the up-and-up."

"Of course. It's all in the works," Mavis lied, so sure she could persuade Peter to do anything she wanted. "It will be marvelous with Lauren onboard!" Mavis pronounced. "Absolutely marvelous! We'll have to celebrate." She glanced at her watch. "But at another time, I'm afraid. I've got an appointment." She quickly canvassed the pool area. "Wherever is that beautiful daughter of yours?"

"She's probably out running."

"I need to dash to my facial," Mavis purred. "I'll catch up with the two of you later."

Charlotte laid her head back and watched Mavis walk away. She and Lauren would have so much to talk about! But what about Toni? She would hardly consider this good news. There was no way she could get involved in any kind of Lavender Lane deal with Toni now. And how could she possibly explain herself -- that Mavis was going to help Lauren and, by the by, that Mavis also had her eye on Lavender Lane? Anxiety quickly overcame her and she was seized with a sudden need for food. She had to put something in her stomach, and not merely a salad. Food -- real food!

Charlotte hurled herself from the chaise and marched back to the café, but it was closed due to the funeral. There was a tea sandwich service set up in the lounge near the reception area, but what she had back in her room tucked into one her suitcase's zippered compartments would be far more satisfying.

She had managed to resist temptation for nearly four days now, but there was no way, at this moment, she could avoid the impending fall from grace. She headed back toward the main house, preoccupied with the thoughts of the budding conflict in which she would soon be enveloped.

When she passed the tennis instructors' cabin, neither the sounds of raucous laughter nor the smell of marijuana caught her attention. She barreled straight ahead, never noticing the bare-chested tennis instructor and an equally bare-chested Lauren, laughing as they peered out at her from the open window in a drug-induced haze.

Chapter Fourteen

Nadia Demidova began her journey through life in a run-down house on Dimitri Prospect, in the marginal and dismally gray meatpacking district of Moscow. She ended her journey at the foot of a magnificent green mountain, continents away. Per her wishes, she was laid to rest at sundown beneath a trio of flowering, yellow hibiscus trees that grew at the foot of that mountain, the same one she had gazed at from her office window on thousands of equally glorious evenings.

As it had done, day after day, year after year, a shimmering orange globe drifted its way down, framing the mountain for brief moments against splashes of fuchsia, pink and brilliant coral streaked across a clear blue sky. The air was already beginning to cool and the denizens of the desert evening were making preparations to greet the part of the day they called their own. A distant hoot owl offered a low, early call and some tiny, spotted brown moles popped out from the earth and scampered across the wide, open meadow.

Neither priest nor minister were in attendance at the funeral. God had betrayed her, had taken away the things she loved, Nadia had once explained to Eleanor. She would not let Him have His way with her at the end. There was no reason to pay Him deference. She didn't fear retribution for denying Him the devotion He considered His due. She had endured enough punishment in her lifetime, she felt, to easily last through all eternity.

With Phoebe and Jake Meyers, the lawyer, at her side, Eleanor softly recited the words of Lord Byron.

"She walks in beauty, like the night

Of cloudless climes and starry skies;

And all that's best of dark and bright

Meet in her aspect and in her eyes..."

Jake stood quietly with his head bowed. Phoebe wept softly, dabbing a handkerchief repeatedly to the corners of her eyes.

When Eleanor finished, they each laid a single, long-stemmed, white rose on the burnished mahogany coffin, augmenting the rich, deep red roses nestled on a spray of lavender resting gracefully on top.

The ceremony, was brief, and drawing to a close when Peter Culvane appeared and strode quickly toward the small group. Without prelude, he bent down and laid a gathering of delicate white lilies at the base of the coffin, then lowered his head for a brief moment. When he looked up, he nodded silently to the others, his gaze resting a bit longer on Eleanor's almost recognizable face. Eleanor and Jake easily returned his wordless greeting. Phoebe however, merely glanced at this tall, slender, most attractive man who stood silent and erect and stared strangely at the coffin.

"Rest in peace, dear Nadia," Eleanor said softly. "I will miss you."

"As will I," echoed Phoebe.

"May God take you to his bosom," whispered Jake.

Peter looked briefly at the coffin again then moved forward and extended his hand to Eleanor. "Peter. Peter Culvane."

"Peter -- of course!" Eleanor responded, smiling. "I'm so glad you're here."

He turned to Jake Meyers.

"Jake Meyers," the lawyer said, shaking Peter's hand warmly.

Phoebe was next in line. Peter offered his hand.

"Phoebe Bancroft," she said. "I've worked with Madame Demidova for the last two decades."

Peter nodded.

"And Mr. Culvane," Phoebe continued, "how do -- how did you know Madame Demidova?"

"Actually, Miss Bancroft..."

"Isn't it wonderful to have him here with us? Eleanor piped in, trying to ameliorate the awkwardness of the moment. "This lovely gentleman is Madame Demidova's son."

Phoebe's face drained of color. "Her son!" she blurted out. "I had no idea..."

Peter attempted a smile.

"It's a long story," Jake Meyers interjected, before Peter could say anything. "And not quite appropriate for this moment. Don't you agree, Eleanor?"

"Without question," Eleanor nodded. "There will be plenty of time for getting into details, won't there, dear?" she said to Peter, smiling as best she could within the confines of her restricted mouth.

"Dear friends," she said, gesturing expansively, "we have said 'goodbye' exactly the way Nadia wanted." She turned in the direction of the crew, which was waiting discreetly several yards away. "These gentlemen will lower Nadia to her final rest shortly after we leave. Now, I hope you'll join me for a drink and a light supper in my suite. None of us should be alone at this moment. We must celebrate Nadia's life."

"Please go on ahead," Peter said. "I'll join all of you in a bit. I'd like to stay for a moment."

"Of course," Eleanor responded.

"Certainly," Jake echoed.

Phoebe stared warily at this stranger, this parvenu who no doubt would have a great deal -- if not everything -- to say about her future at Lavender Lane. She barely managed a smile before setting off to catch up with the others, who were already making their way back to the main building.

Peter lingered a bit before turning to face the coffin. It was beautiful, if there could be such a thing as a beautiful coffin, crafted from the finest woods, shimmering with a discreet patina, and enhanced with burnished bronze handles and trim. He looked around at the glorious nature surrounding him and felt a keen sense of disbelief. How could death exist amidst such extraordinary beauty? And how, indeed, could this death exist for him, at all?

His very breathing since the morning before had required a suspension of belief, a letting go of reality as he knew it. And here he was, feeling nothing and yet feeling everything, finding a void where once there might have been love, experiencing pain where there might have been comfort and joy, respect and belonging. It was impossible to understand this moment.

A breeze whistled through the nearby trees and washed over him. He closed his eyes and tried to find the thoughts that would bring him to some semblance of understanding. When the sound of his voice came, it was as though it were not his own. The words materialized slowly, tentatively, having been branded into his brain at an early age, only to lie dormant for years.

"Holy Mary, Mother of God, pray for us sinners now, and at the hour of our death." His right hand reached up and traced a path it had not trodden for years, moving from forehead to chest and back and forth, making the Sign of the Cross, paying deference to the Holy Mother Church he had long ago abandoned, and paying deference, as well, to the passing of an earthly mother --his earthly mother -- who, for whatever reasons she may have deemed were the right ones, had made the choice to abandon him.

■　　■　　■　　■　　■

A small group had quietly watched the proceedings from a distance, waiting for the official mourners to leave. Once the last had gone -- a man whom none of them recognized -- they came: Chef Andre, who had worked at Lavender Lane for fifteen years; his sous-chef, Antonio, who had assisted him for ten; Nicholas, the head groundskeeper, who had tended to the spa's gardens and pathways for twelve years; and the chief chambermaid, Maria, a nineteen-year veteran of Lavender Lane. Many others followed.

Several of the staff were miffed they had not been invited to join in the official final farewell to Madame Demidova, but they kept their dismay silent out of respect for the woman they revered. Into the late evening, they filed in, the entire panoply of brilliant Coachella Valley wild flowers held in their individual hands. One by one, they laid their tributes of pink, white, yellow and violet on the newly sodden ground. Each said their own uninvited goodbyes to a woman whom they had admired, but never really had known.

∎   ∎   ∎   ∎   ∎

The little gathering at Eleanor's was pleasant, for the most part. As is often the case when people come together after a funeral, a kind of forced gaiety set the tone.

No real information was exchanged during the light supper, and Phoebe felt herself the odd man out, so to speak. She had worked with and known Nadia for more than twenty years and had no idea she had a son. It was as though the man had been dropped, this day, from some newly discovered planet. And yet, she could certainly see a resemblance -- the hair, thick and graying from what certainly had a rich, black beginning, and those soulful dark eyes set back over broad cheek bones surely had their derivation somewhere on the Great Russian Steppes. Peter Culvane was very attractive, and despite his potentially threatening status to her future at Lavender Lane, Phoebe had to admit, she felt an unexpected stir.

It had been some time since she had experienced that kind of feeling, the company of women having sufficed for so long. Not that she had a shot at Peter Culvane. Hardly. As soon as word got out about who he was, he would become a piece of prime filet tossed into a den of privileged, preening lionesses. The man wouldn't last more than an hour at Lavender Lane before one of the predatory, rich bitches found their way into those designer knickers of his. If not his heart.

Beyond that, there were more important things to consider. There was so much Phoebe wanted to know and needed to know, but this was hardly the moment. For now, she would simply have to give everyone her most agreeable smile and summon up a very large dose of British patience.

The hour had grown late, and Jake was the first to call attention to it.

"Eleanor," he said, rising from his chair. "Thank you so much for arranging everything."

"The least I could do for my dear friend Nadia…"

"Peter, again, my condolences."

Peter nodded his head, his role as principal mourner clearly an uncomfortable one.

"And Phoebe," Jake continued, "we know we can count on you to keep things rolling around here."

"Yes. Yes, of course," Phoebe found herself saying, wanting to follow it with "Do I still have a home? Do I still have a job?" and "Have I now lost my chance forever of owning any part of Lavender Lane?"

"You can certainly count on me, Mr. Meyers," Phoebe said. "And Dr. Franklin, please let me know if there is anything I can do for you." She turned to Peter. "Mr. Culvane, I offer you my most sincere condolences. Please let me know how I may be of help."

"Actually Ms. Bancroft, there is something you can do for me. If you can arrange to install me in one of the rooms, I would be most appreciative. I didn't book a hotel." He smiled. "Might as well get used to the place."

Phoebe blanched. "Oh, I'm so sorry. I'm afraid we're totally sold out."

"Really?" Peter responded, clearly surprised at her answer.

"Oh, dear. This is so embarrassing. There's actually not one empty room available."

"Well, business must be booming, then."

Phoebe's face grew whiter by the second. "We're always sold out this time of year. It's high season."

"High season. I see."

"Why don't you drive over to the Ritz Carlton with me, Peter?" Jake suggested. "I'm sure my friends at the front desk can find you something."

"Unless, of course, you want to stay in Madame Dem -- I mean your mother's apartment," Phoebe blurted out. "It's very comfortable, that is, if you wouldn't be uncomfortable staying there." The words were not coming out the way she intended. Resolve or no, her nerves were getting the best of her.

Peter hesitated for a moment. "That would be fine."

"How lovely," Eleanor added. "I can escort Peter there and show him some of Nadia's things."

Phoebe felt as though she didn't have one once ounce of blood left in her entire body. If she didn't get away that very instant, she would not be able to breathe.

"Excellent," she said, doing her best to be calm and measured. "I'll have the key brought up to you straightaway. Good night, then," she said, as she advanced quickly toward the door, with Jake Meyers falling in neatly behind her.

Chapter Fifteen

"Her most treasured possession," Eleanor said to Peter as she grasped Nadia's rich persimmon quilt to her chest. "It's one of the few surviving remnants of an earlier life." Eleanor touched the quilt to her nose and breathed in. It was perfumed with the sweet, spicy aroma of Nadia's signature scent. "Shalimar," she whispered to Peter. "It was her favorite."

"May I see it?" he asked, reaching out to take the quilt. "It's quite beautiful." He admired the bright, theatrical color and the strong silk fabric that had served its owner well for more than half a century. Peter hesitated for a moment then drew the fabric to his nose. The aroma was subtle but still very much in evidence. Strange, he thought, how I can smell her fragrance and hold this quilt, when I never even touched her. Or had I? I wonder how many times -- if ever -- she held me before giving me away.

His temples began to throb and he found himself gripping the cloth too tightly, but it was as close as he would ever get to the woman who had given him life. He loosened his grasp. It would be insane to be angry with a person who never existed for him. Thankfully, he had not lacked for a mother or a father or a complete family. Had Nadia elected to leave well enough alone, he could have continued to live out his life in a blissful state of ignorance. But she hadn't kept her secret to herself, and now her son knew the truth. This unexpected sojourn to Lavender Lane was his only chance to glean the information he lacked, to ferret out the shards of buried truth so he could eke out a place for this newly birthed hurt to install itself and settle in for permanent occupancy.

"Eleanor, may I ask a favor?"

"Certainly."

"I'd appreciate if you would tell me everything you know about Nadia. I Googled her but didn't come up with much of anything other than information about Lavender Lane." He looked at Eleanor tentatively. "And of course, I want to know about Nadia and me. What was our history, if there was any? I'm afraid you're my only source."

Eleanor reached up and put her hand on Peter's cheek, gazing into his eyes with compassion and understanding and no short measure of increasingly transparent longing.

The gesture took Peter by surprise, and he recoiled a bit.

Color flooded Eleanor's face and she quickly removed her hand. "You must be starved for information," she said, backing away. "I'd be happy to tell you everything I know."

"Thank you. I'd appreciate that."

There were some awkward seconds, then Eleanor ushered Peter to a nearby sofa, where she picked up the cut crystal decanter on the table in front of them and poured aged Armagnac into two matching snifters.

"Nadia loved Armagnac. We shared many night caps, over the years." She handed Peter a glass then touched the side of it with her own. "In honor of my friend, Nadia, and to her son. She would have been so proud of you."

"Thank you. And to your kindness," Peter responded.

Eleanor took a long, slow sip then leaned back into the plush velvet cushions of the sofa and cleared her throat. "Well, then, I'll begin. You know, of course, Nadia was Russian."

"That's about all the information I could find on the Internet," Peter said. "Nothing more…"

Eleanor nodded. "She was born in Moscow just as the war was ending in 1945. Nadia told me the family didn't have much money and that her mother died giving birth to her. Nadia's father Boris blamed his only child for his wife's death. He went into a total rage. If the old "babushka" who lived in the basement apartment hadn't been there assisting the midwife at the birth, Boris might actually have killed the newly born Nadia. At least, it's what the old woman later told her."

Boris worked as a butcher and when he wasn't at the slaughter house, he was out drinking. Most of the time Nadia was left with the old lady. One night, as the story went, when she was about three or four, Boris showed up intoxicated and raging. He went after her with a meat cleaver. The only reason Nadia survived the tirade is because the old woman hit him over the head with a large iron frying pan and knocked him unconscious." Eleanor paused and took a sip of brandy. "This feels strange -- I've never repeated to anyone what Nadia told me in confidence a number of years ago."

"Trust me, it feels strange as hell hearing it," Peter said, with a hint of humor in his voice. He took a sip of brandy as well. "But I do appreciate your taking the time to fill me in on all of this. I hope you know that."

Eleanor nodded. "Yes…"

"Please continue," Peter said.

Eleanor began again, "Nadia told me she never forgot that horrible night and had recurrent nightmares. She seemed to have them until the day she died."

"I can imagine," Peter said. "What a horrendous thing for a child to go through." He looked down, lost in thought for a moment, then looked back up when Eleanor continued.

"While her father lay passed out on the floor, the old woman wrapped Nadia up in a blanket and took her to the nearest monastery. She begged one of the brothers to take Nadia in, explaining that she was no longer safe with her father. Before the monk had the chance to say no, she kissed Nadia on the forehead and turned away. Nadia told me she always remembered watching the babushka walk quickly away down the dark, icy path. She called after her, but the old woman did not respond. She said she always remembered feeling totally abandoned, seeing the only mother figure she had ever known go out of her life."

Peter stiffened.

Eleanor drew back at bit. "Oh, dear. I hope this is not too difficult for you."

Peter hesitated for a moment. "No, no." He shook his head. "Please go on."

Eleanor nodded and took another sip of brandy. "According to Nadia, the monk was always concerned that the abbey was no place for a little girl, but the brothers were all very good to her and they began to look upon her as their special little angel, teaching her to read and write and to worship in their faith, which, at the time, was regarded by the state as a political pariah."

"What about the old woman? And her father? Boris, I think you said his name was." Peter's interest was piqued.

"She never saw her father or the babushka again -- never heard a word about or from them. It was as though they had never existed. But she told me the pain that had begun almost from the day she was born grew, little by little, until it created a cavern she couldn't fill, until she met your father."

Father. Peter took another slow sip of brandy…

"Nadia began to blossom, as young girls do, and apparently her growing allure proved to be too much for one of the monks. Her patron -- I think she said his name was Brother Patrimas -- found the monk trying to force himself on Nadia. He had been afraid something like this might happen. Your mother was only twelve years old at the time, but it was clearly the moment for her to move on. Brother Patrimas brought her to the Ballets Russes in Moscow, where his older sister Manya was the wardrobe mistress. He told Nadia that not only would the childless Manya give her a loving home at the ballet, she would teach her how to sew, so she would have a way to earn a living when she grew up."

"Nadia -- my mother -- was a seamstress?"

"She definitely learned to sew, but it wasn't sewing Nadia took a real liking to, but rather dance, and as fate would have it, she had natural ability. At first, she merely darted around trying to imitate the grown-up ballerinas, but it quickly became apparent she possessed grace and real talent. Before long, she was performing in the young corps de ballets. One of the principal male dancers, Valery Demidov, took special notice."

"What was he -- what was Valery like?" Peter asked. It felt odd to hear and say the name of the man who apparently was his biological father.

"Tall and handsome, like you," Eleanor said, leaning forward to put her glass down. "Hang on a second. I think I know where Nadia kept a picture of him."

They locked eyes and, as she stood up, Eleanor veered a bit too close to Peter, brushing his knee with hers. The moment was more than a bit awkward, as the grazing of bodies had not been entirely innocent. Eleanor smiled demurely, clearing a non-existent irritant in her throat. She crossed the room to a handsome dark French mahogany chest and withdrew a framed photograph from the top drawer. She handed it to Peter. "Your father."

Peter took the photograph and looked down at the image of a graceful young man in flowing shirt and ballet tights. His body was tall and slender, yet well developed, and his face was an eerily familiar image: intense dark eyes, broad cheekbones and thick black hair brushed back from the forehead, except for a few errant strands which escaped to the brow. Peter smoothed back the hair on his own forehead and stared at the picture. The image made every bit of sense, and yet it made no sense at all.

He laid the photo down and, voice cracking, asked, "Is he still alive?"

"Valery was several years older than Nadia. Seven or eight, I think."

"That would put him in his eighties. It's possible, I suppose."

"If he is still alive, he's probably in Russia. We tried an Internet search, but nothing came up and he and Nadia had not been in touch over the years. He had known of your impending arrival all those years ago, but of course, he didn't wait around for the birth."

"Yes. I remember you mentioned that in our initial phone conversation. How was Nadia able to remain here?"

"They were in the States on a tour of at least a dozen cities. By the time they reached New York, Nadia was in her sixth month. The troupe was at the point of returning to the Soviet Union when he persuaded her to defect with him. It was a ruse, of course. He checked her into one of the shabby hotels near the theater, and never came back."

Peter shuddered and shook his head.

"The troupe sailed that night. Nadia was left alone and pregnant in a foreign city with very little money and minimal knowledge of the English language. She found a Russian Orthodox church in and went there to beg for help. The Metropolitan -- the Bishop -- took her in and arranged for asylum. After the baby...you...after you were born, he took care of all the necessary papers and the adoption."

"How old was I?" Peter asked, his jaw clenched. "Did she know me at all, or did she just hand me off...send me away?"

Eleanor sighed. "Peter, she was very hurt and confused, and barely eighteen years old with no means of support. She hadn't danced at all during her pregnancy and was totally out of shape. And she didn't have the resources to get her body in shape again and make the transition to an American ballet company. She probably had what today we would call a 'nervous breakdown.' She was convinced that any child would be better off with a family who could offer it a future."

Peter met Eleanor's eyes. "She had her love to give," he said softly.

Eleanor reached over and touched Peter's arm, then quickly withdrew it. "I know how you must feel, but apparently it was not that simple. With Valery, she thought she had finally found a home, finally found someone to love and care for her. But like so many others in her young life he, too, treated her terribly. She had never fully healed from the cruelty of her father, or the lack of a mother, or the disillusionment of being accosted by someone she had trusted. Valery's betrayal was the final blow. Once she knew you were being properly cared for -- I think she told me you were only a few weeks old -- she tried to commit suicide."

Peter sat forward and looked past Eleanor to the window. He focused on the darkness of the night, letting the thoughts and images of Nadia and Valery and an unknown tale of time and place spill out of his brain and mingle somewhere in the colorless distance. He needed blankness, nothingness, if only for a few seconds.

"Peter," Eleanor said gently, "you need to know that once she recovered her health, she realized she had made a mistake and tried to get you back. But it was too late. The adoption had long been sealed and you were with your new family."

"Thank God for them. They are wonderful people…"

"It's so good to know that, Peter. Nadia would have been so relieved. She always regretted her decision. We talked about it many times. She wanted so much to find you, but felt it wouldn't be right to disrupt your life. As she got older, she had to meet you, see you, finally embrace you and tell you that she did what she thought was best for you. Thinking about it often reduced her to tears."

"As difficult as it is for me to absorb all of this, I need for you to continue. Please. "

"Are you sure? We can certainly do it another time."

"Best I learn everything now."

Eleanor breathed deeply. "Nadia's story eventually becomes a lot more positive. After she recuperated from her suicide attempt -- slashed wrists, I think -- her early training came in handy and she was able to find work as a seamstress, in the garment center at a place which made uniforms. She was living with a Russian family, parishioners, and many members of that community held jobs in the sweatshops. It was the early 60s, I guess.

"One day, she was sent to make a delivery to an uptown address. It turned out to be an exclusive exercise studio run by Sonya Pleshinka, who, in her day, had been a world-renowned ballerina. As luck would have it, Madame Pleshinka answered the door herself and when Nadia began to speak, her Russian accent piqued the woman's curiosity. It was a very cold day and she invited Nadia in for tea. Whether it was because Nadia was Russian and had also been a dancer, or because she had beautiful brown eyes and a sweet smile, the older woman took to her and in a few weeks, offered her a job. Nadia went to work there, where she easily translated her dancing skills to the exercise world. Madame Pleshinka, who had no children of her own, grew to care for her like a daughter. At long last, your mother had found a safe haven, a real home. In time, she took over from Madame Pleshinka, and the rest, as they say, is history."

"How did she get to California? Where did she get the money to build this place?"

"Madame Pleshinka willed the studio, which had been very lucrative, to Nadia. Some of the clients who spent their winters in Palm Springs persuaded Nadia to have a look at the area, hoping she might open a small auxiliary studio. She came out here, fell in love with the valley and subsequently closed the New York operation. She started small, and then expanded. She was entrepreneurial, like you."

"I suppose so," Peter nodded, his eyes involuntarily closing. Aside from the trauma of the day, it was nearly midnight, and he was still on east coast time. Exhaustion was beginning to take hold, and that was just as well. Sleep would be a most welcome hiatus. He needed to step away from all of this.

Eleanor put her hand on Peter's arm, patting it gently. "I think you've had about enough for one day."

Peter opened his eyes and struggled to focus. "Yes," he smiled weakly. "That's a pretty accurate assessment."

Eleanor rose from the sofa. "No need to get up. You must be exhausted, poor dear. I'll see myself out."

"Thank you. For everything. You've been very kind."

Eleanor crafted a flirtatious smile. "I wish we could have met under other, more pleasant circumstances, but I'm happy to have been of help."

"You've been wonderful."

"I'm sure there is more I can do to help ease the transition for you. I would be so happy to do anything I can." She paused. "Perhaps we can have dinner tomorrow evening." Eleanor was half asking, half declaring. "I can have something marvelous sent up to my suite."

Peter hesitated before answering, but there was no way he could gracefully decline the invitation. "Would eight suit you?" he asked.

"Wonderful," Eleanor said. "Eight it is, then."

He laid his head back on the pillow and watched Eleanor glide through the door, wishing there could have been some graceful way to have said no to the invitation. But there simply wasn't. He would make the best of it, he thought as he breathed in the cool air that had swept in from the open window on the other side of the room, and slowly closed his eyes.

When he awoke, it was to the brilliant light of day, and when he moved to get up, Nadia's bright persimmon spread fell from the length of his body. Draped over the arm of the sofa the night before, he had apparently reached for it while in a deep sleep, calling upon it to warm him against the chill of the dark desert night.

Chapter Sixteen

On the surface, everything at Lavender Lane had returned to normal, but that was hardly the case. Madame Demidova, of course, with her steady, focused manner and ability to graciously take care of even the most insignificant grievance, would never be available again, and her long-time clients felt keenly deprived of the expertise for which they were paying so handsomely.

And then there was the anomaly of a most attractive, smartly dressed man making the rounds of the facilities. Clearly not an employee, his presence aroused intense interest and speculation. When Phoebe informed the staff he was Madame Demidova's son, they were astounded. To most, Nadia Demidova had been an enigmatic, professional figure so totally enmeshed in Lavender Lane that they could not imagine her having a private life, let alone a child.

While they genuinely grieved her passing, the rumor mill bubbled over with fear and uncertainty.

"What could he know about a place like this? He'll ruin it!"

"Bet he'll turn it into a golf club."

"He'll probably sell it, or worse. Maybe he'll close it down!"

Hardly secure herself, Phoebe tried to inject calm. "I can only tell you what I know, and at this moment, it amounts to precious little. As soon as Mr. Culvane tells me anything, I promise to share it with you. Rest assured,

I am as eager as anyone for Lavender Lane to continue on, as usual…as usual as possible, that is, without our dear Madame Demidova."

■　　■　　■　　■　　■

"He's who?" Mavis Perkins asked incredulously, responding to the tasty bit of information Toni had just shared at the dinner table. "Well, well, well. Interesting…very interesting."

"Wow!" Lauren piped in. She had deigned to have dinner with the group, primarily at the urging of Mavis, who had advised Lauren to keep her mother mollified. "I wonder if he'll like the idea?"

"What idea?" Toni asked.

Charlotte looked sheepishly at Toni and then lowered her eyes and buried her mouth in a huge fork full of large-leafed Romaine lettuce, as though it would somehow shield her from the bomb that was about to drop.

"Mavis and I are going to be the models for that stuff," she said, screwing up her nose. "You know, the quince stuff everybody around here likes so much."

"Don't make faces, Lauren," Charlotte admonished. "You'll get wrinkles." She quickly glanced at Toni, then continued working on her salad.

"The Quince Creme?" Toni asked, clearly surprised.

"It's really kind of gross," Lauren answered. "I can't imagine why anyone would want it."

Toni was crestfallen but determined not to let it show. "Models for the Quince Creme," she said with enthusiasm. "What an interesting idea. Have you made a deal with the prodigal son?"

Mavis gave Toni one of her most self-assured smiles. "Not yet. I don't think it will be necessary."

"How so?" Toni asked.

"I'm thinking about buying the place." Mavis lifted her chin regally and let the words slowly roll out.

Toni grabbed her glass of mineral water, wishing it were pure-grain vodka. Buy the place! She'd suspected things might move quickly, but not at such lightning speed. She glanced at Charlotte again, who wordlessly continued plowing through her salad. Even if she and Phoebe wanted to counter Mavis's offer, with Lauren involved, it would knock Charlotte out. She hardly felt like smiling but managed to.

"What an extraordinary idea."

"It will be marvelous having a place like this and doing all the ads and promotion -- with Lauren, of course." Mavis shot Lauren a proprietary look. "She's perfect!"

"The whole thing sounds wonderful," said Toni. "Don't you think so, Charlotte?" Of course she thinks so, thought Toni, who felt compelled to ask nonetheless.

Charlotte gulped down the remnants of the greens still on her fork and managed a weak "yes." She looked up tentatively and locked eyes with her friend. "It will give Lauren a real head start in the modeling business."

"What a lucky break," Toni said. Well, *don't expect me to give up on the idea of buying Lavender Lane. No way.* "Good luck with it. By the way, does anyone know anything about this Peter Culvane?"

"Other than all the women here seem to think he's cute," Lauren said. "I don't get it."

Charlotte laughed. "I agree with all the women. He's quite attractive."

"Attractive?" Mavis asked, incredulously. "He's absolutely divine!"

Toni did not react.

"Really, Toni," Mavis scoffed. "Don't tell me you don't find him good looking?"

"He's not my type," she lied.

"He certainly is mine," Mavis proclaimed.

Better hire yourself one hell of a terrific bodyguard, Mr. Peter Culvane, Toni thought, because you are about to be devoured by the beautiful, but not-yet-widowed, black spider.

"Well, girls, I think I'll skip coffee and dessert," Mavis announced. "I've got some reading to do before bed."

"Goodnight then," Toni said, as pleasantly as she could muster.

Lauren pushed away from the table. "I've got a date!" She glanced at her mother who looked less than happy with her exit. "A tennis date."

Charlotte put her hand on Lauren's arm. "Tennis, at this hour?"

"The courts are great at night. You know -- no sun."

"OK, but don't come back too late, honey. You need your beauty sleep more than ever now."

Lauren graced her mother with a smile, then bolted off behind Mavis.

Toni and Charlotte found themselves alone, cautiously breathing the same air, heavy with unspoken thoughts

"Toni."

"You don't have to explain, Charlotte. I understand. Really."

"I feel terrible. When we spoke earlier, I had no idea what was going on with Mavis and Lauren. I would love to get involved in this thing with you. Really, I would. But if Mavis can make it all it come together, this could be an amazing opportunity for Lauren…the chance of a lifetime. There's no way I could oppose it, or even discourage her, let alone get involved in countering any moves on Lavender Lane that Mavis is planning."

"Speaking from a strictly selfish point of view, I would be lying if I said I'm not disappointed. It would have been great fun to work together." Toni sighed. "But I certainly understand about Lauren. It's quite a coup."

"Maybe we could do something else," Charlotte said.

"Perhaps. But the more I think about it, the more I love the idea of owning Lavender Lane. I'm not about to throw in the towel. So, I guess that puts us on opposite sides."

"Opposite sides! I hate the way that sounds."

Toni laughed. "If you think of any better way to say it, I'd be happy to hear it."

"Then we're still talking? Still friends?"

"Of course." Toni patted Charlotte on the shoulder. "Don't fret. It will all work itself out, as my mother was fond of saying."

"Mine, too." Charlotte smiled sweetly.

"Sleep well."

"You, too."

Toni turned and ambled away, leaving Charlotte upset, confused, and fearful her daughter's good fortune would come at the expense of a budding relationship that had the makings of turning into a long, meaningful and good-for-the-soul friendship.

■ ■ ■ ■ ■

Mavis couldn't wait to get away from the group. Her head was spinning with possibilities. The plan for Lavender Lane was one thing; Peter Culvane was quite another. Talk about icing on the cake -- those looks and money to boot! A call to a friend well-connected in Wall Street financial circles told her all she needed to know. Peter Culvane was forty-eight, divorced, no children, an attorney, and an immensely successful mergers and acquisitions specialist. Somebody was going to get their hands on him, and there was no reason why that somebody shouldn't be her.

She hadn't seen Peter in the dining room. Surely a man like that wouldn't keep himself stowed away. She checked out the library and the lounge, thinking he might be browsing through the well-stocked bookshelves or enjoying a leisurely coffee by the fire. No such luck. He was not to be found. She'd try again, first thing in the morning—perhaps invite him to dinner out at the marvelous Casa del Forno. The food was superb, the staff were always solicitous to her and, most importantly, the lighting there was excellent. It always cast just the right glow and flattered her skin tone. Yes. That's definitely what she would do.

Pleased with her plan, Mavis went to her suite to wait for Greg. He'd be finished with Lauren soon, and she doubted their session would include anything more than tennis, especially now that she had promised Greg a promotion to Director of Athletic Activities, once Lavender Lane was hers.

■ ■ ■ ■ ■

Phoebe put down her fork and abandoned the idea of eating. She couldn't focus on the food. In fact, she hadn't been able to focus on much of anything all day. Hoping to be summoned by Peter Culvane, she'd heard only from

Jake Meyers, who'd asked her to carry on, assuring her she would be compensated for all of the extra work. But Jake wasn't giving her any indication of how things at Lavender Lane would go forward. It was all strictly up to Peter Culvane, he explained, and, as far as he knew, Mr. Culvane had made no decisions.

The uncertainty was exhausting, and when Phoebe looked across the room and saw Toni coming toward her, a big, expectant smile on her face, she knew there was no way she could carry on a meaningful conversation. She simply had to get to bed. She waved and mouthed "tomorrow."

Despite her self-confessed burnout, there was something very solid about Toni, and Phoebe liked her very much. With Toni's experience in the business world, and her own background, they could do a smashing job of running Lavender Lane together. But the idea of them buying the spa was more than a bit far-fetched. How could Toni come up with that kind of money -- best friend's rich connections notwithstanding. Truly a pipe dream. At this point, she'd be lucky if she were able to keep her job. She was forty-five years old and hardly desirable in a job market obsessed with youth. If she had to leave Lavender Lane now, where could she go? She'd been insulated for so many years, she really had few, if any, meaningful outside contacts. And she never had the opportunity to get close to any of the well-heeled and well-connected guests who might be helpful.

Then there was the shock of Peter Culvane. She couldn't decide whether to approach him directly now and try to save her job, or wait until he contacted her. The tension was depriving her of sleep and showing up on her face. Dark circles had taken root under her eyes. She couldn't remember ever having felt so tired, and if the previous two nights were any indication, the night looming ahead didn't hold the promise of much rest either. Those blessed little orange tablets she had stashed away for the occasional emergency would come in handy. They could always be depended upon to work miracles when miracles were sorely needed.

Chapter Seventeen

Peter dove into the pool and easily negotiated its Olympic length. He had always enjoyed night swimming, when the lulling warmth of the water contrasted with the refreshing, chilled air. While he was generally able to put his thoughts on hold while swimming, this time his mind wouldn't stop. Eleanor. His dinner with her had been pleasant, enough. She was, after all, an accomplished businesswoman and, as it turned out, a fine conversationalist. She had been more than gracious during this whole unbelievable situation, but he definitely wasn't interested in her romantically. She had to be several years older than he and, while she had once most likely been quite attractive if not beautiful, her conspicuous session with some heavy-handed plastic surgeon had not served her well.

Throughout their dinner, it was apparent that Eleanor had more than just a friendly evening in mind. The way she leaned forward when she spoke and the soulful way she looked at him told him all he needed to know. He had been there before, many times, and it was always uncomfortable. He had no desire to embarrass the woman, but he didn't need this aggravation. He would have to avoid being alone with her in the future. Christ knows he had enough on his plate. There was the huge deal in Japan he'd been working on, and an even bigger one in Germany, not to mention figuring out what to do with Lavender Lane. He'd spent the day observing the operation. While it was definitely a class act and a cursory look at the books indicated it was highly profitable, he would most likely decide to sell. He had no desire to be the head counselor in a sleep-away camp for spoiled, rich women.

Swimming usually helped to clear his head, and he hoped that gift would kick in. He continued doing laps. After twenty-five, he'd call it a night.

. . . . .

Toni couldn't sleep. She tried reading, then watching some mindless television, but there was no drifting off. She called Kevin. She needed to assure him she was feeling well and that so far there were no problems. She was also anxious to talk to him about Lavender Lane, about her idea of getting his help with some deep-pocket investors. She was also looking forward to sharing a laugh with him. He would dine out on the whole Mavis story. She could just hear him: "Cruella...back? Ooh, goody. Alert the National Guard and all those cute men!" But she got his voice mail. She was disappointed. She really wanted to dish about Mavis.

Damn that woman! She had so many toys, why did she need Lavender Lane? And Lauren. There had to be a zillion beautiful, young girls Mavis could recruit. Why did she have to pick Charlotte's daughter?

She tossed and turned for nearly forty-five minutes, then finally switched on the light. It was no use. Might as well go for a walk. Better yet -- a swim. That should tire her out. She pulled on her favorite maillot, threw a terry robe over her shoulders and made her way to the pool.

It was a glorious night and Toni breathed deeply as she removed her robe, relishing the cool, fragrant air. She positioned herself on the ledge at the deep end of the pool and was about to dive in when she realized she was not alone. Someone was swimming the length, gliding easily through the water with long, powerful, nearly soundless strokes.

With all the lights turned off for the night, the pool area was illuminated only by a distant half-moon and a bevy of twinkling stars. But even in the dim light, Toni was able to tell the swimmer was a man. She could see his shoulders were broad and his body tall and slender, and his abundant hair shone with mother-of-pearl luster as he advanced through the water.

She indulged in watching him, and he finished another entire length before it hit her: Peter Culvane! They had not met, but like everyone else at Lavender Lane, she had seen him strolling through the grounds, impeccably dressed and totally assured in his gait. He had looked every bit the man assessing his new domain. Unexpected waves coursed through her body. Was she reacting to him because he held the keys to the kingdom, or because he was so attractive? Maybe it was just those damn hormones!

Toni had lied at dinner when she said he was not her type. That was hardly the case. But why declare it at the table? It was open season on the man, as it was. Aside from Mavis, half the women at Lavender Lane -- half the women in the free world, for that matter -- were probably trying to figure out how to ensnare him. And at this point, she was hardly in a position to follow through on any kind of flirtation. As if to remind her, Kumquat stirred. He put her hand on her belly and stood immobile, unable to dive into the pool.

When Peter made the turn at the far end, he saw her, at the edge of the pool's deep end, the breeze tousling her wavy hair and her athletic body silhouetted against a gathering of gracefully swaying palms and night-darkened flora. It was a beautiful night, but what woman would venture out at this hour to plunge into an indigo abyss? This was not his usual fare of perfectly turned out, never-a-hair-out-of-place women. He smiled, intrigued. This woman was adventurous.

"Come on in. The water's fine!" he found himself calling out, then laughed for having used such a hackneyed cliché.

The sound of his voice startled Toni. It was deep and fluid and tinged with the Bostonian. In the dim light, she thought she perceived a smile. Toni hesitated before responding, "Yes, I think I will." She drew herself up on her toes and dove seamlessly into the depths of the inky water.

When she surfaced, she was about a third of the way to the other end, where Peter Culvane lounged casually, his arms stretched out against the side of the pool. His face was more clearly discernible now. The smile she thought she had perceived was more like a grin. She propelled herself forward, more conscious of every movement her body was making than since the first time she wore a bikini on a trip to the South of France, when she was nineteen and had a perfectly flat belly.

"Well, hello there," Peter said, a widened grin now covering his face. "Come here often?"

His voice was friendly and he put Toni at ease almost instantly.

"I don't usually hang out here at midnight, but I do swim every day."

"That's healthy."

"Every day I've been here, I mean," Toni said.

"You mean you don't swim in Massachusetts?"

Toni looked at him with mild disbelief. My God, did he know her? "How in the world…?"

"Judging from the way you pronounce some words, somewhere not far from Boston, I would suspect."

"Well, yes." She grimaced slightly. "Newton, actually."

"Newton. Nice town. No need to be ashamed."

"I'm not ashamed, but I thought I had lost my accent by now. I've been living in New York for years."

"New York? That big, bad, wicked town?"

"It's not nearly wicked enough." She smiled coyly, surprised at her own flirtatiousness. First that young staffer, now this man. *Get a grip, girl.* "But listening to you, I would guess you might be from Boston yourself."

"You're quite right, Miss…"

"Etheridge. Toni Etheridge."

Peter slid down into the water and took her hand. "Peter Culvane."

Toni smiled up at him.

"What do you do in New York?"

"Buyer -- designer sportswear buyer at Gillam's Fifth Avenue."

"So, you're the one responsible for those big bills I used to get every time I took my wife to New York."

His wife? It was chilly and Toni had already submerged herself in the water up to her chin. She wished she had gone completely under so he couldn't see the disappointment that was surely crossing her face.

"I can't be blamed at this point." She managed a smile. "I'm no longer working there."

"Why is that?"

"I couldn't stand it for one more minute."

Peter laughed heartily. "And I couldn't stand being married for one more second -- so I guess neither one of us has to worry about Gillam's any longer!"

So, he was single!

"Any children?" Toni asked, perhaps a bit too eagerly.

"No. Missed out. Always regretted it."

The world was suddenly a much nicer place.

"You?"

"Ah, no…" Toni wasn't quite sure what to say or how. She was relieved when Peter moved on from the topic and asked what she would do when she got back to New York. "If I had my way, I would never go back."

"How so?"

"If I could choose, I would stay right here." Her pregnancy and the arrangement with Kevin notwithstanding, it was the truth. She let her gaze linger a moment before continuing. "I've fallen in love with Lavender Lane."

"How perfectly wonderful for me!" Peter responded. "Seems I own the place."

"So I've heard."

"You have?"

"My dear Mr. Culvane, you're not exactly the average Lavender Lane guest, and there's nothing quite like the all-girl gossip network for speedy transmission of information."

"Yes. I suppose," he said with a laugh. "But tell me, do you really like Lavender Lane all that much?

"Yes. I really do."

"I find your enthusiasm intriguing, Ms. Etheridge."

"Lavender Lane is hardly difficult to like. The grounds are magnificent, the facilities, treatments, classes, staff -- all superb. And the food, even though it is all dreadfully nutritious, is delicious."

Peter laughed. "You look like a girl who's into healthy eating."

You have no idea, Toni mused to herself. "Oh I am. Most definitely."

"Good to hear, and I like what you are saying about the spa. It's very encouraging. Very encouraging, indeed." He looked at her thoughtfully. "It's rather late at the moment, and I'm afraid I've interrupted your swim long enough, but perhaps tomorrow you might take some time to tour the facilities with me. I'd love to get your perspective -- learn what you like, what you think could be better. You know, that sort of thing."

Oh my God. Had she heard correctly? "Certainly." She smiled. "It would be my pleasure.

"Wonderful! Shall we say ten a.m.?

"Ten should be fine," Toni said, without hesitation.

"Why don't we meet back here?"

"Works for me."

"Terrific," Peter said as he hoisted himself up onto the edge of the pool.

They exchanged "good nights" and then Toni quickly swam toward the opposite end of the pool. When she reached the other side, she looked back, half hoping to see Peter still there, but he had already gone.

Toni had planned to do at least ten laps, but now all she wanted to do was return to her room. She was tired, at last, but also giddy with possibilities -- no matter how far-fetched -- that earlier in the evening had been unimaginable.

．　　．　　．　　．　　．

Eleanor sat at the dressing table and stared into the mirror. She was becoming accustomed to the image glaring back at her. Perhaps she had been overreacting, and it wasn't really that bad. Or possibly, as Dr. Kashani had promised, the tautness had begun to diminish and she was on her way to looking more like a younger version of herself rather than the feared epitome of some tightly pulled matron.

Whatever the case, hers was clearly no longer the face to represent youth and vitality. If the board had wanted her to step down before, once they get a look at her now, they would surely want her to disassociate herself completely from Franklin Nutritionals. A face like hers could sink a stock price faster than an insider trading scandal, and no one, herself included, wanted that to happen.

She had no choice. She must step down. Of course, it wasn't the end of the world. Eleanor's life was hardly over. She had many good years to look forward to, and with her financial resources, so much more to explore and do. She would move aside gracefully, and never let anyone know just how broken-hearted she was.

After carefully removing her eye makeup, she smoothed Lavender Lane's Quince Creme on her cheeks, forehead and chin, painstakingly moving her fingers upward and outward to prevent tugging the skin. When she continued on to her neck, the strap of her Montenapoleone ecru silk nightgown slipped from her shoulder, revealing the top of her full right breast. She stared down at her bosom, then moved the other strap. The gown slipped further, leaving both breasts bared. She gazed at herself, searching for confirmation that some semblance of her youth still remained.

Eleanor had taken good care of her body over the years, having regular massages and working with personal trainers as frequently as her demanding schedule would allow. Her efforts had paid off. Unlike her face, her body was aging fairly well. The skin on her shoulders and arms, chest and legs still had nice tone and elasticity, and while her breasts were not those of a young girl, they were full and pleasantly firm. She cupped them in her hands, running her fingers over each nipple. The sensation surprised her. She had forgotten how sensitive her breasts were.

Suddenly, without warning, she began to cry. Her tears were modest at first, but quickly became to flow heavily. "Damn him!" she yelled into the emptiness of the room. Why did he have to be so goddamned attractive? What could I have been thinking? I must have been out of my mind. He wouldn't be interested in a woman my age. A day over thirty-five is probably pushing it for him," she said out loud to no one but herself.

She slammed her fist down on the table in front of her with such force that the jar of creme fell from its perch, distributing some of its contents on the spotless, light peach carpet. She grabbed a tissue and attacked the spill. *It's mortifying. Absolutely mortifying. How stupid could I have been?* She studied herself in the mirror again -- her pulled, manipulated skin looking even more tender through red, crying eyes. *He would never want a woman like me. I see now who I am and I will not soon forget it. I will never let something like this happen again -- of that I am quite sure.*

She dabbed carefully at her eyes and then smoothed the remaining creme from her face and neck and rubbed in into her hands. I simply have to come to terms with the facts and move on with my life. There will be some men, I expect, but they'll all be card-carrying members of the Viagra club. None of them will be even remotely like Peter Culvane.

Eleanor walked over to the window. Her face was flushed and hot from crying and the breeze cooled her. She looked out to the mountains, to the glade where Nadia had been buried only the afternoon before. Forgive me, my dear friend, for letting myself get lost in the moment, lost in a foolish romantic dream. You can rest well, Nadia. Your Peter is smart and charming and so attractive. Lavender Lane is in good hands...very good hands, indeed.

■　　■　　■　　■　　■

Lauren couldn't wait to get to Greg's and finish what they had started. Maybe it was a good thing Mavis had shown up the other night. She could tell he really wanted it, but she wasn't about to give it to him. Not then, anyway. She didn't want to make it too easy.

And boy, that sure did work! Not getting what he wanted made Greg want her even more. She could tell, because earlier in the afternoon things had gotten really hot. They'd both been naked and smoking dope and he had taken it out and put his fingers up her and everything. It was great. He was begging for it. She loved that.

Lauren had wanted him too, but it being the first time and all...well, she had never let anybody actually put it in. But she had to do it sometime soon. After all, she would be sixteen in a few months. And she was going to be a famous model.

Greg had told her to come over about ten. The courts had only been booked until nine thirty. They would have the place all to themselves by then.

When Lauren arrived, it was dark. The only light came from the glow of a small lamp in the instructors' cabin. She liked that. It was sexy, and she was ready. Anticipation permeated every zone of her slender, young body.

"Greg," she called out, trying to affect her most adult, sophisticated tone. "Oh Gregory!" She pushed open the door, but the cabin was empty. A computer was streaming Stones classics and there were two joints and a pack of matches on the table. There was also a note.

"Hey Lauren, had to run an errand. Be back in a nano. Why don't you get a head start and have one of these? Really good stuff. There's some cold Coors in the fridge and some Ranchos in the cabinet, in case you get the munchies. I won't be long!"

Munchies. Isn't he cute? Lauren put the joint to her lips and lit it. She felt a bit full of herself, enjoying a newly found sense of power in her ability to turn a guy on. It was fun, and so was smoking weed. She drew the smoke in, trying to act like a veteran, but quickly gagged. "Shit!" she yelled out between gasps. I've got to learn how to do this.

She drew on the joint again, more modestly this time. The intake was smooth and measured. She leaned her head back and let herself be taken, the sensation seeping into every part of her body. I wish Greg would get here right now, she thought. This stuff does make you want it.

She took a beer from the fridge and began gulping it down, prancing around the tiny cabin, looking for something to amuse her, but there was nothing of interest...just piles of sports magazines, a bunch of old tennis rackets, some dirty shorts and a few cans of fresh balls. What about the munchies, the big bag of Rancho Cheese chips? She ripped one open, but drew back, assaulted by the smell. The combined odors of Monterey Jack, cumin and rancid cooking oil made her gag.

She tossed the chips aside, paying no attention to the dozen or so that spilled out onto the floor. She sang along to the Stones, gyrating her body to the beat. "Can't get no, can't get no..." After downing some more beer, she took another toke, pleased with herself that she had mastered the art of smoking dope. Her self-satisfaction was premature, however. The room quickly began to spin.

She steadied herself with the table, nearly knocking the lamp down in the process. The small cot, a couple of feet away, suddenly loomed huge and inviting. She dove into it, collapsing into a torrent of giggles. "Oh Greggy, where are you? I'm here. Waiting for you. Come 'n get it!"

She grabbed at her polo shirt and pulled it up toward her head. "No satisfaction," she continued to sing. "Can't get no satisfaction..." The room was moving more quickly now, and there were vibrating colors colliding everywhere. She saw reds, blues, and yellows on the floor, on the walls, on the ceiling. Vivid splashes of purple and green, bright spreads of fuchsia and orange. The colors began to run into one another, blending into a torrent of toneless forms and meaningless shapes.

"Greg," she called out, amidst the diminishing vibrations in her head. "Greg!" But the pulsations were beginning to dull, the shapes starting to fade and soon the black nothingness coaxed her into a dark, mindless sleep.

■　　■　　■　　■　　■

Charlotte lay curled up on the couch in her room, a Snickers Bar on the table next to her. Despite doing her best not to succumb to her usual antidote, she sank right after dinner. She felt bad disappointing Toni about joining her in a possible bid for Lavender Lane, and the feeling bad about that spiraled into feeling bad about everything, period. Inevitably, she started to think about her husband and the forthcoming divorce.

She wasn't sure what had gone wrong, though she had been not at all surprised to discover Jerry cheating. She'd often felt lonely when he was right there in the room with her. Perhaps he had felt the same way. It had to be more than her weight. A marriage doesn't break up because one of the partners has an eating problem and put on some extra weight. But maybe it does, because without her beauty-contest looks, she was nothing.

Charlotte stumbled to her bed and sat down. It was true. Jerry's attraction to her had been merely based on her looks, and the more weight she put on, the less attention he paid. Matthew, her first husband, had been the same way. When she didn't lose weight after Lauren was born, he began to turn away, and in less than two years was gone. They had never talked about anything meaningful, either, and that probably was because there was nothing meaningful in her beautiful, so-called head.

She knew she wasn't stupid, only that she had never been encouraged to cultivate anything but her looks. Her parents had meant well, wanting her to have what they felt was the best life had to offer. They were simple people, seduced by the media and the lives of celebrities. In their way of thinking, a girl's best assets were her looks, not her brains.

Charlotte had always felt inadequate around many of the women she met, with their college educations and high-toned conversations. Even though she read the papers and had joined a book club, she never felt up to their standards. When she had a relevant thought or an original idea, she was afraid to speak up, afraid she wouldn't measure up.

She never discussed her interest in investing with her friends, or the women she socialized with at the club. She was proud of the prowess she had developed and was sure Jerry would be as well, but when she tried to engage him in discussing finance and the stock market, he dismissed it with, "Sure, in no time you'll be giving Warren Buffet a run for his money!" Then he laughed and walked away, humiliating her.

Jerry never wanted to talk to her about much of anything, but she had excused his lack of attention because of his drive to build a successful dental practice. Frankly, she had wanted his success every bit as much as he had, but why had it taken her so long to face the truth? Why had she not wanted to? She was too busy decorating their perfect home and trying to make friends with all the right women. Underneath it all, she surely must have sensed the marriage had an empty core. Why else would she have been stuffing herself these past few years?

She glanced over at Lauren's empty bed. She hated this whole modeling thing. It was certainly the opportunity of a lifetime, but would it leave her daughter with that same empty core? She was too young for both the catwalk and the cattiness, and what about her education? She had to convince Lauren not to give up on going to college, not to make the same mistakes she had. But this wasn't the time to talk to her about it. Lauren was caught up in the excitement of Mavis's offer, and she didn't want to put a damper on that.

It was time to stop obsessing, or she would never get to sleep. She clicked on the television and flipped through the channels, looking for something to lose herself in. She landed on a classic musical: An American in Paris, with a handsome, virile Gene Kelly pursuing a lovely, young Leslie Caron amid the magic and color of Paris in the 1950s. Why couldn't real life be like that? Full of beauty, love and romance? She leaned her head back, succumbing to the spell of the lush Gershwin music, allowing it to lull the tension from her body and brain. I'll close my eyes for just a few minutes, she thought. Want to be up when Lauren comes home…

Sometime later, Charlotte awoke with a start. "Good morning," the local news anchor said. "It's 4 a.m. and here's what's happening in the area." 4 a.m. Darn! She had wanted to speak to Lauren before they went to sleep. How could she have allowed herself to drift off? She looked over at her daughter's bed. It was empty. Untouched. How could that be? Where could Lauren be at this hour? Something must have happened to her. Something terrible! She propelled herself out of bed.

Oh my God! What should I do? She started to perspire. *I'll go down to the office. They'll help me. There must be somebody on duty all night.* She grabbed her robe and slippers. *They can send out a search party.* She was sweating profusely now. *Please, dear God. Please don't let anything happen to my baby.*

She stepped into her slippers, threw on her robe and ran out into the dimly lit hallway. A moment later, a young man emerged from a room two doors down. It was Greg, the tennis instructor, and he was coming from Mavis's room. She stopped dead in her tracks. What in the world was he doing with Mavis at this hour? The woman's got to be twice his age! I thought he liked them young, like my daughter, in fact. I'm sure Lauren told me she was having a tennis lesson tonight. "Greg!" she called out, lunging forward. "Greg. Wait! Please…"

Greg flinched, startled by the sound of his name in the dim hallway in the middle of the night. He turned and peered down the hall. "Yes," he said, focusing on Charlotte. "Mrs. Tanner, is that you?"

"Yes, it is," Charlotte answered, advancing quickly toward him. "And I'm worried sick. Lauren didn't come home tonight." She stopped in her tracks. "I thought she was with you."

"Well, she was, I mean she was supposed to be," he stammered. "I was supposed to meet her at 10 o'clock for a lesson." He lowered his eyes. "But I never got there."

"You mean you haven't seen her?" Charlotte blurted out.

"No," Greg said, looking up sheepishly.

"My God. Now I'm sure something must have happened to her. She never came back to our room tonight."

Greg moved toward Charlotte and put his hand on her shoulder. "I'm sure she's all right, Mrs. Tanner. Don't worry."

"How can you be so sure?" Charlotte's voice had now risen several decibels. "This is terrible. Absolutely terrible. And I hold you responsible. She's only a child."

"Calm down, Mrs. Tanner. Nothing could have happened to her. This is private property, and it's patrolled. It's very safe around here. Really." He took hold of her elbow and coaxed her toward the stairs. "Come on. We'll have a look around."

Charlotte's robe began to open. She tugged at it awkwardly, wrapping it more tightly around her body. "I won't even ask what you were doing in Mrs. Perkins's room," she said, looking at Greg directly in the eyes.

Greg met her stare head on. "I would sure appreciate that."

They moved quickly to the end of the hall, rushing down the stairs and out through the side door onto the path leading to the athletic area. The night was cool and without sound, save for the intermittent hooting of the resident desert owl. The sky was dark, tinged with only the slightest hint of the morning light to come. They hurried along in silence.

As they neared the tennis cabin, they became aware of the faint sound of music. That gave Charlotte hope and she hastened her steps. Seconds later, she pushed the door open and let out a "Thank you, sweet Jesus!" at the sight of her daughter sprawled diagonally across the small cot, one arm stretched out, hovering near the floor. Lauren was apparently in a deep sleep and, other than the fact that her T-shirt was hiked up around her midriff, she looked all right. Charlotte's jubilation was short-lived, however, when she noticed two empty beer bottles lying on their sides and the remnants of a hand-made cigarette on the floor below Lauren's dangling fingers. It didn't take her long to realize what kind of cigarette it was.

Charlotte glared at Greg. "Are you responsible for this?"

"I don't know what you mean, Mrs. Tanner."

"You know darned well what I mean. She's not just sleeping. She's passed out."

Greg spotted the note he had left for Lauren on the table and shifted his body in an effort to obscure it. "I told you I didn't see her tonight," he protested, but Charlotte had already spied the piece of paper.

"What's this?" she asked, pouncing on it. She read the words slowly, carefully, then looked up, meeting Greg's eyes squarely. "Look here, young man. If you want to drink beer and smoke garbage, that's fine, but it's not fine for Lauren. Frankly, I don't give a hoot what you drink or smoke or who you do it with -- Mavis Perkins or anybody else, for that matter -- as long as that person is not my daughter."

Greg stared at the floor. "Yes, ma'am. It won't happen again."

"It certainly won't, because you won't be seeing Lauren again."

Lauren stirred and let out a soft moan. "Where am I?" she whimpered, struggling to sit up.

"Not where you should be, young lady," Charlotte said, in a sterner tone than she had used with her daughter in some time. "And you are going back to our room to sleep this off."

Even the dim light offered by the small lamp was too much for Lauren. She turned her head away, covering her face with her hands. "What does she mean, Greggy?"

Greg stared down at Lauren but did not respond. "I know you're angry at me, Mrs. Tanner," he said, looking back at Charlotte, "but at least let me help you get Lauren back to the main house." He smiled weakly. "There's a bellman's cart out back. We can drive. It will be so much easier for you."

Charlotte appraised her daughter. Lauren was hardly in shape to walk. She had no choice but to accept Greg's offer.

"I suppose you're right," she snapped.

Greg nodded and dashed out of the cabin. In minutes, he had deposited Lauren in the back seat of the cart and after a silent ride to the main house, carried her up the stairs and laid her gently on her bed.

"Thank you," Charlotte said, with a definitive lack of warmth.

"No problem," Greg answered, moving briskly toward the door.

"Remember, Gregory," Charlotte said, as he was leaving, "now that this nasty night is over, you won't be seeing Lauren again."

Greg turned around sharply. "But..."

"There are no buts. My daughter is only fifteen and inexperienced and I won't allow her to get into things that could end up ruining her life."

"Mrs. Tan..."

"I said no, Gregory. Period. The end."

Greg locked eyes with Charlotte for a moment then nodded silently before leaving, letting the door close quietly behind him.

Charlotte turned and gazed at her daughter, who was sleeping a seemingly peaceful sleep on the bed where Greg had placed her. She looked so beautiful, this child of hers—this exasperating, willful child. The last few months had been so difficult, and now this.

She walked over and sat down on the bed next to Lauren, reaching out to stroke her long, disheveled hair. How long had it been since she had done that? The girl had taken to shunning any gestures of affection from her mother. Charlotte gathered Lauren's hair and swept it to one side.

Sleep well, my dear daughter, she thought as she bent down to kiss Lauren's forehead. "And have sweet dreams," she continued out loud, "because when you awake tomorrow morning, it will be a whole new ball game. I've let you have your way with me for far too long. I'm still your mother and things are going to be a darn sight different from here on in, Mavis Perkins and your new modeling career notwithstanding. I never wanted to be a stage mother, but it looks like you've left me little choice."

She covered Lauren, then leaned down and kissed her forehead once again before collapsing into her own bed to take advantage of what precious little was left of the pre-dawn darkness.

Chapter Eighteen

Peter patted his freshly shaved face with the bespoke citrus cologne he had mixed at L'Apothicaire in the Marais district of Paris and smoothed back his hair. He really liked the cologne. It was light and refreshing, and didn't overpower like so many of the branded products. He was looking forward to touring the facilities with Toni Etheridge, hoping his first impression would be borne out -- that she was not the kind of woman one would usually find at a place like Lavender Lane. She seemed genuinely unaffected, which surprised him, considering the career in fashion she had mentioned. He had dated a few women from that world and had found most of them to be more trouble than they were worth. Toni didn't fit the mold. She was smart and savvy but didn't have that damned jaded edge. A welcome surprise.

It would be good to see Lavender Lane from her perspective, he thought, and she wasn't too shabby to look at, either. Spending a few hours with her would be no hardship, no hardship at all.

He finished dressing, his mind humming. Perhaps his thoughts of selling Nadia's oasis had been premature. Perhaps he should hang out for a while and really get to know the place before making any definitive decisions. After all, Lavender Lane was hauling in a damned good profit. They had topped eighteen percent last year. If he were to put it on the market, it should bring in a cool thirty million. With valuations so sky high at this point, there was nothing else on the horizon ripe for the infusion of that kind of money. He'd have to park if offshore somewhere, and that was always problematic. Maybe he should just keep the place.

Peter was on the verge of leaving when one of the staff knocked on the door and handed him an envelope. He looked down at his name rendered in an unfamiliar script and then eased the envelope open. Inside was a hand-written note on Lavender Lane stationery.

Dear Mr. Culvane,

How wonderful to learn you are here, although of course, the circumstances are so very sad. Madame Demidova was a most unique and dedicated woman I had the pleasure of knowing for several years. Please accept my most sincere condolences.

I don't believe we have ever met, which is curious, since our paths surely must have crossed at one time or another. Let's do correct that! Please join me for dinner, this evening -- just the two of us. I have a most interesting business proposition I'd like to discuss with you.

I've made a reservation at Casa Forno at eight. As I have some earlier appointments in town, I'll meet you there.

Till this evening,

Mavis Perkins

Peter laughed out loud. It was quite the invitation -- more like a command performance, with no provision for him to decline. Mavis Perkins… The name was familiar, but he couldn't quite place it. He picked up the phone and dialed Phoebe.

"Good morning. It's Peter Culvane. How are you this morning?"

"I'm fine, thank you." Phoebe hesitated a moment before continuing. "And I hope you are as well."

His call clearly unnerved the woman and he would have to do something to put her at ease, not just for the moment, but in general. After all her years at Lavender Lane, she deserved that.

"Phoebe, we'll have a chat about your future very soon. I'm sure it must be on your mind."

Phoebe's breathing was audible. "That's putting it mildly, sir."

"Please, don't worry. We'll see to it things work out for you."

"That's very good of you, Mr. Culvane. Thank you. Thank you so much."

Peter could hear the slightest bit of relief in Phoebe's voice. "We'll talk soon, I promise. At the moment though, I need to ask you about one of the guests: Mavis Perkins."

"Mavis Perkins? Yes, of course. What would you like to know?"

"Her name sounds familiar, but I can't place it."

"You would know her face, though. She was a very famous model several years ago."

"That Mavis. Of course! She only used her first name, as I recall. She was quite beautiful."

"She still is."

Well, well. Isn't this interesting. This Lavender Lane thing isn't turning out so badly, after all. "Thank you, Phoebe. You've been very helpful. And Phoebe, I'll be in touch soon about setting up that meeting."

"That would be splendid, Mr. Culvane."

Peter hung up the phone, grabbed his jacket and headed for the door.

∎　∎　∎　∎　∎

Phoebe didn't know whether to be relieved or concerned. He said he would see that "things worked out for her," but what actually did he mean? Was he simply going to pay her off and send her out to pasture? He hadn't said a thing about her staying at Lavender Lane -- not one word -- and those were the words she wanted desperately to hear.

And what was this Mavis question all about? The creature had obviously made herself known to Peter Culvane, and that did not augur well. The last thing she needed was the glorious Mrs. Perkins giving Peter Culvane advice on how to run the place, or to complicate things by getting into his knickers, which she assessed was pretty much a foregone conclusion.

Phoebe reached for the phone. Toni hadn't come down to breakfast and she really wanted to speak to her. She was about to dial when the phone rang. It was Eleanor Franklin, inviting her to have lunch.

Phoebe was hoping to have lunch with Toni, so they could get started on putting some kind of plan in place, but there was no way she could refuse Eleanor Franklin's totally unexpected invitation. She had been a regular client, not to mention Nadia Demidova's friend, for so many years.

"Of course. That would be lovely."

"Wonderful! Shall we say one o'clock, at your table in the dining room?"

The dining room. Well, it looks as though our Dr. Franklin is overcoming her fear of being seen in public. "One o'clock, then. I look forward to it."

Phoebe ran through the gamut of things Eleanor Franklin might have on her mind. Perhaps she was dissatisfied with one or more of the spa's services, although she had rarely, if ever, complained in the past. Or perhaps she wanted to be reassured that since Mme. Demidova was no longer there to look after her, she would still have priority booking privileges for her frequent visits. There was no way she could have known that what Eleanor Franklin really wanted was a good deal more than a mere service upgrade or any special attention. Eleanor Franklin wanted Lavender Lane itself, and she was prepared to put up the money to get it.

■　　■　　■　　■　　■

"Now that's what I call a good meal," Peter said with a big smile as he sipped his coffee. "And much to my surprise, I have to admit. To be perfectly frank, I was skeptical."

"It was good, wasn't it?" Toni agreed. She couldn't help but look around and notice that the other guests at the poolside café were doing their best not to stare. *Eat your hearts out, ladies! He's mine -- at least for the moment.*

"This is normally about the time I would light up a cigarette," Peter said, almost wistfully. He put his long fingers to his mouth as though he were about to inhale smoke from a no-doubt pricey, imported brand.

"When did you give them up?"

"Years ago, thankfully."

"Me, too. It was really hard. Stopped and started a couple of times before I was successful."

"Understandable, but bet you didn't have the magic secret!" Peter said mischievously.

"And what might that be?"

Peter leaned forward. "I need a rock-solid promise you will never reveal what you are about to see."

Toni leaned forward as well. Their faces were close now and she wanted to close her eyes and not open them until he kissed her, but that was not about to happen -- and even if it did, wouldn't it just complicate her life? *Don't even go there...* "Of course," she whispered, trying not to sigh. "I'll never tell." She raised two fingers. "Scout's honor."

"You're not going to tell me you were a Girl Scout, now, are you?"

"Actually, yes, I was. And I am about to sell you a whole lot of cookies." *Flirting? Really!*

Peter let out a full-throated, belly laugh.

Toni loved the way he laughed. It was down-to-earth and totally unexpected. It was wonderful to be with him, and she hoped she didn't wear her enjoyment too blatantly on her face.

"OK, fess up. What's this big secret of yours?"

He hesitated for a moment, then put his hand in his jacket pocket, pulled something out and plunked it down on the table, keeping his palm firmly on top of it. Toni tried to pry his fingers open, but to no avail. Peter was playing it to the hilt, toying with her mercilessly.

"No fair," Toni chided. "Your hand is bigger than mine!"

"I should hope so!"

Toni tried once again, then pulled back and laughed. "I give up."

"In that case, I'm ready to share my secret."

Peter lifted his hand to reveal an American icon -- a pack of pink Double Bubble Chewing Gum.

"No way!" Toni blurted out.

"I'm afraid so. My niece Ashley turned me on to it. She was only five years old at the time and wickedly smart. Saw the public service commercials about smoking being bad for you and promised to share her Double Bubble with me if I quit. No way I could say no to that deal."

He pulled out his wallet and showed Toni a photo of an adorable little girl with bright red Orphan Annie curls and a knowing look that said I may be five, but don't sell me short.

"She's adorable," Toni said. "I can see why you took her up on it. She could probably have persuaded anybody to do anything."

"Well, she sure persuaded me and let me tell you, seeing me blow bubbles at a corporate takeover meeting is not a pretty picture!"

"You didn't!"

"Nearly. Was unconsciously blowing a big one while I was walking into a meeting. My assistant called me on it."

"Bless her!"

"I owe her, for sure! But truth be told, I still chew the stuff when nobody's looking."

Toni covered her mouth to stifle a hearty laugh of her own "I can actually picture you with a huge bubble coming out of your mouth!" The laugh she was trying to stifle came out full force.

"Well, I'm pleased I've succeeded in amusing you."

"You have. You most definitely have," Toni said, continuing to laugh.

"That's good, because I really did want to do something for you in the way of thanks for this morning's tour."

Toni's heart quickened, and her laugh subsided. "It was my pleasure."

"Seeing Lavender Lane through your eyes has been very helpful. Truth is, I was planning to sell it. But now…"

Peter's remarks were interrupted by his cell. "Sorry. I was wondering when they'd start harassing me."

He grabbed the phone from his pocket. "Hey Charlie...how's it going? ...You don't say?" He glanced at Toni and smiled. "Well, that's excellent!...

No, not at the moment." He glanced at Toni again, then looked at his watch. "Two-thirty...Yes...Give me a few minutes...Good. Three o'clock, then. I'll expect your call."

"I'm afraid I have to run. A conference call is coming through in a few minutes and I need to review some numbers first." He reached over and took her hand.

For a minute she almost brought up the no-cell-phone rule, then laughed to herself. The man owned the place. He could do whatever he damn well pleased!

"Thanks again," Peter said with a big smile.

"You're more than welcome," Toni responded, hoping her face didn't broadcast her disappointment. He hadn't said a word about seeing her again -- and that might be a good thing, from a personal point of view, but business was something else. There hadn't been the right moment to bring up how she and Phoebe might fit in at Lavender Lane. Truth was that during the four and a half hours they had spent together, she had been too busy enjoying him as a man to even look for that moment.

Peter got up from the table and began walking away, then stopped and looked over his shoulder. "Don't forget, now...you promised. Double Bubble is our secret. If you ever tell, I may start smoking again!"

"Oh, don't ever do that!" she called back, smiling weakly. "Mum's the word. Truly. I would never let your niece Ashley down."

Peter Culvane was full of surprises. Toni never would have expected a man like him to be so present in a child's life. She closed her eyes and sighed deeply. Don't go there, Toni, she admonished herself. Please! You'll only drive yourself crazy. Crazier than you already are, that is. She laughed and leaned back in her chair. She'd stay for just a few more minutes, breathe in the beauty of the Southern California desert and perhaps allow herself some of those daydreams, regardless of how farfetched they might actually be.

■   ■   ■   ■   ■

Well, well, well, Mavis carped to herself as she watched Toni and Peter from a table a discreet twenty-five feet away. Being at the cafe was serendipitous, because she rarely, if ever, ate outdoors. She detested bugs of any sort and there were always some, no matter how careful the staff was. She brushed her hand in the air to swat away something that was flying perilously close. The annoying little creatures always managed to be in residence when she was there. Nonetheless, it was better being outdoors. She hadn't felt like having lunch with the blonde Texas cutie, even though she was the mother of the world's next young supermodel, thanks to her. No. Today, she felt like a little fresh air. And then there they were: Peter Culvane and Miss What's Her Name from New York City. How cozy. How goddamned, fucking cozy. Whatever was he doing with her?

Mavis was sitting where she was not likely to be glimpsed by them, but if Peter noticed her, all the better. It would be a perfect prelude to things to come. But he hadn't even glanced her way. Perhaps it was just as well. There would be plenty of time later. Yes, by the end of this day, he would more than just notice her -- she would see to that.

Chapter Nineteen

The woman who walked into the dining room dressed in a turquoise linen shirt and trousers with a large, matching straw hat was wearing huge sunglasses which hid not only her eyes but managed to cover a good deal of her face as well. She paused and slowly surveyed the space before heading toward Phoebe's table at the front. "There you are, my dear," she said gaily, sliding into a chair.

So little of her face was exposed that, were it not for the voice, Phoebe might not have known who it was. "Dr. Franklin," Phoebe smiled warmly. "Nice to see you."

"Thank you for accepting my luncheon invitation," Eleanor said, settling herself in the chair. "Or, should I say thank you for allowing me to invite myself to lunch?" She toyed with her sunglasses for a moment, then, much like one would remove a Band-Aid in one rapid swipe to minimize the pain, she yanked them off abruptly. She looked from side to side, gauging the reactions of the lunching women. Some stared intently, others were less obvious, but nearly all were looking at her in one way or another. She felt more than hideous but she had made the right decision. The moment had to come eventually, and this was as good a time as any.

"Forgive me," she said, looking imploringly at Phoebe. "This public outing is not easy for me."

"I understand..."

Eleanor relaxed a bit in her seat. "Nadia -- Madame Demidova -- used to speak very highly of you."

Very highly. The praise echoed sweetly in Phoebe's head, surprising her with how much feeling it evoked. Her eyes quickly filled, and she blinked back a tear. "That's so good to hear. I appreciate your telling me, Dr. Franklin."

"Please, call me Eleanor," she said smiling, her tightly pulled, misshapen eyes bright and her constrained mouth quivering in its attempt to create a full, natural expression.

At that moment, the waitress appeared with bowls of chilled gazpacho topped with sprigs of fresh, green parsley.

"I took the liberty of ordering for both of us," Phoebe said. "I think you'll like my selections."

"I'm sure I will."

The server presented the soup, acknowledging them both by name as she placed the bowls on the table. "Dr. Franklin. Miss Bancroft."

Eleanor looked up from under her hat, eyes brimming with tears. "Thank you, dear."

Phoebe put her hand on Eleanor's arm. "Are you all right?"

Eleanor nodded then picked up the glass of ice water at her place and took a long sip. "It's just that I was so relieved the waitress recognized me."

"How could she not? She's served you many times over the years."

"That's kind of you, but I don't exactly look like myself."

Phoebe felt herself in a most uncomfortable position. It was true. Eleanor didn't look like herself. But dare she agree? The woman clearly needed reassurance. In truth, her face wasn't really all that bad…a tad too tightly pulled, perhaps. Perhaps it would get better as time progressed. She thought it actually looked a bit better than it had a day or so ago.

"Of course she recognized you."

"And the changes?"

Oh God, Phoebe thought. She's not going to let me off the hook. "The changes, well, there certainly has been a slight modification."

"It's OK, dear. I shouldn't put you in the position of having to lie. I appreciate your sensitivity. Now I know we'll get along well."

Get along well. What was she talking about?

"Nadia shared something with me not long before she died, and I think you should know about it."

Phoebe found herself leaning forward anxiously.

"She had been thinking of taking in a business partner, someone who could infuse some cash into Lavender Lane. There were some major renovations, expansion, and the like, she was planning to do."

"I didn't know she had intentions along those lines."

"I'm sure you also did not know she was planning to give you a percentage of Lavender Lane, as well."

"A percentage of Lavender Lane!" Words that meant everything to her! Words she had been waiting for so long to hear.

"I had no idea," Phoebe said, covering her mouth with her hand. She wanted to scream, to shout, to spew forth the frustration that had been gnawing at her for months. She sighed deeply and audibly. "It's ironic. I had been trying to summon the nerve to speak to Madame Demidova about what I had been wanting and hoping for, and I had finally mustered up the courage on the very day..." She paused. "I never had the chance."

"No, you didn't, and unfortunately, she hadn't yet made the changes in her will, but I do know she was planning to give you ten percent as a reward for your loyalty and service for so many years. You have been a great asset to her, and she knew it."

Phoebe suddenly felt overwhelmed. The words of praise continued to ring gloriously in her ears. She was being given confirmation of a job well done, a validation of her worth, and her reward would have been possible after all, if only...

"I know you must feel cheated."

"At the moment, I am feeling a whole host of things, but I'm grateful Madame Demidova had my interests at heart."

"I'm sure her death has been very difficult for you, on many counts."

Phoebe nodded. "Indeed, it has."

"Perhaps what I have to say will come as welcome news, then." Eleanor paused for a sip of water. "I've been fortunate to have earned a good deal of money, and to have had the expertise of a fine financial advisor over the years."

Phoebe listened in silence, anticipating what was to come.

"I was the partner about whom I spoke a moment or so ago. I've always loved this place, so when Nadia mentioned her plans, I thought it would be a wonderful opportunity for me. I still think it would be. Now, perhaps even more so."

"How so?"

"I am planning to approach Peter Culvane with an offer to buy Lavender Lane."

"Buy Lavender Lane! Surely it must be worth millions many times over!"

"Without question, but raising capital isn't that difficult when you're in the business community, as I've been for years. Plus, there's my own money, of course. I don't anticipate any problems."

No problem coming up with millions, Phoebe thought. How extraordinary!

Eleanor smiled, reaching out to cover Phoebe's hand with her own. "That said, I'd like you to assume the Directorship of Lavender Lane. I'd also like to offer you your ten percent, just as Nadia had intended to."

"My God! Phoebe gasped. I don't know what to say."

"Say you'll accept the offer and continue on as Director."

Phoebe couldn't believe what had just transpired, but she had no desire to delay her response. "Directorship...of course. I would be delighted."

"Wonderful. Then it's settled!"

Yes, but even as she was acknowledging her good fortune, she had other thoughts. Toni. What about Toni? She couldn't negate either the discussions they had had, or the skills Toni could bring to Lavender Lane. She had to mention her.

"Eleanor, may I ask you about a couple of things?"

"Certainly."

"What if Mr. Culvane doesn't want to sell?"

"That's unlikely. He's into making deals, conducting business on an international scale. I can't imagine he would have any interest in running a health resort. I'm sure he must be planning to put Lavender Lane on the market." She paused. "Was there something else?"

"Yes, there is. Toni. Toni Etheridge. She is the woman who came to our rescue when Madame Demidova had the heart attack."

"I do recall someone being there, helping. But frankly, I wasn't in fine shape myself, so I'm afraid my recollection is a bit fuzzy."

"As it turns out, I've gotten to know Toni these past several days and I find her quite bright. She knows a good deal about fitness and has an excellent business background. Worked for years in New York City retail, which, I understand, is as tough as it gets." She hesitated, then looked at Eleanor straight on. "In fact, we've seriously discussed trying to figure out a way of buying Lavender Lane ourselves."

Eleanor regarded Phoebe skeptically. "Does she have access to the kind of money it would take?"

"She has well-heeled connections in the garment business and is pretty sure she could raise it. Big time designer, as I understand it."

"I see."

"Toni would be a wonderful asset to Lavender Lane. She's prepared to take the leap. Isn't there some way to include her?"

"Let me think about it."

Eleanor lowered her eyes and silently sipped her water.

Phoebe couldn't let the subject drop. "Incidentally, Toni has her ear to the ground and tells me there are others who also have their eye on Lavender Lane."

"Is that so? Well, I'll certainly take that and all you've shared with me tonight under advisement." Eleanor smiled at Phoebe, but her tone clearly indicated that she did not care to pursue the conversation any further. "In the meantime," she continued, "this soup looks absolutely marvelous."

Eleanor picked up her spoon and began sipping the gazpacho. There was little left for Phoebe to do but shelve further discussion about Toni and enjoy a pleasant meal with the woman who might hold the key to her now slightly less uncertain future.

Chapter Twenty

Mavis had her plan all mapped out. A leisurely candle-lit dinner, a cozy drive back to Lavender Lane, and then the *piece de resistance* -- the session with Hilda. Given what she knew about the woman's unauthorized sale of Lavender Lane Quince products, there was no way Hilda could refuse. Yes, the evening would end on an absolutely perfect note.

She arrived at Casa Forno twenty minutes before eight to make the special arrangements with the parking valet, and to make sure the table was to her satisfaction. As instructed, the valet parked the car on the other side of the street, and once certain all was in place, Mavis installed herself in her car to wait. When the evening was underway, the valet would move her car to the lot, where the engine supposedly would "die," ensuring that she would make the trip back to Lavender Lane with Peter, giving her more time with him in the unlikely case the dinner didn't suffice. But, for now, her parking spot provided the perfect vantage point from which to watch Peter's entrance.

He arrived shortly before eight o'clock. Once she saw that Peter was safely ensconced inside the restaurant, Mavis checked her makeup one last time, dabbed on a *soupçon* more of the hypnotic perfume she had picked up in Abu Dhabi on a recent trip with her husband, and then proceeded with her assault. She swept into the restaurant with her customary panache, garnering glances with each step. The staff greeted her effusively -- no matter that she had been there less than half an hour before to make all the arrangements. It was incumbent upon them to treat her royally. Not only was she a frequent customer and a one-time darling of the media whom many of their diners would still recognize, she was the wife of one of the most important men in Chicago. Tyler Perkins was a regular for lunch at their flagship restaurant on Michigan Avenue, and he routinely brought with him some of the most important and visible dealmakers on the global scene today. Nothing was too good for Mrs. Perkins.

Mavis never tired of the expansive greeting and deemed it especially welcome on this particular occasion. She had chosen her outfit very carefully, and her efforts were rewarded. She looked perfect in a stunning white silk shantung Versace suit. The jacket revealed just enough cleavage before dipping to a nipped-in waist, the skirt hugged her well-toned thighs, continuing to a discreet top of the knee, and the white, high-heeled slings paid homage to her long, world-class legs. She still had it, and it was all beautifully displayed.

Peter Culvane was already seated when she arrived, and from the expression on his face, Mavis could tell the evening had gotten off to a sterling start. She followed the Maître D' and, as she approached him, Peter eased himself out from behind the corner table. He smiled broadly and extended his hand. "Mrs. Perkins, wonderful to meet you."

Mavis took his hand, held it for a moment, then slowly retreated, letting her long, slim fingers brush softly across his palm. "And wonderful to meet you," she said, looking into his eyes as though she were peering into the center of some celestial vortex.

She slid into the seat and when Peter sat down next to her, she leaned toward him so that her thigh grazed his briefly, letting it linger for a second or two before she carefully eased it away. The evening was young, but there was so much to accomplish. For now, she wanted to create the slightest tremor. The sexual tension would grow exponentially as the hours went by, she had no doubt.

The captain arrived with abundant suggestions. "Whatever you suggest, Mr. Culvane," Mavis cooed.

"Then let's leave it up to the captain," Peter responded. I'm sure he'll choose wisely for us."

Although Casa Forno was a four-star restaurant, food clearly was not the primary objective of the outing. Mavis had her sights set on much more, and Peter appeared amenable to any digressions.

"I must say," Peter began, "this was a most unusual dinner invitation. You made no provisions for me to decline."

Mavis threw her head back and laughed, showing off the long, graceful neck which had, on many occasions a decade prior, worn some of the world's most precious gems in a series of ads for Harry Winston. "I don't believe in negatives," she said.

"I can see that," Peter commented. "It's curious, as you pointed out in your note, we have not met before, because I do, in fact, know your husband."

Mavis tensed up ever so slightly. "Is that so?"

"Nice chap. We were on opposite sides in a real estate deal a few years back."

"Who won?"

"Nobody. The deal fell through."

"I'm not like my husband," Mavis said looking at Peter intently, her body returning to its languid posture. She moved closer and gently squeezed his arm. "I would never let a good deal slip through my hands." The "my" emerged as little more than a whisper, but it was a powerful declaration in every way.

Peter shifted a bit in his seat. "I wouldn't doubt that for a minute." The waiter arrived with beautifully presented Mediterranean duck for two in a wine and berry reduction. His presence was a relief to Peter, but his relief was short-lived. Mavis continued to press close to him, touch him on the arm more than once, and speak in a whisper so he was obliged to move quite close in order to hear her. She was provocative and persistent and against his considerable will, he was succumbing.

"Whatever was it that prompted you to invite me this evening?"

"It actually was strictly business, but now I'm not so sure," Mavis said, once again pressing her thigh to his.

"Business, now that's interesting. What did you have in mind?" At that moment, business could not have been further from his mind.

Mavis toyed with her wine glass, running her fingers up and down the stem in a slow, continuous caress. "Let's talk about Lavender Lane."

Peter shifted his body. "Lavender Lane?"

"Yes," she said. "But why don't we chat on the ride back? I'm sure you won't mind giving me a lift. The rental I drove here died as I was pulling up. The parking valet said it was something about the carburetor. He's such a dear. Said not to worry. He'd get the Palm Desert Auto people to deal with it."

"Well, I'd be happy to give you a lift. It will be my pleasure."

They had coffee and then Peter called for the check, but there was none. Mrs. Perkins had already signed for it, the captain informed him.

"Mavis, you must let me take care of this. I can't let you," Peter said. "It would be ungentlemanly of me."

"Relax. Enjoy being spoiled a bit," Mavis said.

She had taken care of the bill, and Peter would soon learn she had also taken care of some other arrangements for the evening.

On the ride back, Mavis refused to discuss the specific business agenda to which she had referred. "I can't tell you about it," she said, punctuating her remark with a soft caress of his arm. "I have to show you."

"Show me?"

"Have you ever heard of Lavender Lane's Quince Creme?"

"I can't say I have."

"All the better. I promise you won't be disappointed."

When they arrived at the spa, Mavis led Peter to the Beauty Center. It was well past eleven, and the place was dark, the last facial and massage having been given two hours before.

"Where in the world are you taking me?" Peter asked.

"To a new and unforgettable experience." She laughed softly and linked her arm through his.

They were met at the door by Hilda. "Welcome, Mr. Culvane," she said in her Bavarian accent. "We have everything ready for you."

Peter looked at Mavis with a mix of amusement and interest.

"Go on, now," Mavis insisted, prodding him through the door. "You are about to have the treat of your life -- a Lavender Lane Rejuvenating Quince Facial and Body Massage."

"You don't say," Peter said skeptically. A body massage is one thing, but a facial? I haven't joined that boys' club yet!"

"You are the owner of the world's premier spa, Peter. You need to know about these things."

"I suppose so," he laughed.

"Facials are not just for women. More and more men are having them these days -- but none, you can be sure, have ever had one like you're going to get."

"I don't know whether that sounds promising or ominous."

"You are going to love it!" Mavis assured him.

They proceeded down the dimly lit hall to Hilda's treatment room, where the masseuse handed him a towel and instructed him to take off his clothing. "Wrap around waist, then make yourself comfortable on table, with the face down." She patted the tabletop and then gave him a re-assuring smile. "When you are ready, call. I am right outside. I come and we start with back massage."

Peter shot Mavis a look.

She laughed. "You won't be disappointed. I promise."

Mavis and Hilda left the room. When they returned, Peter was on the table as instructed. Mavis hovered as Hilda prepared to begin her ministrations.

He turned his head and glanced up at her. "Now that you've gotten me into this, are you just going to stand there and stare at me?" he asked, half-jokingly.

"Actually, no. I have a couple of calls to make, then I thought I might come back and fetch you so we can have a night cap, and perhaps our discussion." She turned to Hilda. "How long will it be?"

"One hour and twenty minutes. Precisely."

"I'll see you then." Mavis touched Peter gently on the shoulder and left the room.

"We now dim the light, Mr. Culvane, so you relax." Hilda bent over Peter and began spreading warmed Quince Body Oil onto his shoulders and upper back, working it deep into his flesh and muscles. "Ach. The trapezius. They are tight. A big sign from the stress. Massage do you good! Just close the eyes. Do not think about anything but leaving all the tension to go from the body."

The room was warm and fragrant and redolent of an aroma completely unfamiliar to Peter. The sounds of Mozart's Second Piano Concerto wafted softly overhead as Hilda stroked and kneaded. Peter contentedly let his body go and surrendered to the sensations. Mavis was right. The woman was a pro. She gave one hell of a massage.

Hilda finished working on Peter's back and legs, then asked him to turn over. "We do facial now. That way, quince can do work for few minutes. Then I do rest of massage."

"Is that what I've been smelling? The quince?" Peter asked.

"Ya. Is good creme. Excellent for the skin. Now close the eyes so I can start facial."

Peter did as he was told and was rewarded with a series of heavenly barrages to his forehead, cheeks and chin, each step feeling better than the last. No wonder women like this stuff, he thought, surrendering to the pleasure.

Hilda put fresh pads on Peter's eyes. "Now we let you rest for twenty minutes. Then we finish facial and do the rest of massage. Good?"

"Very good."

"I turn off light. Try to take nice snooze."

Peter felt relaxed, unburdened and unabashedly pleased with the pampering. He had no problem letting himself drift off into a light sleep.

Hands drew him back to wakefulness. How long had he dozed? He had no idea. He reached up to remove the eye pads but was stopped.

"Not yet," a barely audible voice instructed him.

He complied and the masseuse continued working. She removed the creme from his face and applied a cool liquid. It tingled as it washed over his skin.

"I do like the smell of that stuff. Wonder how my face looks."

"Ssh. No talking."

"Sorry." This one's all business, Peter thought. Bet the clients like that.

She spread creme on his shoulders and chest and deftly worked it in, massaging his biceps and pectorals, then moved steadily down his torso. She worked the creme in slowly, rhythmically, almost tantalizingly.

What he felt was not the same as he had felt during other massages he'd had, and he was no stranger to the process. He frequently topped off his workouts at the club with a session of pummeling and muscle easing. This one however, felt more like the massage one of his business buddies had treated him to in Tokyo. He smiled at the recollection. That massage had merely been a prelude to an extraordinary night of beautiful women and pleasure. But this wasn't Tokyo, and Hilda sure as Hell wasn't a dainty, feminine Japanese courtesan. Nevertheless, the huge Bavarian knew what she was doing.

She cradled his feet, and then, one by one, manipulated each toe. Then she slowly spread creme on his legs and deftly advanced up each side, kneading and caressing every inch of skin until she reached the top of his thighs. Christ, he thought, as he felt a strong stirring. This is a more than a bit too much for me. I hope I don't embarrass myself.

"Now, now," a voice crooned. "What have we got here?"

That voice! There was no Bavarian accent. But no sooner did he have that realization than he felt the towel being pulled away from his body. He reached down to cover himself, but his hand was met by another.

"Relax," the familiar voice whispered.

It was Mavis, for Christ's sake! He ripped the pads from his eyes and in the dim light, Peter made out her short-cropped black hair. Her head hovered close to his body and her hands were continuing to press the flesh on his thighs, moving steadily upward.

Peter shot up. "What in God's name are you doing?"

"Don't be ridiculous, darling. You know very well what I'm doing." She reached for him, and let out a low, throaty laugh. "And from the feel of you, I'd say this is exactly what the doctor ordered." With that, she bent down and closed her mouth over his rapidly growing erection.

"Oh, Christ!" Peter moaned.

"Just go with it, darling," she managed to croon, while pursuing her mission.

"Go with it?" Peter groaned. "Go with...ah, you...oh, what the fuck?"

"Precisely," Mavis said, momentarily pulling back. "Let's say, shall we, that no good deed goes unrewarded."

Peter had a full-blown erection now, and she tightened her grasp on it, flicking her tongue around the top and then sucking the tip with a skill honed by years of practice.

"Good deed. Aah… but I haven't done anything. Oh, Jesus!" He caught his breath.

"But you will, my pet. You will."

Mavis grasped his testicles and squeezed them with her long, agile fingers.

Peter moaned again, and then surrendered to the inevitable.

Chapter Twenty-One

"Say it isn't so!" Toni said as she burst into Phoebe's office, startling both Phoebe and Eleanor Franklin. "Oh, dear," she said, as she saw them glance at one another. "I shouldn't have barged in like that. My apologies."

"No apologies necessary," Phoebe said. "Are you quite all right?"

"I'm fine." Toni said. "Really. I can come back later."

"Do come in. Dr. Franklin and I were just discussing you."

"Yes," Eleanor said. "Phoebe was telling me what an asset you'd be in any future management of Lavender Lane."

Toni moved cautiously into the room.

"Yes," Phoebe said. "Dr. Franklin expressed interest in joining our effort to buy Lavender Lane, but apparently Mr. Culvane has decided not to sell."

"Moreover," Eleanor chimed in, "it looks as though he and Mavis Perkins are, as they say in the business world, in bed together."

Phoebe groaned.

Toni nodded. "I'm sure you're right. Last night, I couldn't sleep, so I decided to go for a dip, and as I was heading down the path to the pool, I saw them together, walking arm in arm, laughing up a storm. Looked pretty damn cozy to me."

"I learned the news from Peter himself. I had a chat with him this morning." Eleanor cleared her throat. "A business chat. I made him a serious offer to buy Lavender Lane, and he turned it down flat. Said he's not selling. And, not only is he keeping Lavender Lane, he plans to expand it. He credits his momentous decision to Mavis Perkins, no less."

"It figures," Toni said.

Eleanor looked at the expression on Toni's face. It told her all she needed to know. "He is terribly attractive, isn't he?"

Toni blanched.

"Not to worry," Eleanor sighed, her mouth forming a modest smile. "It seems many of us found him attractive." She let out a soft laugh.

"Among other things Mavis Perkins apparently did for Peter," Eleanor continued, pausing theatrically for effect, "was pointing out to him that he was sitting on a veritable goldmine with the Quince Creme. He has now decided to aggressively market Lavender Lane Quince products, and he's also thinking about opening branch spas not only on the east coast, but in Europe and Latin America as well."

"He sure plans quickly! And how does the grand Mavis figure into all of this?"

"Seems as though she'll be the signature model for both the Spa and the Crème."

"Did he mention a younger model, too?" Toni asked. "Mavis had made some promises to the daughter of one of the women here."

"As a matter of fact, he did. Some idea of Mavis's about women of all ages using the creme. I hate to admit it, but it does sound like a damned good ad campaign."

"Now, not only will Mavis get her face in all the ads, she'll get her other parts in his bed -- and she won't even have to buy the place. He'll probably just give it to her!" Toni's whole body practically screamed. "I'm sorry," she whispered, shaking her head. "It's ridiculous to get overly excited about all of this."

"Why don't you sit?" Eleanor offered her chair. "I'll be returning to my room momentarily, anyway. I've got some reading to do. The board of my company Fed-exed some papers for me to look at." Her eyes radiated a surprising twinkle. "They're not expecting it, but I'm about to give them the fight of their lives."

She rose from her chair. "So, it's back to New York for me. But I intend to do everything I can to convince Peter Culvane to work with Franklin Nutritionals to develop a line of private label Lavender Lane vitamins and supplements to sell here at the spa and later, elsewhere, and certainly in all the other locations he is sure to open." She smiled at Phoebe. "Thanks for the suggestion. It's a natural. Don't know why I never thought of it before, myself!"

She turned to Toni. "Now don't you give up. From what Phoebe tells me, you two women would make a dynamite business combination." She paused, appraising Toni. "Don't give up on the man, either. He's bound to see through that one, sooner or later."

Toni didn't know how to respond. She was hoping she was not so transparent. She was wishing, too, that things were not so complicated. She smiled, but said nothing.

Eleanor graciously returned the smile. It was the most natural smile she had been able to achieve in weeks. "On that lovely note, I'll take my leave," she said, making her way to the door.

"He asked me to stay on as Director," Phoebe told Toni, once Eleanor had gone. "He's offering a fifteen percent increase in pay. I had to accept. Lavender Lane is my home. Where else would I go at this point?"

All of their previous discussions about owning Lavender Lane together hovered in the air between them like a complement of clouds waiting to burst.

"And nothing about a percentage partnership?" Toni asked.

"No. Why would he just give it to me? I'm afraid I'll have to be content with what I've got and be grateful." Phoebe locked eyes with Toni. "We may not be able to own the place, but we can still work together."

"How so?" Toni asked skeptically.

"I am the Director, and that includes hiring staff."

Staff? There was no chance of that. She would work from home, if they were able to form a partnership…be a work-from-home mom. Working on the premises was not an option. Maybe this was the moment to tell Phoebe about her pregnancy. Something, however, stopped her, and she opted for humor, instead.

"What would I be? The pool attendant? I had envisioned working from New York. Not re-locating.' She laughed. "All the big money stuff is done in New York."

Phoebe reached out and touched Toni's arm. "Toni, let's not give up so easily. We'll find a solution. Let me give it some more thought. You still have a couple of days left here. In the meantime, why don't you take advantage of everything Lavender Lane has to offer?"

"I wish I could, Phoebe. I really wish I could."

They both knew that what Toni was referring to had little to do with the fitness equipment or taking over the spa, and everything to do with one Mr. Peter Culvane.

■　　■　　■　　■　　■

It didn't take long for the gossip mill to grind into full gear. By lunchtime, the entire staff had learned their new employer and Mavis Perkins were an item, and most of them didn't know which of the duo to dread more: an unknown entity like Peter Culvane, who knew nothing of the spa business and would probably run it into the ground, or his new consort, the infamous Mavis Perkins, whom many of them had had the distinct privilege of serving over the years. The thought of her close to the seat of decision-making made even the most stalwart of them shudder. She was beautiful and famous, but she was also demanding and frequently nasty. As one of the manicurists recalled, in her lilting Irish accent, Mavis always scrutinized every swipe of the nail file as though she were shaving off a piece of the True Cross. She was, as the manicurist had so succinctly put it, "a royal pain in the arse."

When Phoebe entered the dining room that evening accompanied by Mavis and Peter, the friendly, animated chatter so characteristic of meals at Lavender Lane ground to a halt. Everyone watched the trio stroll in, Phoebe appearing somewhat uncomfortable, Peter eager to be seated as quickly as possible and Mavis, gazing slowly around at what she was certain would soon be her personal domain.

For most of the guests, it was odd enough seeing any man other than a server in the dining room. Merely knowing who he was and how he had come to be there would have caused enormous interest and speculation. But the sight of the new owner and the well-known Mavis Perkins together at what used to be Nadia Demidova's table, caused many a fork to be put down mid-mouthful. Peter Culvane was a man at whom more than one among them would have liked a shot. To a woman, however, they realized that the glorious Mavis Perkins had not wasted the proverbial minute and had succeeded brilliantly in precluding any possibility.

Phoebe smiled with relief when Toni beckoned to her, grateful for the opportunity to extricate herself from an awkward situation. She certainly had no wish to eat with Mavis and Peter -- not that she had been invited.

There was another wave coming from Toni's table, but it was met with neither recognition nor response. Lauren was gesturing eagerly at Mavis, but Mavis merely glanced at her and continued to fawn on Peter.

Charlotte looked up from the menu. "With him around," she said to Lauren, "Mavis won't be paying too much attention to you or anybody else tonight."

"Oh, I don't care," Lauren said. "Mavis and I have a date to start work tomorrow, anyway."

"If she can pull herself away from what she's really working on," Toni said.

"Of course, she will!" Lauren snapped. "She promised we would do test shots tomorrow. She really wants this project to happen."

"Undoubtedly," Charlotte said. "But don't expect to be the focus of her attention. Mavis hasn't suggested you for the ads out of the kindness of her heart. She thinks it's a smart business move." She glanced at Toni, then turned to Phoebe. "What do you think, Ms. Bancroft? You certainly know Mavis better than we do."

"I would so love to comment, but it would be frightfully unethical for me to discuss any of the guests."

"I'm so sorry!" Charlotte said. "I didn't mean to put you in a compromising position."

Phoebe smiled devilishly. "Quite candidly, it is hard not to succumb. I will tell you, she is onto something with the creme. How the advertising campaign will do remains to be seen." She looked at Lauren. "Frankly, even though Madame Demidova thought women should begin taking care of their skin at an early age, I don't know that she meant using the Quince Creme. It might be a bit heavy for teenagers. Young skin tends to be oily and blemished."

"My skin's not oily," Lauren barked. "And no way do I have pimples!"

"I'm here to tell you it's entirely possible to have both dry skin and pimples," Toni chimed in. "Trust me: there's nothing quite like a nice big, juicy, adult whitehead. It invariably pops out on a morning when you have a big meeting, or just before a date." She paused. "Date? Did I say date? I must be losing my mind. Haven't had one of those in ages!" Well…not a conventional one, at any rate, she thought.

"You will soon!" Charlotte chirped. "You're looking wonderful!"

"Indeed!" Phoebe added. "You're looking so fit and trim, and your skin is glowing."

*Glowing. Again…*Toni narrowed her eyes and pursed her lips. "Forget about *my* skin." She nodded in the direction of where Peter and Mavis were sitting. "It's Peter Culvane's skin we should be worried about."

They all turned to look and it certainly seemed as though Toni's appraisal was correct. Their business relationship notwithstanding, Mavis was doing little to disguise her personal interest in Peter, gazing boldly into his eyes, her shoulder pressed up against his. The tablecloth obscured what was going on underneath, but Mavis' body language left very little doubt that her thigh was glued directly to Peter's.

"Come on, girls. Let's eat. If you can stomach it!" Toni said. "I'm sure there'll be ample opportunity to watch the Mavis and Peter Show ad nauseam from here on in."

They all took one last look at Mavis and Peter, then Charlotte dove into the steaming bowl of vegetarian chili that had been placed in front of her.

"I'm not hungry," Lauren announced, her mouth fixed in its customary pout.

"As you like," Charlotte said. "But if you don't have a proper dinner, there will be no photography tomorrow." She said it dryly, calmly, without emotion.

"What?" Lauren screamed, glaring at her mother.

"You heard me, Lauren. I want you to have this opportunity, but the food thing has gone too far. And besides, if you don't look healthy, you won't make a good model."

"Look what food has done for you, Mother. I wouldn't exactly call how you look 'healthy.'"

Toni and Phoebe glanced at each other, then quickly lowered their eyes.

"Not to worry, ladies. I'm used to this kind of disrespect. What did we say when we were kids? 'Sticks and stones can break my bones.' Lauren can embarrass herself by speaking to her own mother this way in front of people. She's certainly had enough practice. But at this point, I'm pleased to report, I don't feel a thing. And besides, the fact is I've lost nearly five pounds so far on this trip."

Lauren glared at her, but Charlotte continued to eat as if though there had been no exchange of words.

Lauren looked away from Charlotte and picked up a fork. She clenched her teeth and began stabbing the large yam which dominated the plate of vegetables in front of her. A small burst of trapped steam escaped and quickly dissipated, leaving in its wake the singular, thick aroma of the deep orange sweet potato. *I can't wait to be a famous model, Mother, so I can get away from you, and all your disgusting food.* She looked admiringly at the slender Mavis who held a glass of sparkling water to her lips. Lauren noticed that her mentor had barely taken a sip, choosing instead to drink in every one of Peter Culvane's words.

Part 3

Chapter Twenty-Two

Mavis paced imperiously in the lobby, the front desk phone's long, coiled cord trailing snake-like behind her. "I don't care what their problem is!" she growled. "They should have been here hours ago. We're going to miss the best light."

"Mrs. Perkins," a young staffer called as he ran in through the entrance. "There are some people here to see you."

Without so much as an explanation or a goodbye, Mavis thrust the phone at the receptionist, leaving her to end the call. "Well, there you are!" she said, rushing to embrace a tall, bearded, middle-aged man in black T-shirt and pants with a well-worn Yankees cap that covered a crown of thinning and graying brown hair. "It's been ages, hasn't it?" She gave him a faintly audible air kiss. "There, let me look at you." Her eyes went to his boots, distressed black lizard cowboys which, in their day, must easily have gone for $1500, but which now looked as though they had been retrieved from the bottom of a pile at a suburban yard sale. "Still getting mileage out of those boots, I see."

Ian Graebert laughed and responded with a critical gaze of his own. Incredible. Mavis still looked damn good. And while he had small enthusiasm for thrusting himself back into her clutches, the fact remained that neither the new, young photo editors, nor the up-and-coming ad directors were exactly breaking down his door. It had been quite some time since he'd had a major assignment. There was nothing to lose by doing this shoot on spec. He had taken some extraordinary photographs of Mavis in the past, and with any luck, the magic would still be there. If this scheme of hers gelled, he could get back on a much-needed gravy train.

"Mavis, you look exactly the same as when we shot your last Vogue cover."

"Cut the horseshit, Ian," she said with a low laugh. "We both know that's a crock." She paused and licked her lips. "But I've held up pretty well and I'm itching to get back in the game. I'm bored silly, and the rules are different now. The world is ready for Mavis again." She tilted her head back, smiling with satisfaction. "And Lavender Lane is exactly what I need for my re-entry."

Ian appraised her for a long moment. "Well, then," he said waving his arms expansively, "let the games begin!" He gestured to Dex and Eric, his two young assistants, and Roberto, the seasoned hair and makeup man with whom he had worked frequently in the past. The trio was hovering on the sidelines, drinking in the drama of the Mavis-Ian reunion.

They gathered their gear and proceeded to the pool, where they found Lauren waiting on a lounge, her bikini-clad body wrapped in a towel, with Charlotte hovering protectively behind her. Dex and Eric exchanged approving glances. Their assessment was not lost on Mavis.

"Let's move it boys," she said impatiently. "We haven't got all day."

"Is this really where you want to shoot, Mavis?" Ian ventured. "It's certainly a gorgeous pool, but what are we selling here, sun tan lotion or the face and body creme you were telling me about?"

"The face…" Lauren began to say.

"I'll do the talking, Lauren," Mavis snapped. "You just sit there and look pretty" She turned to Ian and smiled coyly. "Perhaps you're right. What did you have in mind?"

"Some spot where they do facials or something."

"That might not be so easy to arrange, at this point. I'm sure the service areas are all booked."

"Knowing you, Mavis, it won't be much of a problem."

Mavis studied Ian's still-interesting face, trying to remember if she, if they, had ever… but she had never been one to keep count. "You're right, Ian. Problems were made to conquer."

She strode over to the house phone and called Peter. Moments later, she returned, self-satisfaction etched clearly on her face.

"Everything's taken care of. We're on for the Beauty Center." She looked icily at Charlotte. "By the way, we won't be needing you during the shoot. Lauren can tell you all about it later."

Tell me about it later! How dare that woman declare she was not welcome at the shoot. She was hardly planning to interfere. She only wanted to be there to see her daughter move into a world she had never attained. No wonder Mavis Perkins had the reputation of being so awful. She most certainly was.

■   ■   ■   ■   ■

When Mavis called, Peter was ensconced in Nadia's office trying to deal with Lavender Lane while managing his high-flying mergers and acquisitions business, with its entirely different cast of characters. He had been on the phone with Tokyo for hours trying to iron out some problems in an impending deal. As for Lavender Lane, he'd been ready to put it on the block, but Mavis had changed his mind. She made a very convincing argument for him not only to keep it, but also to expand.

She had been very convincing in other areas as well -- perhaps too convincing. While he was not in the market for a long-term, committed relationship -- two failed marriages had sworn him off so-called meaningful relationships for the foreseeable future -- neither did he have any real desire to get involved with a married woman. He had done that once, and it had cost him his first marriage. He'd promised himself never to succumb again.

But this married woman's powers of persuasion were exceptional. Not only was Mavis one of the most beautiful women of any age he had ever met, she knew her way around a body with the kind of skill he rarely, if ever, had encountered. She was nearly impossible to resist, and she had not only lured him into a physical relationship, but also managed to convince him to make her a very key part of Lavender Lane going forward.

When she asked him to see to it that the Beauty Center be cleared, it seemed reasonable enough. After all, she was trying to get a potential Lavender Lane blockbuster off the ground.

■   ■   ■   ■   ■

When Peter gave her the instructions, Phoebe was incredulous. It was 10:30, well into the morning, and the masseuses and facialists were already on their third or even fourth clients of the day. How could she clear out the beauty center with no notice? The guests would be furious. Bloody Hell! He might be handsome and successful, but the man didn't know a farthing about how to run a spa. If this were any indication of how things would be in the future, they were in a lot of trouble. And all because of that damn bitch.

■   ■   ■   ■   ■

Toni took a leisurely walk and found the perfect place for her big act of defiance. a large, beautiful weeping willow tree far enough away from the main house, with a sweet little bench in front. It was perfect for her catch-up call with Kevin. She punched in his number and was almost relieved when she got his voice mail. She began to ramble about how, complete with resident kumquat, she'd developed a teenage crush on one of the world's most eligible single men, and was one of several, including his fave, Mavis Perkins, who wanted to get their pampered paws on him…and it was all so ridiculous because, even if he were interested, which he probably wasn't, once he found out she was pregnant, he surely would run as fast as he could…but then again, maybe he wouldn't because he sounded like he regretted not having had children and it would kinda be like adopting… except that the kid's Uncle-Daddy Kevin would be coming in and out and would be there for holidays and school activities and everything else…and oh, did I mention that I'd like your help in raising several millions dollars so I could buy Lavender Lane?

Her head was spinning. "Sorry I went on and on. Call me back…oh, Kev. I forgot. You can't. I'll have to try you again. Love you." She clicked off and walked slowly to the gym where a Pilates session and some time on the treadmill would help clear her mind.

■　　■　　■　　■　　■

Eleanor hummed contentedly while packing her things. It was unfortunate she had to cut her stay at Lavender Lane short, but she didn't want to take even the slightest chance of losing her resolve.

She glanced at herself in the mirror. The image that looked back seemed less strange to her now. The work she'd had done on her face was still a far cry from what was expected, but she had to admit, it had gotten a tad better. Perhaps what the doctor had promised would still come true.

She closed her last suitcase and rang the front desk. The death of her friend Nadia and the unavailability -- to her -- of Peter Culvane notwithstanding, things were looking up. By the next time she visited Lavender Lane, she would be ensconced more firmly than ever as the Chairman of the Board of Franklin Family Nutritionals. She liked the addition of the word "Family." Not only did it sound more inclusive, it told anyone who needed reminding just where and with whom the company had originated.

Chapter Twenty-Three

Roberto, the hair and makeup man, studied Mavis's face with appreciation. Some of the models he worked on were merely blank canvasses, leaving him free to create whatever woman the moment called for. There was no such mission with Mavis Perkins. Her beauty was incontrovertible. His job was merely to enhance it.

He deftly applied a creamy, pale liquid foundation, dusted on muted tones of mauve and violet eye shadow and then generously coated Mavis's lashes with ebony mascara. He carefully lined her lips with a neutral pencil and then used a soft shade of raspberry to fill them in. Remarkable. Her lips were still full. If she'd had any fillers, it was impossible to tell. Mavis's short, cropped hair had no need of attention. It fell naturally, beautifully into place. She was ready for the camera in a mere thirty minutes, an anomaly in a business in which it generally took several hours or more to get a model ready for the camera.

"Ian and I will get started on some test shots," Mavis informed Lauren. "You just sit down and let Roberto work his magic."

Lauren sat back, waiting for Roberto to morph her into some desirable creature. He turned her face from side to side and examined its structure, then ran his fingers through her hair, using both hands to lift, pull and fan, only to finish by pulling it back into a long, sweeping pony tail.

"Is that all you're going to do with my hair?" Lauren whined.

Roberto backed away and gave her the exaggerated, arched-eyebrow look only an aging queen would give an enviably beautiful, young woman. "These are body shots, sweetie, not ads for Clairol's color of the month. But not to worry. We'll get to the Miss Teenage America look for the close-ups." His expression darkened. "I do need to smooth out those skin tones though, even for the long shots." He lowered his eyes to her chin.

Lauren grimaced. 'Smooth out those skin tones?' What's he talking about?

"Now, now! No unpleasant faces, little girl." He wagged his finger in front of her. "Don't try to screw up what the universe so generously gave you."

What's his problem? Ugh. She wanted to barf, right then and there, but she had to be nice. "I'll try," she said as sweetly as possible. "I never had my makeup done professionally before."

"Really? I never would have known." Roberto glared smugly at her.

Lauren didn't like him. She didn't like him at all. But she would have to put up with his shit. Were all makeup artists like this? She hoped not -- not with all the hair stylists and makeup people she'd have working on her once she became a top model.

Roberto gave Lauren's complexion an even, glowing tone, softly enhanced her eyes with taupe and mocha shadows and tinted her beautiful, full mouth with a light cherry gloss. She checked herself out in the mirror and had to admit she liked what she saw. She favored Roberto with a smile, and he favored her back with an "I told-you-so" look that slid neatly down his surgically attenuated nose.

Ian decided to do the test shots in the solarium to take advantage of the natural light. He positioned Mavis and Lauren on the tiled floor, facing in opposite directions, love-seat style, their torsos aligned and their respective long legs stretched out in front. Behind them, brightly colored wild flowers and a running brook were softly visible through the clear glass windows.

"This is so uncomfortable!" Lauren groaned. "The floor is too cold."

Mavis shot her a sharp look. "We haven't even finished the test shots and you're already complaining. Not a good sign, Lauren." She made no effort to keep her voice down.

An audible hush came over the group, but Roberto could plainly be heard snickering in the background. Lauren looked away from Mavis's critical gaze and straightened her posture.

"All right, people," Ian called out. "Simmer down. We have a full day's work ahead of us."

The preliminary shots showed that Mavis hadn't lost it. Her fifty-two-year-old body, while certainly not one of an ingénue, was lean and firm and she still knew how to move in front of a camera.

The shots also showed that Lauren had more than the right kind of body for the business. One look at Dex or Eric neatly told the tale. "This girl's got it," their expressions proclaimed as they navigated the room.

Ian moved on to the regular shots and Lauren's potential did not go unnoticed by him, either. "Let's go, ladies," he commanded. "More chest, Mavis. That's it. Drop your left shoulder," he said softly. "Good. OK, Lauren, move your right leg up and wet those lips. Beautiful. Now give me a fantastic smile," He raised his voice a bit. "Come on, give it to me, Lauren. Yes! "That's it," he sang out. "Dynamite!"

Ian was paying an inordinate amount of attention to Lauren, and Mavis was not happy. The girl was meant to be an adjunct to her -- not the newest fucking star in the whole fucking galaxy.

"Break time!" she commanded. "I'm famished, aren't you?" She reached for her jumpsuit and slipped it on over her bikini. "Let's get something to eat. We can do the head shots later."

"I'm not really hungry. You go on without me," Lauren said.

"You know, Lauren, you can take this not-eating thing too far," Mavis shot back. But, as you like." She linked her arm through Ian's. "As for me, I need a little, shall we say sustenance, to keep me going." She threw her head back and let out a knowing laugh.

God, Lauren thought, does she flirt with every man in sight?

After Mavis and Ian left the room, Lauren picked up a hand mirror and examined her face. She actually liked the natural way Roberto had done her eyes, but she wasn't sure about the lip-gloss. She studied her mouth. It was too gooey, especially her lower lip. Not...and then she saw it -- a small, discolored bump sitting neatly on her on her chin. It had appeared from out of nowhere and was red and raised and forming a head. "A pimple!" she mouthed incredulously. "No way! I've never had a stupid pimple in my whole life!"

Her eyes darted around the room in a panic and landed on a table with a tray containing some bottles, cotton and menacing-looking implements. She grabbed a piece of cotton, soaked it with antiseptic and attacked the thing. The mound in front of her merely grew redder and more swollen.

I've got an hour break, she thought. Maybe if I get some fresh air, it will go away. She threw on her clothes and Nikes and sprinted out the door.

■   ■   ■   ■   ■

When the group returned, Lauren was nowhere to be seen. "Not to worry," Mavis crooned. "She probably decided to get something to eat after all. Why don't we just get started on me?"

After a quick makeup check, Ian positioned Mavis on a large, wicker peacock chair. He framed her with graceful, lilting palm fronds, and the mating dance between model and photographer they both knew so well began anew. Ian adjusted the lighting, moved his tripod closer, then peered down into the Pentax's viewfinder. Regardless of what the new crop of young photographers, who all used digital cameras thought, nothing yields the nuanced results of good, old-fashioned film.

A minute later, Lauren wandered in and stood transfixed at what she saw: Mavis posed and postured and made long, lingering love to the camera. It was incredible. No way she could ever do that -- not today, not next month, not next year. She felt a sudden pang of terror.

"Great work, Mavis," Ian called out. "Take a few minutes." He turned to summon Lauren. "Ah, there you are. Perfect timing." He gave her a big smile. "Out of those clothes, quick, like a bunny," he said, clapping his hands. "Put on the white shirt that's hanging over there. Roberto's been an angel to work up some wardrobe for us. Mrs. Perkins didn't exactly give us a whole lot of time to hire a stylist, not to mention having to drop everything and get cross country overnight."

"You love it, you old goat," Mavis scoffed. "Where else are you going to get a chance like this?"

Ian held up his hands in surrender.

"Right," Mavis said, savoring her ability to remind him how totally beholden to her he was. "Let's hurry up and get Lauren's singles done so we can move on to the two-shots. I've got other things to do around here."

Roberto was hovering a few feet away, one hand on his hip, the other daintily dangling the white shirt.

Lauren quickly pulled her T-shirt over her head, but left her bra on.

Roberto snickered. "What do you think you're doing, missy?"

"Getting ready for the shot."

"First of all, we have to touch up your makeup and fix that hair. Secondly, you can't leave your bra on. It will show through."

Lauren felt the color rise in her face. She must seem so stupid, so inexperienced! She removed the bra, covered her chest with the T-shirt and plunked herself down in Roberto's makeup chair, a knot growing in her stomach. She had dreamed about modeling for as long as she could remember, but right now she wanted to be anywhere else and doing anything but.

Roberto loomed over her, makeup brush in hand. "What is that thing?" he shrieked.

"What thing?" Lauren whispered, knowing full well what he meant.

"The thing on your chin!" He let out a huge sigh of exasperation. "It's the biggest god-damned pimple I have ever seen. There's no way I can cover it up enough for a close-up."

"Roberto, stop overdramatizing," Ian said, quickly moving toward them. "Let me have a look." He took Lauren's face in his hand and peered down at her chin. "Hmm," he said, fingering the brim on his cap. "It *is* rather large and quite red."

This couldn't possibly be happening, Lauren thought.

"Let me see it," Mavis called out, taking no measures to mask the irritation in her voice. "You know, Lauren, your mother is probably right.

If you ate properly, you wouldn't be having this problem." She peered at Lauren's chin. "This thing is hideous. Simply hideous. We can't shoot you today. The boys will simply have to stay another day."

"I suppose," Ian sighed.

"Don't suppose, Ian. Just damn well do it. Pull out your cell and cancel all those other great bookings you no doubt have."

He shrugged and nodded. She had him.

"As for you Lauren, put yourself in the hands of a facialist before the day is out and for God's sake, get a good night's sleep. We can finish up tomorrow morning."

"I'm sorry. I've never had a pimple."

"There's a first time for everything," Roberto snickered.

Lauren kept her eyes lowered, not daring to look up. Her stomach was on fire and she was close to tears.

"Run along everyone," Mavis directed. "I'll see to it that we have this space again in the morning. I trust you boys have accommodations in town."

"If you can call a sorry excuse for a motel 'accommodations.'"

"With the tons of work you'll be getting as soon as this thing takes off," Mavis retorted, "it'll be the Ritz Carlton all the way."

While the others were packing up and leaving, Lauren sat transfixed on the stool. She wanted to run as fast as she could and as far away from all of them as her well-practiced legs would carry her, but she was unable to budge. It was as though lead had infused her entire torso.

"Are you coming, Lauren?" Mavis called, leading the exodus.

Lauren barely uttered a response.

"Suit yourself," Mavis answered coldly. "But be sure to be back here well-rested, pimple-free and ready to go at 9 a.m. tomorrow."

"I will," Lauren responded faintly.

The lead in Lauren's torso poured down into her legs like molten lava, and a rush of tears was close to spilling out all over her face. She squeezed her eyes tightly.

"Are you going to be all right?" Dex, the last to pack up, called out. He hesitated a moment, then added, "Want to come out with Eric and me for a beer?"

"No thanks." Lauren answered softly.

"OK, then," Dex said, letting the door close gently behind him.

Lauren looked slowly around the room. Everything in front of her began to blur, to move around like shimmering images in a desert mirage. The heat in her legs and torso had traveled up through her chest and into her head. She felt as though she were suffocating. She needed to be free, to be outside in the fresh air. She forced her body off the stool, struggled to get her clothes on and then stumbled out the door into the rescuing breeze of the late desert afternoon.

Chapter Twenty-Four

Mavis placed her hands on the table in front of her.

"Would you like them any shorter?" the manicurist asked.

"No. Not one iota."

"Shall I cut your..."

"No, Iris! I've told you over and over again: I never cut my cuticles. Ever. Just smooth and polish and be quick about it. I have important things to attend to."

"But..."

"Do as I say, Iris."

"Yes, Mrs. Perkins."

What is wrong with these people? Can't they listen? Mavis sighed with exasperation. And then there's Lauren...

She closed her eyes and let the afternoon play out in front of her. The girl had begun to irritate her. She was impossibly immature and annoying. Lauren was no more capable of being a model than that other little bitch Andrea was. Why hadn't she seen it before?

Mavis thought back to a time many years before, when she was at the height of her career. She had spotted a lovely young thing in the waiting room of an ad agency. It was a "go-see" for a hair commercial. Her own hair was quite long then, black and luxurious, and she was always in demand. The wannabe's mane was deep brown and long as well, but in need of some tender loving care. They struck up a conversation, and Mavis was taken with the young Andrea, barely seventeen. Unlike Lauren, Andrea was a street kid trying to parlay her looks into a meal ticket. She was savvy and smart and prickly in the way only someone who didn't have a great childhood can have. The girl had reminded her of herself. She felt unaccustomed pangs of empathy and decided to mentor her.

Mavis took Andrea under her wing, and taught her all she had painstakingly learned about the business. She introduced her to the right people and got her signed with Bella, her long-time agency. With her continued help, the girl took off and in no time, was doing major fashion spreads and covers. Did she ever thank Mavis? No. Not even once. And did she ever make time to see her once her star had begun to ascend? The disgusting girl never even returned her calls.

Ingrates, she thought, shaking her head. All of them, Lauren included, with her pouting and complaining. You might think I'd have learned my lesson. Well, being nice doesn't pay, and I'm not about to do it again. Time to nip this thing with Lauren in the bud. I'll tell her that on second thought, Nadia Demidova was wrong: the Quince Creme really doesn't make sense for young women. It's way too rich. After all, she'd sprouted a pimple, hadn't she? I'll let her think that somewhere down the line, we'll develop a lighter creme and use her then. Yes. That should work. She'll be upset, but she'll get over it. They'll be leaving in a couple of days anyway, and I won't have to see Lauren or that mother of hers ever again.

Mavis opened her eyes and scrutinized the application of deep red polish Iris had been painstakingly applying. Now she could settle back and think of much more pleasant things, like what her newly-lacquered nails would do later in the evening to Peter Culvane's gorgeous, well-tuned back.

■   ■   ■   ■   ■

Charlotte made her way back to her room. She didn't know what to do with herself. Should she go to exercise class, shop at Lavender Lane's chic little boutique, or start the latest Elena Ferrante novel? There was so much she could do here, but nothing moved get her mind away from food. The generous bowls of fresh fruits and vegetables stationed all around the spa didn't do it for her. These healthful reminders may have helped others stick to their diets, but when Charlotte was really upset, only one thing could abate the gnawing in her stomach. She had only fallen off the wagon once since arriving at Lavender Lane and despite that earlier transgression, had succeeded in losing five pounds. She was now in danger of totally destroying the inroads she had made.

Why did being shut out from watching the photo shoot affect her so strongly? Probably because Lauren hadn't even protested. Being dismissed that way made her feel unneeded, unnecessary, exactly the way she had felt around her daughter the last few years. This was such an exciting time for Lauren and Charlotte just wanted to be a part of it. She looked at herself in the mirror and tried to be objective about what she saw -- a clearly overweight but still attractive thirty-eight-year-old woman, with good skin and a hairdo that needed some updating and styling.

But beyond those looks, Charlotte saw herself as a failure at controlling her eating and a failure at being a mother. No ten-day stay at any pricey fat farm was going to change that. A torrent of tears suddenly spilled down her face. She stumbled into the bathroom and lunged at the tissue box on the table, yanking out the last one.

She went into the other room and dove into her handbag, looking for the pack of tissues she always carried. Instead, she found the small box of See's chocolates she had bought in the airport "just in case." A few days before, she had polished off the emergency Snickers Bar she had stashed in the side zipper compartment of her suitcase. She had hoped the candy bar would be her only indiscretion.

She fingered the shiny white carton of See's. She quickly ripped through the cellophane covering and the distinctive aroma of cocoa filled her nostrils. If ever there was a time for the kind of soothing only good chocolate could deliver, this was it.

She plucked out an Almond Royal and bit down through the dense coating of creamy dark chocolate into a thick nut core. She closed her eyes and chewed slowly. Bits of crunchy almond swam in the rich chocolate rendered into liquid velvet by the warmth of her mouth.

She selected another piece: A swirl of solid mocha hosting a creamy filling. With these candies, it was always a thrill to imagine what surprise might be inside -- tantalizing white mint truffle, divine maple caramel, heavenly cherries jubilee. Charlotte worked her way slowly and steadily through the box, visualizing all the possible flavors, numbering her favorites as she went, and then finally biting into the next treat awaiting her tongue.

Apricot cream, it was flawlessly smooth and quintessentially piquant. She let the taste linger in her mouth, savoring the texture for as long as she could, before giving in to the need to consume it in its entirety. Charlotte closed her eyes and sighed, luxuriating in the singular comfort and contentment that would last a mere moment or two more, before the siege of guilt and self-recrimination which always followed.

■　　■　　■　　■　　■

Toni was doing her best to think positively, but she had come to the conclusion that the whole notion of partnering with Phoebe to run Lavender Lane was a pipe dream. Less than two weeks before, nothing even remotely like it would ever have entered her mind, nor would meeting someone like Peter Culvane. She had other priorities now, a little life who was depending on her to bring him or her into the best personal world she would be able to create. She decided she must stop thinking about Peter and start figuring out what kind of work she could do in the future, and even though the thought of having to return to fashion sent a sharp pain through her neck, it was what she most likely would have to do.

Maybe she should accept Kevin's offer. Shortly after she called him and left a message, he texted her back, begging her to call him ASAP. She returned to the bench under the weeping willow.

"Thank GOD," he oozed. "I was worried that with the spa's ridiculous rules, you would have your phone off."

"You can take the girl out of the city," Toni laughed. "Are you OK? What's going on?"

"What's going on," Kevin said, "is that my prayers have been answered and my partner's niece, the anorexic little bitch who's been running our showroom, has quit. Hard to believe, but she's actually landed a guy, and wants to try being a homebody while she plans the no-doubt most over-the-top American wedding since Carrie thought she was marrying Mr. Big at the Fifth Avenue Library."

"Oh, dear. Hope her guy shows up," Toni laughed.

"What I hope, my little chickadee, is that you will take her place at my esteemed establishment."

"Me? But Kev, you know I had so hoped to get out of the *schmatta* business."

"Are you calling my glorious creations *schmattas*?"

"You know what I mean. I wanted to try something completely different."

"Like starvation? Honey, when they can have their pick of skinny, 22-yeal-old Harvard MBAs, who's going to hire a 35-year-old pregnant woman these days

Toni laughed. "Thanks for shaving off a few years."

"Seriously, it's rough out there. You know my clothing line. God knows, unless you've been lying to me all these years, you actually like my stuff."

"I love your clothing! You're a great designer."

"And your best friend, and, dare I mention, the father of your coming attraction -- a brilliant, talented, charismatic and gorgeous little creature?"

"Gorgeous, without doubt -- and all of those other things, too!"

"What could be better, Toni? A pleasant working environment -- well, except, maybe for my partner -- all the divine clothing you can cram into your closet, once you get your figure back, that is. And me all day long. It's a win-win! You can even bring our sweet little one to work. Oooh...I would sooo love that!"

"It's tempting, I'll admit..."

"Toni! Come home to Papa! You know it's the right thing, especially now. We're family."

"I'll think about it Kev. Really, I will."

"OK. But don't wait too long."

"I'll think long and hard."

"I know you will. Love you, Antoinette."

"Love you too, Kevin. You're the best."

Toni ended the call and heaved a huge sigh. Would she ever escape the fashion rat race? Kevin's offer was really a good one. She'd be running the showroom of one the country's most sought after sportswear designers, who just happened to be her best friend and the father of her child. Child care would be less of an issue. It could really work out pretty well. Personal considerations aside, it was so much more than a cut above working at Gillam's or any other store, for that matter. And she was a little long in the tooth to even think about one of those young and trendy on-line retailers.

The pool, only a few feet away, beckoned, but as she removed her robe, she heard Peter and Phoebe coming down the path. She couldn't bear to see Peter at that moment. She was sure one look at her would reveal her disappointment that nothing more than business chat had happened between them. She didn't want him to have a clue at how annoyed she was with herself for even thinking there could ever have been anything between them -- pregnancy notwithstanding. There was simply no way to compete with Mavis Perkins.

She walked quickly to the pool's deep end, and just as Peter and Phoebe approached, she dove in and swam the length underwater, hoping by the time she surfaced, they would be well out of sight.

Chapter Twenty-Five

"Do you think the Beauty Center is adequate?" Peter asked, as he and Phoebe walked.

"Well, yes."

"And the massage rooms. Are they comfortable enough?"

"I should think so," Phoebe replied.

"Perhaps the clients might prefer choosing their own music."

"That might be nice, but wouldn't it complicate things a bit?"

"I suppose so," Peter said. That was stupid of me, he thought, hoping his question didn't reveal his undue familiarity with the Lavender Lane massage area. He was not about to discuss any aspect of his rather special Beauty Center experience the other night.

On painstaking reflection, truth was he would have preferred not to have had the pleasure of that experience at all. Her considerable attributes notwithstanding, Mavis was becoming way too proprietary for his tastes. The fact that he knew her husband gnawed at him. He should never even have gone to dinner with her, but he had no way of knowing she'd had more than business on that wicked little mind of hers.

No question he found Mavis difficult to resist. Moreover, the business aspect of their budding "relationship" had lots of merit. While skin cremes were certainly not Peter's forte, research reports he'd run detailed the enormous sums of money and the extraordinary profit margins companies like Lavender Lane were pulling in. With its cachet, Lavender Lane should be able to out run the best of them.

He had heard nothing but glowing reports about the Quince Creme. Thanks to word of mouth and the social media chatter of ecstatic clients, orders were coming in from all over the country. Phoebe was confident she would be able to take over Nadia's relationship with the private-label lab in Covina that manufactured it. No doubt: Lavender Lane Rejuvenating Quince Creme had great potential written all over it. Peter really liked the addition of the word "rejuvenating." It gave it better buzz value, and the darned stuff was actually good. Peter had never used a serious moisturizing product before -- although he had noticed in locker rooms around the world that many men did -- and his skin had never looked so fresh or felt so soft. Maybe, he thought, there would be a men's line in the future.

Peter's phone rang and he excused himself. When he returned to Phoebe's side, he told her he'd be taking a flight to San Francisco for an unexpected important meeting the following morning.

"There's a whole contingent from Tokyo arriving even as we speak. Will you be all right here without me?"

Phoebe was about to reply when Peter began to laugh.

"How ridiculous of me! Lavender Lane managed to get along rather nicely without me for quite a number of years. Then, of course, you had Madame Demidova."

"Yes, we did. God rest her soul." Phoebe sighed, but recovered quickly. "When do you expect to return?"

"Hard to say. Sometimes these things are over in a couple of hours, and other times they drag on for days."

"Better hurry then. Have a good trip."

"Thanks!" Peter called out as he sprinted down the path, leaving Phoebe totally in charge for at least a day or two, but still not in possession of the partnership that always seemed to be just beyond her reach.

.   .   .   .   .

"Say it isn't so," Mavis cooed into the phone.

"I'm sure you'll have no problem surviving without me," Peter said a bit coldly.

"I'd prefer that I did not have to."

Peter waited a moment before answering. "That's terribly flattering, Mavis, but I've really got to go. Business is business, you know. If I don't hurry, I'll miss my flight."

"That wouldn't bother me."

"You're cute. I'll ring you when I get back."

"And when do you expect that will be?" Mavis asked, her honey-sweet delivery tinged ever so slightly with impatience.

"Could be tomorrow. Could be three days. At this moment, I really can't say. Take care," Peter said, quickly disconnecting the call.

Mavis couldn't believe Peter had hung up. *He wasn't so goddamned detached the last time I had his dick in my mouth and was sending him on his way to heaven.* She toyed with the phone for a few seconds and then put it aside. She walked over to the full-length mirror and loosened the tie on her dressing gown. The black silk kimono slipped from her shoulders and fell to the floor in front of her. Her nearly flawless white skin appeared incandescent in the golden rays of late afternoon sun. Stepping back at bit, she let her eyes slowly drink in the image in the mirror. She never tired of lingering over what peered back at her. He'll be back, that's for sure, she thought. *And it won't be for any short-lived tryst. I have big plans for this man, and I am not planning to take no for an answer.*

She bent down, picked up the robe and flung it over her shoulder. In the meantime, there are other toys to play with. I'm not going to waste a perfectly good night sitting around with a bunch of boring old hens. And no fucking way am I about to have dinner with that pouting Lauren and her plus-sized mother. She walked over to the phone and dialed the tennis courts. Yes, indeed: When it comes to room service, Gregory can be counted on to deliver the best.

Chapter Twenty-Six

"I absolutely hate that this is my last full day at Lavender Lane," Toni said to Phoebe at the breakfast table. "It seems as though I just got here."

"Your last day this time around. I may not have been able to convince you to change your mind about working at Lavender Lane, but I certainly meant it when I said you'd always be welcome here."

She was bursting to tell Phoebe about the kumquat but it was still too early. She'd have to punt.

"My friend Kevin Gavelli offered me the job of running his showroom and I might take him up on it -- second best to being a partner in Lavender Lane, but not shabby. And if I do take the job, I can probably afford to come back here at some point. It is rather expensive, you know."

"That's part of its charm. Most of the women who come here like the fact it's so expensive. Being able to afford it makes them feel superior." Phoebe blanched and quickly put her hand over her mouth. "Oh dear. I should not have said that!"

"Probably not," Toni said, letting out a howl. "But I'm glad you did!"

They exploded in laughter. Phoebe tried desperately to maintain her British decorum, but it was an exercise in futility.

"Are there enough funnies to go around?" Charlotte asked, approaching the table. "I could sure use a laugh. I've totally fallen off the wagon."

"I thought something might have been wrong when you didn't come down for dinner last night," Toni said.

"By the time I polished off an entire box of chocolates, even I was too full for dinner."

Phoebe reached across and patted Charlotte's arm. "Not to worry, my dear. Today is a brand-new opportunity to start again. And you will!"

"And I was doing so well…"

"I totally agree with Phoebe," Toni said. "And you will again. "Now where's Lauren this morning? I thought for sure she'd join us for the last group breakfast."

"She's got the photography thing with Mavis again."

"How exciting!" Phoebe said. "What are you doing here with us? Don't you want to see everything?"

"The Grand One has banished me from the set. What I want apparently means nothing to her. After all, I'm only the girl's mother."

I could have told you, Toni thought, but said, instead, "Don't fret. There will be plenty of opportunities to see Lauren in action. She's bound to have a long and successful modeling career."

"I don't know. She didn't seem all that enthusiastic when she left the room this morning. She seemed upset, whining about some pimple. But of course, when I asked to see it, all I got was 'Oh, Mother.'"

"Her skin looked clear to me when I saw her last," Phoebe said. "She'll be fine."

Sure, she will, Toni thought. No doubt the divine Mavis will go totally out of her way to make the experience as wonderful as possible for her budding young protégé. "Come on, girls, let's eat," she said. "There's a beautiful day waiting. And It's our last. We don't want to waste it!"

■　■　■　■　■

Lauren's exhibited no enthusiasm as she made her way to the solarium. She'd found the previous day's experience so much different from what she'd expected. Modeling wasn't fun. It wasn't fun at all.

After tossing fitfully during a night plagued with disturbing dreams, she'd woken up in a sweat. And the pimple that everyone seemed so concerned about, had blossomed even more.

"Shit!" she screamed, staring in the bathroom mirror in disbelief.

"What did you say?" Charlotte called out from the other room.

"I said 'shit' and if you must know, I have a horrendous pimple."

"That's hardly the end of the world."

"Like you really know what you're talking about, Mother," Lauren barked. "Have you forgotten I'm posing for photographs this morning? A pimple is not exactly what a model needs on her face."

"They can re-touch it out."

"Don't you now anything, mother? They're not doing much of that anymore. Everyone wants natural."

"Well, then. Let me see. Maybe I can help."

"Just leave me alone!"

Of course, Charlotte thought to herself. What do I know about anything? She wiped away the tear that had formed in the corner of her eye.

When Lauren arrived at the solarium, Mavis was already in the makeup chair, with Roberto prancing around her, brush in hand. Ian was fiddling with his camera and Eric and Dex were busily rearranging the plants. They barely acknowledged her arrival.

"There you are," Mavis called out sharply. "Come over here. I need to talk to you."

At the sound of Mavis's voice, they all quickly looked up, then just as quickly looked away.

"Roberto, love," Mavis crooned, affecting a look of disappointment at having to stop his masterful work for even a second. "Can you give us a few moments?" She reached up and patted his cheek.

"No problem. Sing out when you're ready."

What won't take long? Lauren thought.

Mavis didn't waste a moment before saying, "Well, Lauren, it seems as though we've had a change in direction."

"What do you mean?"

"We won't be needing you anymore," Mavis said matter-of-factly.

A tremor jolted through Lauren's body. *What is she saying? This isn't happening...* She lost her balance and fell against Mavis's arm. Mavis pushed her away.

"I don't understand."

"It's quite simple. On further consideration, the Quince Creme really is entirely too rich for young skin. It wouldn't make any sense to try to market it to anyone your age."

"But..."

Mavis shook her head. "There are no buts. It won't work, and we need to move on."

Move on... Lauren's eyes began to well up with tears.

"Now, now. Be a big girl. You're very young and you're a good type. There will be plenty of opportunities for you in the future."

"But I wanted to work with you. Now."

"Well, as the business moves along, perhaps we'll do another creme, a lighter one that's appropriate for teenagers." She gave Lauren her most patronizing smile. "We will be sure to consider you when the time comes."

Consider me? Lauren couldn't believe it. Just hours ago, she was co-starring in an exciting ad campaign and the world was waiting for her. She stared at Mavis, unable to respond.

"I have to get back to work now, Lauren," Mavis said coldly. "Roberto," she trilled, turning away. "Ready!"

Lauren didn't move. She stood there, shivering in her skimpy shorts and T-shirt against the chill of the overly air-conditioned room.

"Excuse me, dearie," Roberto said, as he advanced toward Mavis, wielding his brush. "Time to move on." He wedged his narrow body between Lauren and Mavis and returned to applying a subtle shade of light violet shadow under Mavis's chiseled brow bones.

Time to move on?

Lauren couldn't speak, but it didn't much matter as neither Mavis nor Roberto seemed the least bit interested in her presence. Roberto was totally engrossed in making up one of the world's most beautiful faces, and the woman beneath his brush had apparently already removed Lauren from her radar screen.

Lauren began to back away, disbelief governing each small step she took. Suddenly, her body was seized with the need to move -- and to move quickly. She spun around, darted to the door, and thrust herself out into the warmth of the day.

The early morning sun was beaming with a vigor that foretold the intensity that would blanket the valley later in the day, but it felt good on Lauren's chilled skin. She reveled in the warmth for a moment, then tore down the path leading to the foot of the mountains.

The air was clear and clean and she drank it in, and with every breath, the need to run became even stronger. She picked up speed as she moved along, each increase between paces fueling the next. She could focus only on the need to run and keep on running. Nothing existed other than the movement. Save the occasional cry of a soaring desert hawk or a darting jack rabbit's rustling in an adjacent bush, the only sound Lauren could hear was the crunching of gravel as her feet landed, first one and then the other and then the first again, in a litany of repetition.

The path began its incline up the side of the hill and the sun's rays grew stronger, but Lauren's feet continued to pursue their mission, further and further, higher and higher, until the trail became nothing more than a winding thread making its way amidst a covering of stones, rocks and prickly cactus, until the heat of the sun finally gave way to the cooling shade of the mountain's abundant trees.

Lauren had been running mindlessly for some time, but the mounting incline slowed her and jarred her consciousness. She recounted the events of the last twenty-four hours and a tidal wave of anxiety washed over her. She realized she had been running in fear. She also realized how tired and thirsty she was, and even a little hungry.

She slowed to a stop and looked around. A few hundred feet ahead, the darkened, narrowed path gave way to a small, sunny meadow, then it narrowed and darkened, once again, on its pilgrimage back up the side of the mountain. She began to run again, and as she drew closer, she could hear the sound of running water. She pressed on, propelled by the thought of a cool drink from a fresh mountain stream.

Only a few yards away from that drink, Lauren mis-stepped and her foot sunk into a hole. There was an audible crunch as she felt her ankle give way, and then the thud of her body as she fell to the ground.

"Shit!" she screamed, trying to push herself up. Her arms were covered with scratches and blood trickled from a cut right below her elbow. Great. Just great. I'll probably have scars all over my arms and my legs -- not that it will matter much anyway. Nobody will want me as a model now that Mavis Perkins has dumped me.

She tried to stand but fell back down. "Je-sus!" she yelled, as the pain ripped through her ankle and up the side of her leg. *It's the same damned ankle I turned last week. This really sucks.* She tried getting up again, but it was no use. The pain shot through her leg once more. The sun was at full intensity now and beating down mercilessly. Without benefit of sunscreen, Lauren's skin began to burn quickly. Somehow, she had to get herself out of the sun while she figured out what to do. She knew prolonged exposure at midday might lead to sun poisoning or sunstroke and, without water, severe dehydration.

Each time she tried to balance herself, the slightest pressure on her injured foot delivered searing pain. She started to hop, but the path was full of large stones and pebbles. She looked around for a loose branch to use as a walking stick, but as she moved forward, she landed on a barely exposed rock, and toppled over.

As she felt herself falling, Lauren was aware of the ground coming up to meet her, but not of the rock that sat at the point where her head made contact. She felt the slightest impact, but then nothing, oblivious to what had happened and to the dangerous consequences that would be wreaked by hours of unprotected exposure, not only to the scorching sun of the afternoon, but also to the near freezing temperatures of the desert mountain night.

Chapter Twenty-Seven

Phoebe was at her desk when Peter called to say he'd probably not be back until morning. He also had a favor to ask. Could she get a discreet message to Mrs. Perkins explaining that he'd been delayed in San Francisco so they would have to continue their discussion the next day, prior to her departure. But Phoebe had news: Mavis was not leaving the next day with the others. She had decided to stay on for an additional ten days.

"Another ten days! I thought we were booked solid, well into June."

"We are, but Mrs. Perkins was in my office when a cancellation call came in. She moved right in for the kill."

Peter burst out laughing. "She would!"

No wonder all these women have crimps in their knickers over him. He is totally charming.

"Well, in any event, please tell Mrs. Perkins I expect to be back sometime tomorrow."

"Of course..."

"Thank you. And, is everything else OK? Any problems?"

"Nothing out of the ordinary. Nothing I can't handle."

"Good to know! On that note, I'll return to my meeting. See you tomorrow."

"Yes...see you tomorrow."

Phoebe hung up, but her hand remained on the receiver. God knows, they always shoot the messenger, she thought, wondering how she was going to get the information to Mavis without being subject to the dreadful reaction bound to come.

■ ■ ■ ■ ■

"Damn it!" Mavis shrieked as she slammed down the phone in her room. Phoebe had left a voice mail relaying Peter's message. What business meeting was more important than a delicious evening *à deux*? Well, she would just have to make do. There was always Gregory, but she'd had her fill of him this trip. Enough little boy games. He could barely hold a candle -- so to speak -- to Peter, who was entirely grown up. And anyway, she was tired. She'd forgotten how exhausting all that posing for the camera was. So be it. She'd settle for a good night's sleep. `

She checked her watch. The girls were probably all fluffing for their last dinner together. She could go down and eat with them, but then she'd have to deal with Lauren. No. A nice hot bath, a divine massage and a little something sent up from the kitchen would be fine. She dialed the Beauty Center. If no massages were available, she was prepared to throw Peter Culvane's name around sufficiently enough to make one materialize ASAP.

■ ■ ■ ■ ■

"I can't believe this is our last dinner together." Charlotte sighed deeply. "It's too awful!"

"My dear," Phoebe said, looking at Charlotte's sad face. "It's not like we are expiring at any moment. We'll see each other again."

"I certainly hope so," said Toni. "One doesn't get to meet such quality people very often."

"I'll drink to that," Charlotte said, raising her glass of peppermint iced tea.

"As will I!" piped in Phoebe.

"To us!" Toni said as they lifted their glasses in a toast.

The bitter sweetness of their last dinner together was animated with lots of laughter and delicious girl talk. They even managed to joke about how Mavis and her scheming had come between them, and of course, how The Grand One had pounced on Peter Culvane before he had even gotten his bearings. At one point, they got a naughty chuckle out of Phoebe who protested that she shouldn't, really couldn't, discuss any of the clients. But trashing Mavis Perkins was just too much of a temptation for any red-blooded British-American woman to resist.

Charlotte confided that after giving it a great deal of thought, she was going to go back to school to earn a college degree. "Better late than never," she said. "It's either school or becoming a pastry chef, and we know where that would get me -- back to size 16."

"Good for you, Charlotte," Phoebe said. "That's wonderful!"

"And you, Ms. Toni. Have you decided what you want to be when you grow up?" Charlotte asked.

A mother, Toni thought. *Definitely a mother.*

"I don't know," Toni groaned. "Just when I thought I was sure I wanted to give up the razzle dazzle of the fashion world, the allure of the old glitz 'n glamour is rearing its head -- not to mention the money that comes along with it. As I told Phoebe before, my friend Kevin -- you know, the designer I've mentioned to you -- has offered me the job of running his showroom. I adore him, and his offer is quite generous. It's the proverbial offer I can't refuse."

"Ooh. Do I smell a romance brewing?" Charlotte asked?

"No, not in the traditional sense," Toni said. "I'm not his flavor, if you know what I mean, but Kevin and I have a very special relationship." *Special doesn't even begin to describe it!* "We're really like family."

"Well. He's lucky to have you as his friend. And so am I -- to have you both as friends. Isn't it wonderful we had this time together at Lavender Lane?"

"I'll drink to that," Toni said, lifting her glass of sparkling water."

"As will I!" said Phoebe.

"Me too," said Charlotte.

They enjoyed a wonderful last evening together. The only sour note was that Lauren never showed up and, even though Charlotte was sure her daughter had simply decided, yet again, not to eat, she couldn't help but worry. Lauren had not obeyed the "no cell phone rule" and it was always with her. Charlotte called Lauren repeatedly, but the call went straight to voice mail every time. As much as she hated to encounter the dreaded Mavis, right before dinner she mustered her courage and checked the Solarium to see if they were still shooting. Strange -- the room was locked, the photography session evidently over. She went on to check the pool, the tennis courts, the steam and locker rooms. No sign of Lauren. The only conclusion she could draw was that her daughter had gone running.

After the women said their goodbyes and Charlotte finally returned to her room, she opened the door expecting Lauren to be slouched on the sofa watching television or texting some friend. Instead, she found the room dark and empty. When she turned the lights on, it was obvious that no one, other than the maid who had turned down the beds, had been there in the last several hours. It was also obvious that Lauren didn't want to be found: she had left her phone in the room. It sat there on the bed stand almost as a taunt. Now I have no way of reaching her, Charlotte thought. Heaven only knows where she is.

The digital clock on the nightstand glared 10:20 pm. The same bottomless panic she had felt two nights before enveloped her, and she wasn't able to focus. *Think, Charlotte! Think!* She began to pace. Surely Mavis would know something. They were together all day. She must know where Lauren is. As much as Charlotte hated having to call her, she bit the bullet and dialed Mavis's room.

"No, Charlotte," Mavis said curtly. "I have not seen Lauren since early this morning."

"I don't understand. I thought she was with you all day, to do the photographs."

"It seems we've had a slight change of plans." Then, without skipping a beat, Mavis continued. "We are going forward without a younger model."

Charlotte's breath caught in her throat. She wasn't sure she had heard correctly. "I'm not sure I understand. You're saying that you're not using Lauren?"

"Precisely."

"Oh my God. Lauren must be devastated."

"She's young. She'll get over it," Mavis said, with not even a hint of sympathy in her voice. "I'm quite sure you've had your disappointments, and you survived."

What a bitch! Charlotte chastised herself for allowing the word to even enter her thoughts, but it was so overwhelmingly appropriate. "Yes," Charlotte managed to get out. She drew a deep breath. "And one of the biggest disappointments of them all was having this trip ruined by meeting you."

Charlotte could hear Mavis breathing in the silence. "I should never have allowed my daughter to get involved with you. How could you possibly have built up her hopes, make her think she was about to become an important model, and then drop her, just like that? It's cruel. You are cruel." Charlotte's heart was beating wildly, but she pressed on. "You may have beauty, but you don't have much else. You have no heart, and from the looks of it, you surely have no soul!"

Mavis was now breathing discernibly into the phone. "Have you quite finished?" she asked.

"No, there's one more thing."

"And what might that be?" Mavis sneered.

"You can go straight to Hell," Charlotte said, pronouncing each word slowly and methodically before slamming down the phone. Her body shook as she withdrew her hand from the receiver, but she felt an enormous sense of relief. She was sure God would forgive her. Someone had to tell that woman off, and it was entirely appropriate she be the one to do it!

But Charlotte's relief was short-lived. She still had no idea where Lauren was. She dialed the tennis office. It would not have surprised her if Lauren had disobeyed her and saw Greg again, but there was no answer.

She began pacing. *Think, Charlotte, think!* She walked over to the window and looked out into the darkness. *Dear God. My daughter could be out there somewhere.* She turned away. *Toni. Toni can help me. And Phoebe. They'll know what to do.* She hated to disturb them at such a late hour, but she phoned and both Phoebe and Toni were at her side in short order. In a few minutes more were discussing how Phoebe would mobilize the security crew to canvas the grounds.

Her friends did their best to allay Charlotte's fears, but when, an hour and a half later the crew reported that their search had turned up nothing, Charlotte was hyper-ventilating, in a state of true panic.

"Listen to me," Toni said, grasping Charlotte by the shoulders. "We are going to find her. I promise."

Charlotte nodded weakly.

"Think with me now. Lauren's a runner. You once told me she often takes off for a run when she's upset."

Charlotte nodded her head again.

"I bet she went running after Mavis let her down. Maybe she's tripped or fallen."

"Or worse. There are all kinds of animals out there!"

"She'll be all right We'll find her. Don't you agree, Phoebe?"

"Yes, of course," Phoebe said, but she was merely paying lip service. She understood only too well of the dangers of being out in the dark on some of the area's more obscure trails. Several years prior, a guest who didn't show up for breakfast or morning activities was found badly mauled by a bear. It took her weeks in the hospital to recover. "I think we should phone the sheriff. He's got a helicopter and his men can search areas our people can't get to with their cars."

Chapter Twenty-Eight

Lauren opened her eyes and tried to focus. Every part of her body ached, but the aching in her body was nothing compared to the pain in her head. It was as though carving knives were being jammed through her skull, piercing right through bone to her eyes.

She tried to make out her surroundings, but she could barely see the silhouettes of the bushes and trees. She heard ominous sounds in the distance, and then remembered she had been running and had fallen. She also remembered the blazing sun and searing heat. Now the sky was dark and the air was cold -- very cold.

The noises of the desert seemed to be coming closer -- low, growling, ominous sounds. Lauren tried to shut images of all ravenous wild creatures out of her brain. *I'm trapped.* She shuddered. *What am I going to do?* She tried righting her body but couldn't. Terror washed over her. *I'll never get out of here. I'll never get out of here alive.*

Whatever creature was growling, it was moving closer. Pain relentlessly pounded throughout Lauren's parched and battered body, and a torrent of tears gushed down her badly sunburned face. If only she had her cell phone. It was all Mavis's fault. She had told her not to bring it to the set.

■　■　■　■　■

Peter yawned repeatedly as he sat back in the car, trying to stay awake as the driver made his way from the Palm Springs airport. Nearly midnight, he was bushed. It had been one hell of a day. They were damned good negotiators, that team from Tokyo, but in the end, he had prevailed, picking up the potash site for five million less than his clients were prepared to pay -- not a bad savings, considering that his fees were augmented with a hefty equity position.

He could have stayed the night and made the trip back to Lavender Lane the next morning, but he wanted to get an early start. There were lots of decisions to be made at the spa before returning to Boston, and unless he was prepared to make Lavender Lane his full-time occupation, he had to get back east.

Peter would also have to deal with Mavis, who obviously had decided to make him her full-time occupation. The more he thought about it during the last twenty-four hours, the more he'd realized that he had to extricate himself from the more personal aspects of their arrangement. He hoped it was possible to salvage the business end of their deal, because using her as the Quince Creme spokesperson had a lot of merit. Telling her about his expectations for their relationship moving forward however, was a prospect he did not relish.

As Peter approached Lavender Lane, he was surprised to see flashes of bright light and hear the sound of helicopter blades piercing the calm of the desert night. When he reached the front of the main house, he saw several people clustered around a contingent of police cars, and a copter heading off toward the eastern mountain range that bordered the property.

"What's all of this?" Peter asked, stepping out of his car.

"Can I help you sir?" an aging, overweight sheriff asked. "You're on private property," he added in a well-practiced, official tone.

"Yes, I believe I am," Peter answered smiling. He extended his hand. "I'm Peter Culvane."

The sheriff blanched. He, like everyone else in the area, had heard of Nadia's death and the emergence of the son no one knew she had. "Yes, of course. I beg your pardon, sir. I'd been acquainted with Madame, I mean, your mother, for many years. I had great respect for her." He lowered his eyes. "I was so sorry to learn of her passing. Please accept my condolences."

"Thank you," Peter said.

"Mr. Culvane," Phoebe called from the front steps. "I'm so glad you're here!" She approached at a rapid pace, somewhat out of breath. "We're in a bit of a nightmare."

"It certainly would seem so. What exactly is going on?"

"Lauren, the young girl Mavis wanted to use in the Quince Creme ads, has been missing for hours. She's a runner and we're afraid she might be lost, or heaven forbid, worse. Sheriff Maxwell has been good enough to bring over his tracking team."

"My helicopter is canvassing the trails that go up the side of the mountain. There's a good possibility she might have run up there and fallen. Gotten herself hurt."

"Let's hope not," Peter said. "How long has she been missing?"

"It's difficult to say, Mr. Culvane," Phoebe responded. "Charlotte Tanner, her mother, realized sometime after dinner that she was missing."

"What about Mavis Perkins?" Peter asked. "Weren't they working together all day?"

"For God's sake, what is all this horrendous noise?" Mavis bellowed, almost at the precise mention of her name. She was pushing her way through the crowd of guests who had gathered on the steps. "Whatever's going on, you are making it impossible to sleep!" She advanced on the police cars, glaring at the people who were huddled there. When she saw Peter, her demeanor changed in an instant.

"Oh, Peter darling," she said, quickly and hardly in a whisper. "When did you get back?"

"Hold off, Mavis," Peter said sharply. "We've got a crisis to deal with at the moment."

"Crisis? Oh, dear." She plied Peter with her most seductive smile.

"When was the last time you saw young Lauren?"

Mavis looked puzzled. "About nine o'clock this morning. Why?"

"What happened to your all-day photography session together?"

"That's what my poor daughter expected," Charlotte interjected, approaching the group with Toni at her side.

"I don't understand," Mavis demanded.

"You have destroyed my little girl's world," Charlotte said, eyes flashing. "Now she's run off and God knows what's happened to her."

"Don't be ridiculous," Mavis said. "I can assure you I had absolutely nothing to do with Lauren's going anywhere. She was perfectly fine when I saw her this morning."

"Would someone please clarify what happened for me?" Peter said.

Mavis and Charlotte continued wordlessly glaring at each other.

"What appears to have happened," Toni offered, "is that Mavis dismissed Lauren -- summarily fired the poor girl, who was then so upset, she ran off. Where she is now, I'm afraid, none of us can be sure."

"Don't worry, Mrs. Tanner," Peter said, patting Charlotte gently on the shoulder. "We'll find your daughter. Won't we, Sheriff?"

"Yes, of course," Mr. Culvane. "My crew has it under control. Why don't you all go to the house and I'll report back the moment we know anything. It's pretty dang cold out here tonight."

There was a long silence. "Let's go in and have some nice hot tea," Phoebe suggested.

"Good idea. No point in your standing around out here in this chill,' Peter said. "You ladies aren't dressed for it." He looked pointedly at Mavis.

Charlotte and Toni were in warm-up suits, and Phoebe was still in her working attire. Mavis was in a sheer robe that had fallen open, revealing much of her breasts. She toyed with the folds of the robe but made no attempt to cover herself further.

"Peter," she said, "why don't we have a brandy? I have some lovely Napoleon in my room."

"She's un-fucking-believable," Toni whispered under her breath. "Let's go girls. Time for tea!" She was anxious to get inside. It would be too easy to catch a chill, and she couldn't afford to do that.

"I'd better join my men," the sheriff said, clearly uncomfortable at overhearing Mavis's invitation.

"Thank you, Sheriff. I'll be in the office." Peter's pronunciation of the word "office" left little doubt as to what he was trying to communicate. "I'd appreciate knowing what, if anything, your men find. And please share the news with me before it's given to anyone else. This is especially important if the news is not good."

The sheriff nodded and walked away.

"Peter," Mavis said, putting her hand on his arm.

Peter wrenched his arm away. "What could you have been thinking? That invitation was hardly appropriate given the circumstances, and in front others, including Sheriff Maxwell."

Mavis cocked her head to the side. "Don't be so angry," she said, pursing her lips in a Lauren-like pout. "It was hardly shocking stuff –- and nothing, you can be sure, the sheriff has not heard before."

"Well, Mavis. I can't speak for you, but the sheriff has certainly never been privy to my personal agenda, and I really don't have any plans to change that." He paused, his expression losing any vestiges of warmth. "Now if you'll excuse me..."

"Excuse you!" Mavis said incredulously. "Excuse you? No, I certainly will not excuse you. You run off and have one of your peons leave a voice mail for me and you want me to excuse you?"

"I was called away unexpectedly and there was no time to phone you myself. And, while we're at it, Mavis, let's get some other things straight." Color began to rise in Peter's face. "Because we enjoyed some, shall we say, private time together, does not make you my keeper."

Mavis let out a long, throaty laugh. "Could have fooled me. Didn't seem like it the other night."

"Well, Mavis, you do have some very persuasive tactics. And I enjoyed our time together. I won't dispute that. But, the fact remains, you are married -- and, of all things, to someone I know."

"But you were aware of that."

"Yes, I was."

"Well?"

"Apparently I made a staggering error in judgment."

Mavis studied him for a moment. "You're not going to tell me you've never, shall we say, 'spent time' with a married woman before?"

Peter ran his fingers over his forehead and up through his hair. "I would be a liar if I said I hadn't. And on careful thought, it's not something I'm especially proud of nor is it something I now care to do again."

"And what if I were no longer married?"

"Don't even go there, Mavis."

Mavis looked at Peter long and hard. "I see. And what about our business arrangement? I realize we have nothing in writing. I didn't think it would be necessary, considering the, uh, circumstances." She let her gaze drift down his body before raising her eyes to meet his again.

Peter regarded her dispassionately. "I think we should go forward with the Quince project. If you still want to be the model and spokesperson, we can make it work-- even though letting the poor girl down in such a manner was hardly a smart move, let alone a gracious one. You should have checked with me before deciding to let her go. The younger/older woman positioning would have worked quite well."

Mavis stiffened. "Wait a minute, Peter. I wasn't planning to be merely a model or spokesperson. I thought I was going to have a stake in this project -- points, shares, whatever you call it."

"The Quince Creme belongs to Lavender Lane, and Lavender Lane belongs to me -- no stockholders, no partners, no special interests, and I intend to keep it that way -- with the exception of a percentage I'm planning to give to Phoebe Bancroft."

"A percentage for Phoebe! Are you mad?"

"Hardly. It's a reward for her exceptional work and loyalty to Madame Demidova over the years. She deserves it."

Mavis glared at him. "And how about what I deserve? You know, all my work for the Quince Creme?"

Peter looked long at hard at this woman for whom he had nearly lost his way. My God, she was remarkable. He really had to steel his resolve.

"If and when we come to some formal arrangement, Mavis, you can be sure it will be an equitable one."

Mavis eyed him a moment, then broke into a sardonic smile. "Yes, Peter, I'm sure that it will be." She paused. "But, just in case, I'll have my husband get in touch. He's a marvelous negotiator, as you no doubt remember."

"It will be my pleasure to do business with him." Peter smiled.

"Yes. I expect it will be," Mavis said, shrugging her shoulders. Well, then, I suppose there's nothing else we need to talk about right now, is there?"

"I expect not. We can talk more in the next couple of days."

"Not actually. I'll be leaving tomorrow."

"Oh..."

"Yes. I had planned to extend my stay, but there doesn't seem to be a reason to now, does there?" She leaned forward and kissed Peter on the check, brushing her lips close to his mouth, and rubbing her breasts against him in the process.

"You never stop, do you Mavis?"

"Sometimes I do, Peter, and I guess this qualifies as one of those times." She sighed audibly and mouthed "see you" as she turned on her heels and strode away like a reigning diva exiting the stage, having delivered an arduous and thunderously applauded aria.

.　　.　　.　　.　　.

Lauren lay shivering and exhausted. Each time she felt her tears subsiding, they started again, leaving her more frightened and desperate than before.

Maybe by the time it gets light out my foot will feel better and I might be able to walk, she thought. But even as the words formed in her mind, searing pain bolted through her ankle and up the length of her leg.

The growling she'd heard earlier began to pierce the stillness of the night once more, but this time, the source of the menacing noise seemed much closer. "Mother, please," she begged out loud, looking up as if her mother were some celestial being who could answer her prayers. "Won't you send somebody to come and find me?"

Then she saw him. He was standing on a boulder only a few feet away, his hungry eyes gleaming in the moonlight -- a magnificent, regal and proud mountain lion, poised and ready to pounce. Lauren felt a surge of terror unlike anything she had ever in her young life experienced. "My God," she said, catching her breath. I'm going to die."

Her heart began beating wildly. She tried to calm herself. Stay still. He won't pounce if you stay still. It will be OK, she thought. He's not moving. It will be ok. It will be ok. She repeated the words to herself over and over while the animal kept his eyes fixed on her. After what seemed like hours, she thought she heard a faint, whirling sound. As the noise grew louder, the animal turned, stopped for a moment, then bolted away.

A surge of relief coursed through Lauren's body. Soon, the blackness of the sky grayed and was shattered by a shaft of light. A helicopter hovered over a nearby meadow, spraying light on the ground beneath. *Thank you, God! Thank you.* She propped herself up on one arm, waving frantically with the other and screaming at the top of her lungs: "Here! I'm here!" But there was no point. The crew could neither hear her against the noise of the motor, nor see her as she lay nearly flat against the earth.

"Please," Lauren sobbed. "Please..."

The copter remained in place for what seemed like mere seconds before it turned and began to move away. "No! Don't go," she screamed. She had to find some way to get their attention. She grabbed at her stomach, her fingers grasping folds of the thin T-shirt that had been providing a paltry shield against the chill of the night. She pulled her shirt over her head and began to wave it back and forth. She waved and waved but it appeared to be too late. The copter continued on its course moving out and away. "Don't go...please!" she yelled. She kept on waving, frustration overwhelming her. "Please don't go. Please..."

The copter paused in mid-air, as though it were making up its mind as to which direction to go. Lauren waved the shirt, up and down and high and wide and screamed louder than she thought she was capable of screaming.

And then the bird moved, made a sharp turn and began to double back.

"I'm here! I'm here!" she yelled, flailing her arms, the T-shirt moving back and forth like a flag of surrender on a decimated battle field. "Can you see me? I'm here."

The copter paused directly over the clearing and its light shone brilliantly down on her bruised face and naked torso. She could hear someone's amplified voice calling to her over the din of the motor and the whirling of the blades. "Hang in there, young lady. We're comin' to get you."

A man lowered himself down a swaying rope ladder and, in a few moments, jumped to the ground. Lauren wiped away the tears of relief that had flooded her face and covered her breasts as best she could. Her mother would have a shit-fit if she heard she had no top on when they found her, but, as the man came closer, she heard him say, "Your mom is sure going to be happy when she learns you're safe!" She felt overwhelmed. She didn't think there was one tear left to be shed, but as the man took off his jacket and covered her, the floodgates burst open again.

"It's going to be OK," he said. "We'll have you fixed up in no time."

"Thank you," she whispered. "Thank you so much." As he gently lifted her up and walked towards the hovering copter, she closed her eyes and her body went limp with relief.

Chapter Twenty-Nine

The helicopter took Lauren directly to Palm Springs General, where the doctors put her on a hydrating IV, set her broken ankle, and attended to her badly scratched and sunburned skin. They also sedated her, since she was extremely agitated. Charlotte spent the night in a chair by her bedside, looking at her sleeping daughter. Lauren looked so young and innocent, so vulnerable, this rebellious teenager of hers, just like when she fell off her bike and fractured her arm when she was six years old. Where had those nine years gone?

Charlotte reached over and gently stroked her forehead. Lauren stirred, slowly opened her eyes and blinked. She looked around the room, then back at Charlotte again.

"Mommy, oh Mommy," she cried, as she tried to sit up.

"You're safe now sweetheart."

"I was so scared."

"I know you were, honey, but everything's going to be all right now."

Lauren leaned forward, put her arms around Charlotte's neck and began to sob.

"Thank you for sending them to find me. It was so awful."

"There's no need to thank me. I'm your mother and I love you."

Charlotte cradled Lauren in her arms. amid her own flowing tears.

"I love you, too, Mommy," Lauren said. "So much. And I'm sorry I've been such a brat."

They held on to each other for quite some time, finally letting go when a nurse came in to tell them Lauren would be discharged by noon.

.   .   .   .   .

At mid-day, the doctors released Lauren to the waiting phalanx of worriers -- Toni, Phoebe and Peter, all who had accompanied Charlotte and Lauren to the hospital the evening before, stayed for several hours and returned in the morning. Lauren, on crutches, and Charlotte, looking exhausted, appeared with big smiles. The group was assured when the doctor announced that Lauren would be "Good as new in a few weeks."

"This calls for a celebration!" Peter said. "Let's head over to Sal's New York Pizza. The head groundskeeper tells me it's the best pizza west of Brooklyn."

Charlotte glanced at Lauren, who hadn't touched pizza since she'd become obsessed with her weight, but Lauren gave her mother a big smile and said, "That sounds super!"

When the waiter put two huge pepperoni pies on the table, Toni was hit with a sudden wave of nausea and made a bee-line for the bathroom. When she didn't come back in a reasonable amount of time, Phoebe went to check on her. She found Toni leaning against the sink, breathing heavily.

"I'm fine, Phoebe. Really. I didn't mean to take you away from the group."

"I was concerned. You've been in here far longer than it would take for a normal potty break."

"Tummy issues. Sorry."

Phoebe watched Toni wipe her face with a fresh towel and freshen her lipstick.

"Hope it was nothing you ate at the spa. We are scrupulous with our cleanliness standards in the kitchen."

"Oh, no." Toni shook her head. "Nothing like that."

Phoebe appraised the woman who, in only a couple of days, had become much more than a client or mere acquaintance. The appraisal turned into a stare.

"Whaaat?" Toni asked, her face still flushed.

Phoebe crossed her arms and nodded at Toni. "I'm going to take a wild guess here, my friend." She paused. "I'm going to say you're pregnant."

Toni let that roll around in her brain before deciding how to answer. No point in denying it. She was at the 11th week and all was well -- and aside from a couple of bouts of morning sickness and now this nausea, she was feeling really good. She could push the 12-week rule just a tad.

"Well," Toni finally answered. "Guess you found me out."

"Oh my God!" Phoebe yelled out, forgetting her usual British reserve. "Such lovely news!" She embraced Toni. "I need to hear all the details -- when, how and most of all who?

At that moment, the door opened. "Is everything all right in here?" the waitress asked. "The gentleman at your table sent me to see."

"Peter...how nice," Phoebe said with an arched brow. "But I guess it can't be him. Not enough cooking time. And anyway, don't think Mavis let anybody else near him."

"Certainly not near enough to do the deed!" Toni said.

That sent them into spasms of laughter. The waitress didn't get the joke. "Excuse me. Can I tell him you'll be coming out soon?"

"Yes. Of course - and thank you," Phoebe said.

"Okey-dokey." The waitress said as she turned and left.

"One quick question before we go back to the table," Phoebe said. How could you flirt with Peter knowing that there's somebody else's little bun in that oven?"

Toni's face fell. Phoebe had hit a nerve.

"Sorry, I don't mean to sound judgmental..." She put her hand on Toni's arm. "Really..."

"Chalk it up to hormones. Anyway, it's not like that...I mean, it's complicated -- way too complicated to get into at this minute. Another time. For now, I'll just tell you I am going to be a single mother. It was a well-thought-out choice and it's something I'm very happy about."

Phoebe put her arms around Toni and gave her a big hug. "Then I'm happy too. I'm on your team, you know."

"I do know." Toni gave Phoebe a big smile.

"You must be happy. You're glowing!"

Toni laughed. "A girl can never glow too much…"

"Well, when you're ready, I want to hear all the details. Promise?"

"Promise."

"Wonderful. For now, we had better be getting back to the others."

Peter stood as they approached the table. "Ah, there you are. I was beginning to get concerned."

"Nothing to worry about," Toni said.

"Nothing at all," Phoebe added with a smile.

"That's good, because we are having a wonderful celebration and this seems like the perfect time to share some news." He looked around the table and focused on Phoebe. "I've decided to officially name Phoebe Director of Lavender Lane. And to make it more enticing -- in case she might want to understandably run the other way -- or at least straight back into the women's room, or whatever they call it these days -- I am also awarding her a percentage partnership."

"Wow! Lauren cheered. That is totally amazing!"

"Amazing," Charlotte agreed.

"Brava!" Toni added.

Phoebe tried to speak, but had difficulty in getting any words out. She had worked for this for so very long…had worked so very hard. With a trembling hand, she picked up the glass of water in front of her and took a sip. "I…I…thank you Mr. Culvane. Thank you so much."

"And it's 'Peter,' please.

Phoebe smiled.

"You sure as hell have earned both the title and the perks!" He reached out for Phoebe's hand and shook it warmly. "Congratulations. I hope you don't mind my unorthodox way of relaying this news. Somehow it seemed appropriate to celebrate now!"

"Well, you have certainly made my day!" Phoebe declared.

"It's my pleasure. But be advised," he added with a grin, "you most certainly will continue to earn it!"

"Even if he works you to those elegant bones," Toni said, getting up to hug Phoebe, "it's worth it. Congratulations!"

"Yes, indeed," Charlotte piped in. "Congratulations! And, I can't say it too often, thank you so much for everything you did to help find Lauren."

Lauren gave Phoebe a sweet smile. "Thank you so much."

Phoebe sighed deeply. Thank God, indeed. Her feelings of happiness that Lauren was safe and not gravely injured were nearly overshadowed by her sense of relief that her own personal struggle had finally ended. The smile would not leave her face as she let go months and months of pent-up anxiety and frustration. She was finally a partner in The Spa at Lavender Lane.

"And may I offer gratitude as well to our beloved Madame Demidova, who took me under her wing and into her confidence for so many years." Phoebe wiped a tear from the corner of her eye. "She taught me so much and I will be forever grateful."

Phoebe put a hand to her heart, closed her eyes and said a silent thank you.

"I will join you in that thank-you, Phoebe," Peter said. "I, too, am grateful."

It seemed to Toni that everyone in her Lavender Lane "family" had something to celebrate: Lauren was back safely and had decided to forget about modeling and apply to colleges and Charlotte had lost several pounds, was feeling empowered and making plans to go to college herself. Eleanor Franklin had left early and by now had probably given her company's board the comeuppance they deserved, and Phoebe had gotten her long-awaited percentage partnership. She, too, had something to celebrate but decided to still keep her secret. She didn't want to detract from Phoebe's moment. She and Charlotte had already vowed to stay in touch and she would let Charlotte know about the kumquat in just a few weeks, when she was well into the second trimester.

As for Peter, it probably wouldn't make much of a difference to him. She doubted that after she left Lavender Lane, she would ever hear from him or see him again. He might have been the man of her forty-something dreams, but she doubted that she was the woman of his.

■   ■   ■   ■   ■

Mavis was conspicuously absent, having checked out earlier in the day. As far as anyone knew, she had never even made an inquiry as to Lauren's whereabouts, let alone as to her safe return. Her singular lack of concern was a surprise, of course, to no one.

It was checkout time and the foyer was crowded with suitcases and the bubbly chatter of satisfied clients. Nearly all of the women had achieved their goals of plunging into weight-reduction programs, putting themselves on new paths to healthful living and making some tough and important decisions about their lives going forward. The breakfast tables that morning had buzzed with the news of Lauren's disappearance and subsequent rescue, and when the women saw her hobble in on crutches, they broke into spontaneous applause. They were genuinely happy to see that the beautiful young woman had been returned safely, albeit on crutches and with a bit too much sun, but safe, nonetheless.

"Try to be more careful next time," one woman called out. "You don't want to damage that pretty face of yours!"

"Thanks. That's what my mother keeps saying! She's very smart, you know!" Lauren squeezed Charlotte's arm, exhibiting a warmth and tone which, just days before, would not have been possible.

As busy as Phoebe was, she carved time out of her day to personally attend to Toni's checkout.

"Are you sure you don't want to stay on for another ten days? It's only an additional ten thousand dollars."

"Make it a month! You do have experience dealing with bounced checks, don't you?"

Phoebe put her hand on Toni's arm. "You will promise to stay in touch? "Of course."

"I want that little person to know they have an Aunt Phoebe! And you know, Toni, if I'd had my way, we'd still be working on the partnership we talked about."

"It would have been terrific, I'm sure. But Lavender Lane is in really good hands going forward. I think Peter is feeling very paternal about the place." Toni laughed. "Do you think there's any possibility he might feel paternal about other things, too?"

"You'll never find out, Toni, unless you get to know each other better, and I have a hunch he'd like that."

"What makes you think that?"

"Oh, I don't know. the way he was looking at you at lunch? There was something…"

"I can only wish," Toni said with a huge sigh. She smiled and took Phoebe's hands in hers. "I suspect that with the kind of demands I'll be having placed on me, I'll be ready for some Lavender Lane R&R before you know it.

"Well, any time you return, I'll make sure you get a "friends and family" discount."

"I didn't know there was one."

"There isn't -- but it doesn't mean I can't institute one."

"Sounds good to me!"

Toni had filled her in on Kevin, their years of close friendship starting that day so many years before when, while students, Toni and Kevin worked on a big fashion show and Mavis had been so absolutely evil to her…and their well-thought-out plan to bring a child into the world together.

Phoebe listened with a big smile on her face. She leaned forward and gave Toni a big hug. "Whatever's in store, Toni, I hope it will all make you happy."

"What will make Toni happy?" Peter asked, approaching with travel gear in hand.

"You giving her a lift to the airport!" Phoebe said expansively, seizing the moment.

"Phoebe!" Toni blurted out.

"It would be my pleasure," Peter said with a big grin. "As a matter of fact, I was going to ask you if you needed a lift but my astute director knew exactly what to do."

Toni nodded. "She does seem to have that knack, doesn't she?"

"And, Toni, if you're a very good girl," Peter said, "I might give you a piece of my cranberry flavored Double-Bubble."

Toni threw back her head and laughed heartily, but Phoebe looked at Peter as though he were speaking in tongues. "Double Bubble?" she asked. "As in chewing gum for children?"

"Now, now, Ms. Bancroft. "It's a private matter between Ms. Etheridge and myself. Just because you're my partner doesn't mean I have to tell you everything!"

"And why do I have the feeling it's lucky for me that you don't?" Phoebe retorted. "Have a good trip, you two."

"Thanks," Peter said, smiling. "Speak to you tomorrow."

A shiny black car pulled up to the door. The driver stepped out, took their luggage and stowed it neatly in the trunk. Peter opened the door for Toni. "After you," he said, graciously. He waited for her to get comfortable before sliding in beside her. Then he reached across, pulled out Toni's seat belt and secured it. She gave him a dazzling smile and as Peter turned to secure his own belt, Toni turned and blew Phoebe a kiss.

"Well, well, well," Phoebe said aloud, doing her best Bette Davis imitation for no one to hear but a small fawn-colored rabbit scampering across the path. "It might not be such a bumpy ride after all!"

She smiled and blew Toni a kiss of her own as she watched the car take off down the lavender-lined, sun dappled, and very private road coveted by so many and available to so few.

The End

Acknowledgements

Thanks to my agent and friend Linda Langton, without whom I could not have crossed the finish fine. Linda, you are the gold standard!

Many thanks to the best band of cheerleaders and early readers a writer could have: Vivienne Fleisher, Steve Carbone, Lyn Leigh, Lauren Anderson, Christine Schwab, Annette Green, Judy and Gary Richter, Catherine Ventura, Alice Simpson, Paul Thomas, Mimi Weisbond, Dale Simpson, Lynne Greene, Alvin Chereskin, Joan Bronk, Sheetal Vedi, David Reich, Roxanne Watson, Don Pizzutello, Bonnie Weiss and my life-long friends and fellow writers Ray Fox and Sam Shirakawa. Your friendship and encouragement means everything to me.

To the indefatigable George Christy for always believing and being there to help…and to the amazing Victor Skrebneski for my moment as a super model: Thank you! I am blessed to have you both as dear friends.

A big shout out to Charles Salzberg, The New York Writers Workshop and the talented writers with whom I have had the pleasure of an untold number of evenings of sharing, discovery, and some pretty good critiquing -- not to mention a bit of raucous laughter and a few glasses of wine along the way…and to Cristine Fadden for her knowing editor's eye.

And finally, to my muse Modigliani, my swagalicious Schnoodle who was by my side for endless hours at the computer when he would much rather have been romping in Central Park. Mo, there's a bag of special treats with your name on it!

About the Author

Skrebneski

The former Vice President of Public Relations for *Estee Lauder,* Phyllis Melhado has been published in *Town & Country, Cosmopolitan* and *The Scarlet Leaf Review.* She has also ghosted a best-selling beauty book, as well as a nationally syndicated beauty column. She earned her master's degree in communications from NYU and lives in New York City. *The Spa at Lavender Lane* is her first novel.

Note from the Author

Word-of-mouth is crucial for any author to succeed. If you enjoyed the book -- and I hope you have -- please leave a review on your favorite site. Even if it's just a sentence or two. It would make all the difference and would be very much appreciated.

Many Thanks!
Phyllis

Thank you so much for reading one of our **Women's Fiction** novels. If you enjoyed the experience, please check out our recommendation for your next great read!

City in a Forest by Ginger Pinholster

Finalist for a *Santa Fe Writers Project Literary Award*

"Ginger Pinholster, a master of significant detail, weaves her struggling characters' pasts, present, and futures into a breathtaking, beautiful novel in *City in a Forest*.
—*IndieReader Approved*

View other Black Rose Writing titles at www.blackrosewriting.com/books and use promo code **PRINT** to receive a **20% discount** when purchasing.

Made in the USA
Coppell, TX
27 December 2020

47182462R10146